ST. BENET'S

Proofread by Jay G Arscott

Special thanks to Lorraine Swoboda,
John Kincaid, Ali Dunn, Anna Burke and Kath Middleton

Published by Black Oak Publishing Ltd
2nd edition published in Great Britain, 2020

Disclaimer:
These are works of fiction. Names, characters, businesses, places,
events and incidents are either the products of the author's
imagination or used in a fictitious manner. Any resemblance to
actual persons, living or dead, or actual events is purely
coincidental.

Cover photograph 96943072 © David Martin - Dreamstime.com
Cover photograph 126064957 © Volodymyr Muliar - Dreamstime.com

ISBN: 978-1-9163479-1-5

DEDICATION

For Akiko, Akira and Kai.

BOOKS BY DAVID BLAKE

CRIME FICTION
Broadland
St. Benet's
Moorings
Three Rivers
Horsey Mere

CRIME COMEDY
The Slaughtered Virgin of Zenopolis
The Curious Case of Cut-Throat Cate
The Thrills & Spills of Genocide Jill
The Herbaceous Affair of Cocaine Claire

SPACE CRIME COMEDY
Space Police: Attack of the Mammary Clans
Space Police: The Final Fish Finger
Space Police: The Toaster That Time Forgot
Space Police: Rise of the Retail-Bot
Space Police: Enemy at the Cat Flap
Space Police: The Day The Earth Moved A Bit

SPACE ADVENTURE COMEDY
Galaxy Squad: Danger From Drackonia

ROMANTIC COMEDY
Headline Love
Prime Time Love

"In him we have redemption through his blood, the forgiveness of sins, in accordance with the riches of God's grace."
Ephesians 1:7

- PROLOGUE -

Thursday, 8th July, 1976

CLAIRE JUDSON'S DELICATE bare feet burned against the black sun-scorched path as she sprinted over towards the half-open church door. Once inside, she crouched low, and took a moment to peer around.

The church was empty; at least she thought it was.

There she remained for a moment, basking in the cool stale air whilst relishing the touch of the cold flagstone floor against the soles of her feet.

She'd abandoned her ugly school shoes and the white socks that came with them when she'd been hiding behind a gravestone outside, waiting for the coast to be clear. As painful as it had been to run on the blistering tarmac, the shoes' solid block heels made it impossible for her to walk anywhere without being heard, and silence was imperative. Her clandestine lunchtime rendezvous at the top of the bell tower with her much older boyfriend *had* to remain a secret. The Catholic girls' boarding school that she attended just down the road was well known for its zero tolerance towards pupils having any sort of relations with the

1

opposite sex. If she was caught, she'd be expelled. There was no question about that.

However, with current circumstances as they were, she didn't feel she had much of a choice. The stifling heatwave that had gripped the Norfolk Broads for the last two weeks, as it had the rest of the country, left her in a permanent state of sexual arousal. From the moment she awoke, a thin layer of sweat clung to her, making some of the most sensitive parts of her body stick to the coarse material that made up her hideously unfashionable school uniform.

Not wearing a bra probably didn't help. She'd yet to get used to them. Although they provided her with much needed support, she found them to be insanely uncomfortable, and she was always looking for an excuse not to wear them; the intense summer's heat proving to be the perfect one.

On that particular day, she wasn't wearing any pants either. Gary had asked her not to. After their liaison the previous day, he'd mentioned that the idea of her walking around school without them would be a real turn-on for him. She'd yet to have the chance to tell him, but she was fairly sure that doing as he suggested had aroused her far more.

Since starting school that morning she'd found the combination of the oppressive heat, along with the knowledge that she was secretly strutting around her strict boarding school wearing nothing under her uniform, made thinking about anything other than Gary having his way with her virtually impossible.

It had been purely by chance that their covert encounters had coincided with the beginning of the heatwave. That was also when a deep sense of guilt had started to follow her around school, like an annoying unwanted friend. She'd been brought up to believe that sex performed outside of the holy union of marriage was a sin against God. She'd never understood why, especially after she'd had her first orgasm. How could something that felt so good possibly be against God? Quite the opposite! It made her feel empowered, liberated, alive - at least it did when she wasn't worrying about what would happen to her soul after her mortal existence came to an end. As long as Gary wore a condom, she really couldn't see the harm. The act itself made her feel far closer to God than anything had done before, certainly more than singing insipidly boring hymns, or being forced to listen to never-ending sermons, the sole purpose of which seemed to be to incite perpetual fear of what lay in wait for mankind beyond the grave for all but the most spiritually minded.

Naturally, the Church took offence at the use of contraception as well. Now that *really* didn't make sense! Why ban the one thing that turned sex into nothing more than a harmless act of mutual affection?

But there was one thing that meant what she had been doing with such hedonistic pleasure was most definitely wrong, both in the eyes of God and the law of the land: she was only fifteen. But it was a minor technicality, at least it was in her eyes. She would be sixteen in September, which was close enough.

However, she hadn't been entirely honest about it with Gary. When they'd first met, she'd told him she was eighteen, and that she was about to sit her 'A' levels. In fact she hadn't even done her mock 'O' level exams. In her defence, she *felt* like she was eighteen, and she most definitely looked it. She could probably pass for nineteen, maybe even twenty, or she could if she was allowed to wear makeup and some half decent clothes.

Once she was sure that no-one was there, she padded over the cool flagstone floor towards the narrow door that marked the entrance to the bell tower. Ducking inside, she closed it gently behind her to begin stepping lightly up the narrow stone steps which circled around the outer edge.

As she neared the top, the spiralling stairs became progressively steeper, so much so that with no hand rail, she used the steps in front of her like the rungs of a ladder, placing hand over hand on each as she climbed ever higher.

At last she arrived at the level where the giant domed church bells hung from their massive beams, waiting in patient silence for the next time they were needed. From there, a steel ladder took her up to where the final half-dozen or so wooden steps led out onto the roof.

Breathing hard, her legs beginning to tire, she couldn't help but imagine Gary's smile as he lifted up her skirt.

Directly ahead now was the ancient wooden door that led out to the roof, a band of sunlight filling the gap between it and the frame, like a saintly halo.

A mischievous smile played over her lips as she imagined the door being the entrance to heaven itself. As far as she was concerned, it wasn't far off.

She paused to catch her breath, bracing herself for the intense heat that awaited her. It was supposed to be one of the hottest days since records began, and even though she'd be at the top of a tower over a hundred feet high, she knew it would make no difference. The air would be as listless up there as it was at ground level, as it had been since their very first illicit meeting.

Her breathing may have eased, but her heart continued to pound hard in her chest as she climbed the last of the steps. What she'd been doing with Gary at the top of the very place where she attended Sunday Mass every week was by far the most exciting thing she'd ever done in her entire life.

Inching open the door, she squinted in the sun's glare, and stepped out onto the grey wooden planking.

Gary wasn't there.

He'd normally be waiting for her just beside the entrance, leaning against the stone ramparts, cigarette in hand.

She checked her watch.

She was a little early, perhaps, but she'd never arrived ahead of him before. He only lived down the road, so he didn't have far to come. He was a barman at The Bittern in Wroxham, working the evening shift, and didn't start until three. That was why they were only able to meet during her school lunch break.

From the stairs behind her came the sharp creaking of wood.

Knowing it must be Gary, she decided to strike the exact same pose he always did when she was about to emerge. Without a cigarette, she instead used her free hand to raise up her pleated green skirt, all the way to the top of her legs, exposing her smooth porcelain white thighs along with the perfectly formed curvature of her bum, so giving him proof that she wasn't wearing anything underneath, just as he'd requested.

When she saw the top of his dark head she called, 'Hello stranger!' With amused nonchalance she then turned to gaze out over the village of Horning, shimmering in the breathless heat of the sun, adding, 'What do you think of the view?'

She pictured his wide square shoulders rising slowly up through the roof, and the way he would stop and stare in awe and desire at the half-naked school girl standing ready for his attention.

Turning to smile at him, she was so expecting it to be Gary that it took her a full second to realise that it wasn't. The man who was openly ogling her, and who seemed unperturbed by the fact that she had caught him doing so, was wearing the black cassock of a priest.

Dropping her skirt, flushing in hot embarrassment, she spun to face him, adopting the traditional pose of an innocent young Catholic school girl as she did, legs locked together, her hands clasped in front of her skirt, as if the combination of the two created some sort of impenetrable barrier to her long-lost virginity.

As the man stepped out onto the roof, being careful not to trip over the hem of his cassock, his gaze seemed to linger unduly on her full naturally red lips, and her cute up-turned nose. 'I thought I heard someone creeping around up here,' he said.

Unable to think of anything to say in response, she stared down at her bare feet, attempting to offer the correct level of reverence due to a man of the cloth.

Placing his hands firmly on his hips, in a voice of stern condemnation he asked, 'Shouldn't you be at school, young lady?'

'I am - I - I mean, I should, yes, sorry,' she stuttered, 'but it's my lunch break, you see, so I, er...'

'So you thought you'd sneak up here, did you?'

Claire replied with a single nod.

'To meet someone, I assume?'

She didn't answer.

'Was it Gary Mitchell, by any chance?'

Once more her cheeks flushed, but now with embarrassed indignation.

How the hell did he know about Gary?

As if able to read her mind, the man said, 'Don't worry. I won't tell anyone.'

'You won't?' she asked, lifting her head just enough to send him a questioning look.

'I won't,' he confirmed. Staring deep into her translucent blue eyes, he added, 'As long as you're prepared to do something for me.'

Assuming that whatever that was would involve some insanely boring chore, like having to mop the church floor after school for a week, with an insolent glare she demanded, 'And what's that?'

'Oh, nothing much,' he replied, allowing his eyes to slide down the length of her curvaceous young body. 'My silence in exchange for, shall we say...a kiss?'

'A...*kiss*?' she repeated, incredulous, and began searching his face for a sign that he wasn't being serious.

The intense focus of his eyes, and the salacious grin that now curled his lips, did nothing to allay her fear that a kiss was exactly what he wanted.

Panic began to take hold. There was something about this whole situation that was beginning to make her feel increasingly uncomfortable - the way she'd seen him openly ogling her earlier, and how he'd done nothing to avert his gaze, even when she'd caught him in the act. And to ask for a kiss in return for his silence?

The sense of heightened arousal she'd felt climbing the church tower had now been replaced by one of exposed vulnerability. He'd seen just how naked she was underneath her skirt, and Gary had taught her the effect such knowledge could have on a man.

But a priest?

She stole a glance down at his groin.

Her breath caught in her throat.

Underneath his long black cassock, it was blatantly obvious that the man was fully aroused. But as disturbing a sight as that was, what was far worse was the fact that he seemed to be doing nothing to hide it.

Instinctively, she took a half step back from him, wrenching her eyes away to the enclosed square roof, desperately searching for a way to escape. But she was at the top of a tower, over a hundred feet above the ground. The only exit was the door through which she'd come, and to reach that she had to pass the very man she was becoming increasingly desperate to get away from.

The man glanced down at where her hands remained locked in front of her pleated green skirt, before returning to stare at her face.

As if shocked by the fear he saw written there, he frowned down at her and said, 'My goodness, child, I didn't mean on the lips!'

As a surge of relief flowed through her body, she looked into his eyes to ask, 'You didn't?'

Returning to her what had transformed into a

warm, almost benevolent smile, as if appalled by the very suggestion, he exclaimed, 'Good Lord, no!' His eyes then stopped to rest briefly on her soft inviting mouth, before continuing down the length of her body. Narrowing them at where her hands were again, with a single step forward, he added, 'At least, not on *those* lips.'

- CHAPTER ONE -

MALTHOUSE BROAD SPARKLED gently in the early morning sun as John Tanner ambled over the car park outside Ranworth's village shop. Tucked under one arm was the hefty bundle of papers that made up the Sunday Times, while from the other hand hung a litre of milk.

Reaching the edge of the quayside, he indulged himself by gazing out over the Broad, drinking in the cool fresh morning air as he did.

There were definitely more boats than last weekend, he thought, as he focused his attention towards the middle of the Broad. Moored out there were a handful of sailing yachts, their tall bare masts standing like exclamation marks against the treeline beyond.

He glanced upwards, towards the trees nearest to him, the bright green of their new season's foliage a perfect complement to the azure blue sky. There was movement up there, but not a lot. Certainly not as much as he'd been hoping for.

He continued his short journey, following the path around towards *Seascape*, the traditional 1930s gaff-rigged Norfolk cruising yacht which he considered to be his home. It used to belong to Commander

Matthew Bardsley of the Metropolitan Police, who'd given it to Tanner when he first moved up to Norfolk as somewhere temporary to stay. He'd so enjoyed living on board that he'd put an offer in to buy it just the month before, which had been graciously accepted.

Matthew was a close family friend. He'd joined the Force at the same time as Tanner's late father, after whose death he had kept a close parental eye over John and his family. When John's daughter was murdered, it was Matthew who kept him sane, and who, when the time was right, found him his current position, as a Detective Inspector for Wroxham Police. He'd also been the one to provide a formal letter of recommendation, which had gone a long way towards securing the post only a few months before.

As Tanner followed the path around, paying close attention to the many mooring lines that led from the hard standing to the boats alongside, he occasionally smiled and nodded at the various people he saw in the open rear cabins of what looked to be mostly hired boats. Some were enjoying a lazy breakfast, others were preparing to start fishing, and a few looked as if they were getting ready to spend a day out on the Broads.

Rounding a bend in the path he soon saw his own boat moored up. He'd taken the white canvas awning off before he'd left for the shop, allowing him to admire the varnished mahogany which glowed with reflected warmth.

Seeing a familiar figure stretched out over the starboard side bench, one hand draped over the side of the boat, the other resting on the rounded metal tiller, a smile played over his lips.

'Morning,' he called out, as he stepped aboard. 'Or should I say, good afternoon.'

The young woman lifted the rim of the floppy wide-brimmed hat which had covered the whole of her pretty face, and without moving her head, squinted over at him.

'It's not even half past nine!' she moaned, as if lodging an official complaint.

Checking his watch, Tanner said, 'Actually, it's just gone.'

She dropped the brim of the hat back over her face. 'I suppose that's what you call afternoon in London, is it?'

'Well, people do have to get up very early down there.'

'Is that so they don't miss out on all the worms?'

'Something like that. Anyway, I've got the papers, and some milk.'

'How about the paracetamol?'

'Oops! I knew there was something I'd forgotten.'

'Please tell me you're joking!'

He pulled out a small blue box from the front pocket of his jeans and gave it a shake.

'Now that *was* funny,' she said. 'You really should write that one down.'

'What do you want first, the drugs or the coffee?'

'Which would you recommend?'

'Well, one will take about ten minutes to make, whilst the other will only need a glass of water.'

'Drugs, please!'

'Right you are, miss, but if you want either, you're going to have to move. The cups are under the bench, along with the kettle.'

'Move, as in get up?'

'Unless you've mastered the art of levitation.'

'Hold on. I'm a bit out of practice, but let me have a go.'

There followed a full ten seconds of silence.

'Anything?' she asked.

'You mean, did your body lift magically up in the air, allowing me to retrieve a glass, two mugs and a kettle from under the bench seat?'

'Uh-huh.'

'I'm afraid not, no.'

'Shit.'

'Are you going to move, or am I going to have to hire a fork lift truck?'

'Are you saying I'm fat?'

'If I said yes, would you get up and punch me in the face?'

'Definitely!'

'OK, yes, you're fat!'

'Right, that does it.'

After making a feeble effort to sit up straight, she gave up, raised her arms helplessly in the air and said, 'Give us a hand, will you?'

Dumping the newspaper, milk and paracetamol on the small fold-up table positioned in the middle of the cockpit, he took hold of her hands to heave her into a sitting position.

Straightening her hat, she looked him in the eyes to say, 'Oh, hello, stranger! My name's Jennifer Evans. Didn't we have sex last night?'

'If you mean, did you pass out on top of me whilst endeavouring to take off your coat, then yes, I believe we did.'

'Was it as good for you as it was for me?'

'Unforgettable,' he assured her, before knitting his eyebrows together in apparent confusion to ask, 'Sorry, but - who are you again?'

Jenny sent him an unamused scowl, earning a grin in return.

'Now,' he said, 'are you going to get up, or am I going to have to arrest you for loitering with intent?'

'With intent to do what?'

'With intent to stop me from putting the kettle on.'

Letting out a disgruntled moan, she raised herself onto her feet and removed her hat. As she squinted around the cockpit, she said, 'Tell you what, if you can find my sunglasses, I'll make the coffee.'

'Deal,' and he turned to look down into the yacht's minuscule cabin, which was a mess of bedsheets, clothes, books, and magazines.

'Any idea where they are?' he asked, thinking that he should have offered to make the coffee instead.

'If I knew that, I'd have found them myself,' she pointed out, lifting the lid of the bench seat on which she'd so recently been sprawled.

Ducking his head, Tanner stepped into the cabin to begin tidying up, hoping that doing so would uncover the missing sunglasses belonging to the woman he'd only recently thought of as being his girlfriend.

Two cups of individually filtered premium grade coffee later, while Jenny studied the Sunday Times' Fashion & Beauty section as if she was about to be tested on it, Tanner sat up and began folding up the rest. Despite the many hundreds of column inches featuring the very latest in news, gossip and editorial comment, he'd hardly been able to find anything to engage his interest.

Glancing over to watch a hired motor boat burble past, Tanner asked, 'What do you fancy doing today?'

'Not sure,' she said, still absorbed in the article she was reading.

'Shall we take *Seascape* out for a spin?'

Turning to stare at him over the top of her sunglasses, she asked, 'Seriously?'

'I thought we could, yes.'

'Despite the fact that we spent over twelve hours yesterday attempting to take part in the Three Rivers Race, before giving up due to the lack of wind, having to be towed back here, getting shamefully drunk and collapsing into bed?'

'Speak for yourself,' he said. 'But apart from that, why not?'

Jenny pushed her sunglasses up the bridge of her nose to stare up at the small blue and red flag positioned at the top of the mast.

It was lifeless and limp.

With some effort, she turned to study the tops of the nearest trees.

'Well, there's no wind for a start,' she eventually said.

Following her gaze, he said in nature's defence, 'There's some.'

'A breath, maybe, but I doubt there's even as much as there was yesterday. How about we take that 1980s TV mini-series car of yours out for a drive instead? There are loads of nice pubs around here we've yet to go to, assuming it can make it to one of them without breaking down first, of course.'

'You know, at some stage you'd better start making a few more complimentary remarks about my car, else one day you might find that it's reversed over you when you weren't looking.'

'Are you saying it can go into reverse now?'

He narrowed his eyes at her, leaping to the defence of his beloved 1985 Jaguar XJS. 'The gearbox was fixed last week, as you well know.'

'Oh yes, that's right. Sorry, I forgot.'

'They cleaned it, as well.'

'Really! What colour is it now?'

Ignoring the question, Tanner said, 'We can always take your car, if you prefer?'

'Oh, no. If we take mine, we know we're going to end up at the place we set out for. With yours, we never know which garage we'll end up in.'

Tanner smiled with wry amusement. His rather individual choice of vehicle provided Jenny with a seeming endless amount of comic material. However, deep down, over the two months they'd been together, he knew she'd grown to like it. He reached that conclusion because, when he'd offered to sell it and buy something more German instead, she'd refused to allow him. It hadn't stopped the jokes, of course, but at least he knew then that that was all they were.

'Assuming we get back before dark, maybe we could go for a walk afterwards?' Jenny suggested. 'I've still not taken you to the wildlife reserve.'

'How far is that?'

Pointing over towards the front of the boat, she said, 'It's about ten minutes that way, and we won't even have to risk driving.'

- CHAPTER TWO -

O N THEIR RETURN from a pleasantly uneventful drive through the Norfolk countryside, culminating in a pub lunch, Jenny led the way over to the Norfolk Broads Wildlife Centre.

Following a path through a bank of magnolia coloured reeds, they arrived at a modest building, one with wooden planked sides and a steep thatched roof, all of which jutted out into Ranworth Broad to provide unspoilt panoramic views over the water and the marshland beyond.

There they spent an enjoyable hour, taking it in turns to watch some of the many insects and birds through a freely available telescope. Although they saw kingfishers, dragonflies, a reed warbler and even a marsh harrier, the bird Jenny had been most hoping to catch a glimpse of, the elusive bittern, was nowhere to be seen. Despite having grown up in the area, she'd never been lucky enough to catch sight of one. As the Centre's conservationist explained, in recent years they'd simply become so rare that only the booming call of the male could be heard, and even that was unusual.

By the time they got back to the boat it was only half-past three. With time to kill, and with even less wind than there had been in the morning, Jenny suggested that they drive over to St. Andrew's church in Horning, which she felt was worth a visit. On the way, their thoughts turned to the week ahead, leading naturally to the subject of their new boss, Detective Chief Inspector James Forrester. He'd been brought in to replace DCI Barrington, who'd been encouraged into early retirement after a less than stellar performance in a previous case, one which cost the life of three civilians and a senior officer, and had left Jenny seriously wounded.

'What do you make of him?' asked Jenny, sat in the passenger seat next to Tanner.

'It's too early to tell. He's more hands-on than Barrington was, I know that much.'

'Is that good or bad?'

'I've no idea. Thankfully, we've been pretty quiet since the death of Burgess, and in my experience, you only see someone's true colours when they're under pressure.'

Enjoying the view of the lush green landscape which seemed to slip effortlessly past, Jenny said, 'You know, I still think they were too hard on Barrington. I mean, what happened to Burgess was hardly his fault.'

'Maybe not directly, but I think that had he been more decisive, less concerned about politics and more focused on what needed to be done, then there's a possibility it could have been averted. I never told you, but I did sneak a peek at the disciplinary report's findings, which I agreed with. Burgess didn't have enough experience to lead the investigation. I'm not saying I'd have done any better, but you don't give someone free rein on a high-profile murder case without them having had at least some prior experience.'

They rounded a bend in the narrow tree-lined road, after which Jenny directed him to turn left into an empty gravelled car park.

Leaving the Jag, as Jenny led the way towards the church spire they could see poking up beyond a clump of trees, she said, 'I still think you should have applied for the DCI job.'

'Er, no thanks!'

'Why not? You've got the experience. And if it wasn't for you, we'd still have a deranged serial killer roaming the Broads.'

'Yes, but if you remember, I nearly managed to get you killed in the process.'

'I've told you before, John. That wasn't your fault.'

'But it was. I should never have allowed you to go inside that mill. Neither one of us should have, not without back-up.'

'I seem to remember that we didn't have much choice.'

'Our actions didn't save Burgess though, did they? And you don't seem to understand just how close we came to losing you as well.'

As they took in the view of the many crooked gravestones over to their left, Jenny lifted her hand to her neck to feel the thin three-inch scar which she did her best to keep hidden under the folds of a silk scarf, and which was likely to serve as a permanent testament to the many dangers of the job.

'Anyway, I'm happy enough being a DI,' he said. 'I prefer to be out and about than stuck behind a desk having to deal with station politics.'

Pulling the scarf back into place, Jenny wound her arm around his, saying, 'But you wouldn't have to be behind a desk all the time. Forrester isn't.'

'No, well, as I said, he's more hands-on than most DCIs I've known. But the responsibility remains, and we've both seen what can happen when you screw it up.'

There was no denying it, and for a moment neither spoke.

Keen to change the subject, Tanner eventually asked, 'So anyway, are you still intending to sit your Sergeant's exam in October?'

The horrific events that had occurred less than two months before had done little to deter her interest in pursuing a career in the Force.

'That's the plan,' she replied. She then slid him a sideways look to add, 'You don't sound exactly enthralled by the idea.'

'Only because I don't like the idea of you being in harm's way.'

'We've discussed this before.'

'I know, but it doesn't change how I feel. With what happened... I just worry, that's all.'

'Well, don't! For all we know, I could get hit by a bus tomorrow.'

'What, in the middle of the Norfolk Broads? I think you'd have more chance of being hit by a falling satellite.'

'We do have buses, you know. And they're not bright red like the ones down in London, which does make them harder to spot.'

Bringing Tanner to a halt at the edge of the graveyard, about fifty feet away from the church itself, she looked up at the imposing square block tower, rising into the sky before them. 'So, what do you think?'

'Impressive. Can we go inside?'

'I'm sure we *could*, but I can't say I'm too keen.'

'Don't tell me you're the Anti-Christ, and you'd burst into flames if you did?' questioned Tanner. 'I've certainly not seen 666 tattooed anywhere on your body.'

'You haven't looked hard enough.'

'You'd better remind me to have a closer look tonight,' remarked Tanner, sending her over his own version of a mischievous smile.

She glanced over at him to say, 'Don't let me forget,' before returning her attention to the historic building ahead. As her dark brown eyebrows drew closer together, she continued by saying, 'This used to be my church.' Noticing the confused look on Tanner's face, she added, 'I was brought up a Catholic. I was even baptised here. This used to be where I'd come every Sunday, with my parents, and I went to the Catholic girls' school, just down the road.'

'But…I thought you were brought up in Horning?'

'This is Horning's parish church. The village grew up away from it, probably due to the attraction of the river.'

'I see.' He had no idea that Jenny was a Catholic, and with a little caution, asked, 'Do you still go to church?'

'The last time was for midnight mass on Christmas Eve over ten years ago, and I seem to remember being half-drunk at the time. That's why I'm not too keen to go in.'

'Why's that? Did you throw up on the priest's shoes?'

'Not that I can remember.'

'So…why not?'

'It's a guilt thing, I suppose. And I don't particularly wish to find myself face-to-face with my old priest and have him ask me where I've been all his life.'

'Do you think the same one would still be there?'

'I've no idea, but they do have a tendency to live longer than most.'

After dutifully appreciating the church's 15th Century architecture, Tanner eventually said, 'If we can't go inside, can we at least walk around?'

'That's not a problem. After all, I did want you to see it, but if we meet a clean-shaven white-haired old man wearing a cassock and a dog collar, then I'm off!'

- CHAPTER THREE -

Monday, 17th June

ALUMINOUS LAYER of pre-dawn mist hung over the Broads like a widow's veil. The only sign that the sun was about to rise was the merest hint of blue edging the horizon to the east. The sky above remained as black as pitch.

Stanley Garbett would not normally be up and about this early. He certainly wouldn't have been when he was still working. It was over five years since he'd retired, and at seventy-one, he was finding it increasingly difficult to remain lounging in bed for hours on end, as he used to do when he was younger. His bladder now had him up before four o'clock every morning, and once awake, it was almost impossible for him to get back to sleep. He would lie there staring at the ceiling, becoming increasingly worried about the smallest of things, such as whether he'd turned the gas fire off before going to bed, or if he'd remembered to lock the back door. The longer he remained, the darker his imagination would become. For example, if he *had* forgotten to turn the fire off, was the living room now ablaze with him trapped upstairs, and no way to escape? Or if he *had* neglected to lock the back door, was there someone in the kitchen at that very moment, knife in hand, preparing to climb the stairs and stab him to death?

Foolish nonsense, of course, but six months ago he'd woken to discover that he *had* forgotten to turn the gas fire off; and there had been several occasions when he'd left the back door unlocked, giving anyone the opportunity to wander in.

He blamed his memory for all of this. He'd never admit to it, at least not to anyone else, but it was nowhere near as good as it used to be. Before his wife died it had always been as bright as a button; he'd rarely forget anything. But within just a few months of her passing, he'd noticed it had begun to grow dull. Two years on, and he was lucky if he could remember what he'd had for dinner the day before.

Watching a program on TV about how to keep his brain active had given him the idea of taking up a new hobby. According to the programme, you didn't just have to exercise the body; you had to do something similar with the mind, and apparently one of the most effective ways of doing so was to learn something new.

Fishing was the obvious choice, given his location. He'd lived in and around the Broads all his life, and had certainly seen enough people huddled along the many river banks, hiding amongst the reeds, waiting, watching, or more probably sleeping. He'd often thought about it, but never so much that he'd acted upon it. Before he retired, he hadn't the time, and afterwards, frankly, he couldn't be bothered. But if doing so would help him to keep his mind sharp, then he was willing to give it a go.

Having bought all the gear over the weekend, at some considerable expense, and taking advice as to the best location, and the most suitable time, here he was, just after four o'clock in the morning, trudging his way towards the ancient gatehouse of St. Benet's Abbey, still blinking the sleep from his eyes.

His intended destination was the river bank level with where the abbey's high altar had stood, now marked by a tall wooden cross. That was where he'd been told the best fishing could be found.

According to the map, from the small parking area that served for abbey visitors, it hadn't looked too far to walk. But now he was actually there, on the ground, laden with all his newly acquired fishing gear, it was beginning to seem considerably further than he'd thought.

He could just about make out the cross, silhouetted against the expanding blue light from the not yet risen sun. His plan was to bypass the ruins by following the bank of the River Bure. He knew there was no footpath down there, but he felt more comfortable walking along the river than through the ruins themselves.

The abbey itself was thought to date as far back as the 9th Century, when it was a monastery of the Order of Saint Benedict, hence the name. Like most ancient sites, its history was marked by brutality, disease and death. The very first historical account told of a religious hermit being slaughtered by a group of Danes as they rampaged through East Anglia in 865. Other stories included the summary execution of the site's holy inhabitants after they refused to give up their treasures during the Dissolution of the Monasteries in the reign of Henry VIII. Then there was the tale of a young girl, back in the 17th Century, who'd used the abbey's high altar to sacrifice her baby, before being caught and burned at the stake for the illegal practice of witchcraft. Tradition had it that, on the darkest and most blustery of nights, her screams could still be heard echoing out over the flat unbroken landscape, as her soul burned forever in the flames of hell.

As far as Stanley was concerned, whether or not any of this was true was neither here nor there. He'd always been easily spooked; even the old Hammer Horror productions of the 1960s, which his friends had enjoyed, and laughed off, had been enough to have him checking behind doors on his way up to bed. It was for that reason, along with the many stories he'd been told about the abbey over a pint down his local pub, that he was keen to avoid going anywhere near its crumbling remains. He didn't mind the ruined gatehouse so much, slap bang in the middle of which some 18th Century farmer had, for some unknown and frankly bizarre reason, decided to build a drainage mill. It was a little spooky, but nothing more than that. It was the ruined remains of the abbey itself he had issues with, especially up near where the cross stood, and especially during what was still, to all intents and purposes, the dead of night.

He looked over towards where he could hear the River Bure flowing majestically down towards the village of Thurne, but it was still too dark, and he couldn't even make out where the field ended and the river began. The only thing he could see with any certainty was the cross, and the narrow footpath that led towards it.

Not confident that he could successfully cross a muddy field towards the river without stumbling straight into it, he realised that his only sensible option was to head through the abbey. From there, another footpath was marked on the map, one that should take him safely down to the river's edge, near to the location he'd been advised to try.

Putting tall tales behind him, he hitched up the khaki green carryall he had slung over his shoulder, stood up straight, and with his shoulders back, began to whistle as he marched down the footpath towards the abbey at the end, making a mental effort to look neither left nor right, whilst doing his best to keep his over-active imagination under control.

Within a few minutes he was able to make out the first jagged clumps of time-aged rock where the abbey's walls had stood over a thousand years before.

Reaching the first of the ruined remains he stopped. That was where the entrance used to be, with the high altar at the far end. His tuneless whistling fell silent. It was silly, but he knew that if he took just one more step, he'd be entering the abbey itself. It may have once been consecrated ground, but the local population now considered it to be a godless place, known more for its links to the occult than as a home of divine spirituality.

He stared ahead, towards the cross. The sky was perceptibly lighter now. The translucent line of blue had been replaced by a wide band of crimson red, and the mist that remained suspended in the air now glowed orange, as if it were smoke, lit by a distant fire.

As he searched for the courage to take a step forward, something caught his eye. Lying on top of what remained of the abbey's altar, directly underneath the cross, was a crumpled pile of discarded black bin liners, spewing out waste from their open ends.

Some moronic boat owner has dumped their rubbish here! he thought, feeling his temper rise. *Probably some stupid bloody tourist.* He'd never liked the fact that every year literally millions of holidaymakers would pour into the Broads, half of them taking out boats, most without a single clue as to how to drive them, and many showing little respect for the waterways' fragile ecosystem.

Fuming with indignation, he marched forward, straight down the middle of the ruined abbey, to take a closer look. Hopefully he'd be able to find something that would tell him who'd left it there.

So sure of what he thought he'd seen, it was only when he was standing virtually on top of it, staring down, that he realised what it actually was.

Sprawled out on its back was a man's body clad all in black. From one end jutted a pair of bony white feet; from the other hung a head. But where the man's neck should have been was instead a horrific gash. From there oozed a slow but steady stream of dark coagulating blood, which had soaked his face, and was now clinging to the top of a shaven grey head, waiting to drip into the darkness of the ground below.

Unable to take his eyes off the gaping wound, Stanley took a faltering step back, away from the butchered body, dropping the heavy holdall as he did.

The face twitched.

Stanley's breath caught in his throat.

Wrenching his gaze away, he spun around, hoping to run; but his feet had caught around the bag at his feet. Losing his footing, he began stumbling backwards, realising to his horror that he was falling onto the corpse itself.

It was only when the nearest of the body's arms raised itself up to offer him a cold embrace that he began to scream.

- CHAPTER FOUR -

THE SUN HAD only just cleared the horizon when the call came: a body, throat cut, lying within the ancient ruins of St. Benet's Abbey.

Bleary-eyed, Tanner and Jenny emerged from their floating mahogany cocoon to shower, dress and prepare themselves for a long day ahead. And they did so just as quickly as the circumstances of their living environment would allow, that being a wooden boat that was only twenty-four foot long, one which had none of the most basic of modern day conveniences, like hot and cold running water, or even electricity.

Since she'd been released from hospital a couple of months earlier, Jenny had been spending an increasing amount of time with Tanner on board his yacht. What began as the occasional overnight stay soon drifted into Friday night through to Monday morning, giving them the entire weekend together. The rest of the week Jenny stayed at her flat, offering them a degree of independence. They'd decided fairly early on that some social separation was important, especially as they worked together as well; more often than not, side by side.

They were keen to keep knowledge of their relationship away from work, as best they could. So far, they'd been successful. The only person who seemed to have cottoned on to the idea that something was going on between them was DS Vicky Gilbert, but apart from her dropping the occasional hint that she was aware of their secret, she'd only done so when the three of them were alone together, never in front of anyone else. Assuming she did know, she'd been surprisingly discreet about it, and thankfully hadn't gone around announcing the fact to all and sundry. Most people wouldn't have been able to keep their mouths shut, even if their knowledge was based on nothing more than intuition.

Despite it being cramped, impractical, and not even particularly comfortable, Jenny found life on board Tanner's boat to be the perfect place to help her recuperate from her recent physical trauma. The psychologist she'd met with afterwards had even encouraged it. She so enjoyed her time there that when Tanner floated the idea of offering to buy it, she'd backed him all the way. After all, compared to a flat, it was as cheap as chips. Thinking ahead, if they were to end up living together in more sensible accommodation, then *Seascape* would make the perfect summer weekend retreat.

As they became increasingly at ease with each other, it didn't take long for cramped to become cosy. Although there were no soft armchairs or luxurious settees to recline on, the wooden bench seats in the cockpit area were comfortable enough, at least they were once she'd brought some cushions along from her flat.

After they showered, dressed and had coffee, along with something to eat, for appearances sake they took their own cars. This had become their post-weekend routine; if they arrived at work in the same car on Monday morning, they may as well send an email around, announcing the fact that they were an item.

Although the call had been to attend the scene of a possible murder at the ruins of St. Benet's Abbey, Ranworth, where they were moored, was on the wrong side of the river. The quickest way there, by car at least, was to cross the bridge at Wroxham, and continue on, straight past the police station. In such circumstances they felt it unlikely that Tanner would have driven past Jenny's flat in Horning to pick her up, especially at such an ungodly hour.

What they weren't able to avoid doing was to arrive at the same time, with Jenny's silver VW Golf driving into the already busy carpark near to the abbey's gatehouse, and Tanner's sleek black XJS purring in behind.

Despite the early hour, it was clear that they were among the last to arrive. Apart from an ambulance and two squad cars, a forensics van was also parked up, along with DCI Forrester's black BMW and the more nondescript vehicles belonging to DS Cooper and DS Gilbert.

Stepping out, Tanner took in his first view of St. Benet's Abbey, or at least its most well-known part.

The ancient Benedictine monastery's gatehouse was a giant stone structure which had formed the entrance to the monastic community via a defensive wall, most of which had long since disappeared. If the gatehouse was impressive, it was dwarfed in comparison to the conical brick base of what used to be a drainage mill, constructed in the 18th Century.

Surrounding the site, as far as the eye could see, was

nothing but flat land, shrouded by tendrils of early morning mist glowing yellow in the light from a steadily rising sun. Above and beyond was a wide open blue sky, streaked by long lines of clouds, their soft edges burnished by rich hues of orange and scarlet.

Catching up with Jenny, together they approached a uniformed constable. He was standing in front of a line of blue and white Police Do Not Cross tape, strung loosely between the end of a steel fence and a wooden gate post. In the morning chill he stood with his hands buried deep inside the pockets of a fluorescent yellow jacket, which had been zipped all the way up to his nose.

'Morning sir, ma'am,' said the officer, lifting his head just enough for his mouth to clear the jacket's collar.

Replying with nothing more than a nod and a brief smile, Tanner asked, 'Where's the body?'

'Down by the main abbey's ruins, just under the cross. If you follow the footpath, you can't miss it.'

Ducking under the tape, Tanner led the way along the path as directed. The constable was right; now that they knew where to look, the scene was impossible to miss. Even from where they were, they could see the all too familiar sight of a forensics unit in full swing, busily working in amongst a series of misshapen lumps of weathered rock which presumably marked what was left of the ancient abbey, but now only seemed to scar what would have otherwise been an ordinary field of unkempt grass.

With Jenny just two steps behind him, Tanner followed the narrow footpath, pulling his black overcoat around him as he did.

'I see DCI Forrester is there,' Jenny said, peering over Tanner's hunched-over shoulders.

'As I said - more hands-on than Barrington,' he replied, before lapsing into silence.

Reaching the edge of the ruins a few minutes later, they could clearly make out the shiny bald head of DCI Forrester, who seemed to be deep in conversation with their medical examiner, Dr Johnstone.

As they approached, Forrester looked up briefly before checking the time on his watch to say, 'Ah, DI Tanner, DC Evans. I was wondering when you two were going to make an appearance.'

Although it wouldn't have been possible for them to have arrived any earlier, Tanner thought it prudent to apologise. 'Excuse our tardiness, sir. We both live the other side of the river.'

'As do I, Tanner, but I still managed to get here a good ten minutes before either of you.'

Tempting as it was to point out that Forrester probably had a shower directly opposite his bedroom, could dress himself without feeling like he was playing a game of Twister, and had a kettle that didn't need to spend at least five minutes resting over a gas hob in order for its contents to boil, it was unlikely such remarks would be appreciated. They would also do little to explain why Jenny was also late. So instead, he said, simply, 'Yes, sir. Sorry, sir,' and glanced behind him at Jenny, to give her a stern frown of feigned rebuke, mimicking the look DCI Forrester was giving him.

It took a degree of mental fortitude for Jenny to prevent herself from laughing. She'd always had a problem with taking authority seriously, especially when it was in the hands of a bald fat middle-aged man whose jowls wobbled like a seal's every time he spoke.

Although it was glaringly obvious to Tanner that she was doing her best not to laugh, fortunately, for both their sakes, Forrester seemed oblivious.

'Anyway,' he continued, 'now that you're finally here, you'd better come over and take a look.' Turning to face the man clad in white overalls who he'd been talking to when they'd first arrived, Forrester said, 'He was found by a fisherman in the early hours, but maybe Dr Johnstone can explain the rest.'

'Of course,' the doctor said, nodding first at Jenny, then over at Tanner.

As the doctor turned to lead them down to where the cross stood, Tanner had his first look at the body. It was lying on its back, on top of what would have been an impressive altar, sandaled feet facing them with long white toes sticking out from the ends, like a row of gravestones clinging to the edge of a cliff.

Approaching the body, Tanner found himself staring at the man's feet; the skin of which was paper thin, covered over by ugly brown liver spots, and the toenails were almost yellow, each lined with thick ridges that curled inwards at the ends.

'We have an elderly male,' Johnstone reported, 'white, obviously; probably in his late seventies.'

'Time of death?' asked Tanner, considering the long black robe that enveloped the body.

'I'd say somewhere between eleven o'clock last night and two o'clock this morning.'

'And the cause?'

'At the moment, I'm going with the obvious.'

Only half listening, Tanner began inching his way down the length of the body, making sure to tread on the raised platforms that had been positioned around the altar to preserve any evidence left lying on the surrounding ground.

As he noticed the way the man's arm protruded from the side of the altar, he eventually asked, 'And the obvious is...?'

Johnstone gestured towards the head. 'See for yourself.'

At first glance, Tanner thought the body's head had been completely severed. But when he saw the curvature of a cleanly shaved chin pointing up towards the sky, he realised that the head was there all right, but was hanging off the edge of the altar at an almost ninety-degree angle. It was only then that he realised what the doctor had meant. The man's throat had been opened to such an extent that the weight of the head was pulling the wound open, presenting them with a macabre view of cut tendons and sliced flesh.

'Jesus Christ!' exclaimed Tanner, momentarily forced to look away. Despite his many years' experience working for London Metropolitan CID, he'd never seen anything quite like it before.

'Not a pretty sight, I'd have to admit.'

Regaining his professional composure, Tanner said, 'At least we know it was murder.'

'Not so fast!' warned the doctor.

Moving from platform to platform, Johnstone led Tanner around to the other side, where he crouched down and pointed.

There, resting in the fingers of an open palm that

brushed against the blood-soaked grass, was a knife; its handle carved in elaborate golden scales, and its blade a polished silver which glistened with a deep red sheen.

'Suicide?' asked Tanner, trying to understand what the medical examiner seemed to be proposing.

Joining them on the ground, DCI Forrester said, 'We're thinking more along the lines of some sort of self-sacrifice.'

'You're not being serious, surely?'

'As bizarre as it may sound, Tanner, it's a possibility. These ruins have long been a favoured location for satanic-cult types. If you look around, you'll see where candles have been burned to the wick, marking out a five-pointed star.'

Glancing over his shoulder, Tanner asked, 'Isn't there a law against that sort of thing?'

'Only if the land was privately owned and they were trespassing.'

'If that *is* what happened here,' interjected Johnstone, ever cautious, 'he wouldn't be the first. A few years back, we found the body of a teenage boy in similar circumstances.'

'What, like this?'

'If I remember correctly, he'd opened up his wrists, but he was dressed in similar robes, and his bedroom at home was piled high with satanic books and magazines.'

As the three of them got up, Tanner glanced around for Jenny, hoping she'd been spared the gruesome sight. Relieved to see that she'd had the good sense to remain beside the dead man's feet, he turned back to Johnstone to say, 'Is it really possible for someone to slice open their throat in such a way?'

'Well, it would have taken a degree of determination.'

'And to fall back on the altar like this?'

'Looking at where most of the blood has ended up, I'd say so.'

Tanner studied the body once again, before glancing over at Forrester. 'I don't know, sir, but there's something about it which looks staged to me.'

Returning his gaze, Forrester said, 'That is the other possibility, of course: that it's been set up to look like he took his own life. Hopefully forensics will be able to give us a more definitive idea.'

'There's something else, sir,' Tanner observed. 'How did he get here? I didn't see any unfamiliar cars in the parking area.'

'There's a boat moored up on the river down there. I've just sent Cooper and Gilbert to take a look. Hopefully it belongs to him, and it will give us his identity. Tell you what, as we're all here, we may as well head over there and see if they've been able to come up with anything.'

- CHAPTER FIVE -

ROM THE FOOTPATH down towards the
river, with the sun rising fast, the boat Forrester
mentioned was easy enough to see.

Having gained considerably more knowledge about
watercraft since he'd moved into the area, and
especially since he'd started to live on board a yacht,
Tanner could tell straight away from the heavy use of
wood that it was a traditional motor cruiser. Judging by
the way the entire front section of the painted white
hull swept gracefully upwards until level with its sliding
cabin roof, he thought the design probably dated from
the 1930s.

The boat was on its own. The area was popular
with fishermen; there were no public moorings down
there, though that didn't mean it was moored illegally.
Apart from privately owned areas, there were few
places in and around the Broads' waterways where
boats weren't allowed to stop. However, most people
preferred to use the designated areas as they had fixed
anchor points. When tying up to a muddy grass bank,
as was the case here, boat owners had to resort to
using something known locally as a rhond hook, which
served the same purpose as an anchor.

Spotting DS Cooper's mousey brown head of hair
bob up from the open cockpit, Forrester called out,

'How does it look?'

'I reckon it's his boat all right, sir,' Cooper responded, nodding a greeting over at Jenny and Tanner.

Pleased to have his assumption confirmed, Forrester asked, 'Wishful thinking perhaps, but I don't suppose there's any sign of a suicide note?'

'Well, sort of.'

'Either there is or there isn't.'

'Sorry, sir. It's difficult to explain. Maybe you should take a look?'

His curiosity piqued, making sure not to touch anything with his hands, DCI Forrester hopped onto the boat's side to invite Tanner and Jenny to do the same. Stepping down into the cockpit, the three of them followed Cooper through a narrow doorway, down some polished wooden steps and into a generously sized cabin, one lit by a series of circular portholes cut into rich mahogany panelling.

Initial inspection suggested that the space had been used as a combination of office and lounge, with a mixture of books and files lining the shelves, with more piled up on two opposing bench seats.

At the end of a table that ran down the middle of the cabin, DS Vicky Gilbert was picking her way through an old black box file.

As they gathered inside, Cooper said, 'We believe the boat belongs to a certain Martin Isaac.'

Hearing the name, Jenny shot him a look to ask, 'You don't mean *Reverend* Martin Isaac?'

'That's the one,' replied Cooper, with a note of surprise.

'I take it you know him, DC Evans?' Forrester said,

turning to face her.

'Well, I know *of* him, sir,' she said. 'He's a priest, at least he used to be, back in the Seventies. He was charged with the murder of a girl from my old school.'

Forrester raised an eyebrow at her, sending furrows up one half of his wide forehead.

Taking the look as encouragement, she went on to say, 'He was eventually acquitted, but only after a lengthy trial. Afterwards he left the Church and went on to write some sort of anti-God type book, one which became a best-seller, but which had the Christian community up in arms.'

'Was it called *Christianity in Purgatory* by any chance?' asked Cooper, staring down at a large hard-backed book that lay open on the table in front of him.

'I think so,' she replied. 'After the book's success he went on to set up some sort of a satanic cult, which became very popular, at least it was back then.'

To Cooper, Forrester said, 'I assume you're thinking that the body up in the ruins is this Isaac character?'

'I'd have thought so, sir, yes. We found his wallet in amongst some clothes left on the bed in the cabin at the back, so it looks like he changed into the robes he was wearing before making his way up.'

'And you mentioned a suicide note?'

'Well, as I said, sir, it's not a note as such. We found this book left open at a page, and one of the paragraphs has been highlighted.'

As Cooper pointed down towards the passage in question, Forrester moved forward to see for himself.

Putting on a pair of glasses, he bent down to read. *'Fear not, I am the first and the last, and the living one. I died, and behold I am alive forevermore, and I have the keys of Death.'*

Straightening up, Forrester removed his glasses to look back at Cooper and say, 'It's a quote from Revelations.'

'Yes, sir,' Cooper agreed, although he only knew that because it was credited as such underneath the text.

'You're not seriously telling me that because some old guy left a book open with a quote highlighted from Revelations, that he was therefore intending to kill himself?'

'Well, not on its own, sir, no. The quote is included within a chapter entitled *Ritual for Resurrection*. I've had a quick scan through. It seems to be about human self-sacrifice and ends by saying how he planned to cheat death by offering himself up to - well, to the Devil, sir.'

'The guy sounds like a complete looney!'

'Yes, sir,' said Cooper. 'I suspect he probably was.'

'And so you think he left this page open to signify that that was his intention - to *sacrifice* himself?'

With a shrug of his shoulders, Cooper said, 'It's a possibility.'

'And it was a Blood Moon last night, sir,' interjected DS Gilbert, from the other end of the table.

'What the hell's that got to do with anything?' Forrester demanded.

Looking as if she wished she'd kept her mouth shut, Gilbert cleared her throat. 'It's just that it was on the local news last night, sir, about how a Blood Moon has always had associations with spiritualism and the occult.'

With Forrester's eyes still firmly fixed on hers, she

added, 'And...well, sir. I just thought that if someone was going to sacrifice themselves to the Devil, then last night would have been quite a good time.'

As Tanner and Jenny exchanged an amused look, Forrester shook his head to say, 'So anyway, leaving aside all this Devil worshipping nonsense, I assume you're both of the opinion that the man up there is this Martin Isaac character, and that for whatever bizarre reason he chose to end it all by cutting open his own throat?'

With Gilbert remaining quiet, it was left for Cooper to reply. 'Unless forensics finds evidence to the contrary, then I'd have to go with that, sir, yes.'

From behind them, Tanner entered the conversation by saying, 'Although it would have been easy enough for someone else to have left the book open like this, even highlighting the passage. I mean, it's hardly a hand-written note.'

Nodding in agreement, Forrester turned back to Cooper and Gilbert. 'Was the boat locked?'

'No, sir,' Cooper replied. 'The cabin doors were closed, but not locked, and the cockpit roof was left wide open.'

'So, it is possible then that someone else killed him, and set it up to make it look like he'd done it as part of some sort of satanic self-sacrifice?'

'I suppose so, sir, but he'd dressed himself up for something. His normal clothes are lying on his bed.'

'But for someone to cut open their own throat like that!' exclaimed Tanner. 'I must admit that I've never seen anything like it before.'

'There is another possibility,' Jenny said.

Catching her eye, Forrester asked, 'And what's

that?'

'That he had help.'

'You mean euthanasia?'

'I was actually thinking more along the lines of it being done as part of a group ritual, and that someone else did the actual cutting.'

As Forrester digested that suggestion, he glanced around the cabin before eventually asking, 'I assume we can rule out robbery?'

'There's no sign of it,' Cooper said. 'His wallet still had cash in it, although not much else.'

'Do we know where he lived?'

'Not yet, sir, but we can check with the boat authorities. They should have an address on file.'

Looking back down at the box she'd been going through, Gilbert said, 'There's nothing in here except page after page of handwritten notes, most of which seem to be illegible.'

Forrester thought for a moment, before saying, 'Had he left a note stating what his specific intentions were, and had he taken his life by a less challenging method, then I think we'd be able to move forward on the basis that this is a case of suicide, whatever his misguided reason. But with just a highlighted passage from his book, and his throat cut open in such a manner, I think it's safe to say that it's suspicious enough to warrant further investigation. However, that *doesn't* mean to say we think its murder, so I don't want you all going around telling everyone it is. Is that understood?'

Seeing his four officers nod back in agreement, Forrester continued.

'Until we've heard back from Dr Johnstone, we

can't make any assumptions. Cooper, make sure forensics give this boat a thorough once over. We need to know if there are any signs that anyone else has been on board recently, especially around the table area and where you said he'd left his clothes. Then we're going to need to start talking to his family and friends; cult followers if he still has any. If he was planning to "sacrifice" himself last night, as suggested in his book, then I think it's probable he would have told someone of his intentions; or as DC Evans has suggested, they may have even helped him. Background checks on them all will be in order. If he did set up some sort of weird satanic cult, did he do so with anyone else?

'Cooper and Gilbert, get access to his email and phone accounts. Social media, if he was into that sort of thing. Find out who he's been talking to. See if you can put together his movements over the last two weeks leading up to last night.

'Tanner and Evans, I want you to take a look into his business dealings, especially in relation to this cult organisation. If he *was* heading up some sort of satanic church, we need to know how it was funded, who else was involved, and what their specific roles were.'

- CHAPTER SIX -

BACK AT THE station, the team initially drew a blank in their attempts to discover more about Martin Isaac, in particular who his associates were, and if he still had links to the occult.

For Tanner and Jenny, they couldn't find much in the public domain to add to what they already knew. Google had brought up a handful of results, all of which were in relation to his life leading up to when he published his book, but nothing afterwards. There was a Wikipedia entry for him, but it only contained the barest of information; there wasn't even a photograph.

Cooper and Gilbert hadn't fared much better either. He didn't seem to own a phone, at least not one with a contract, nor did he have an email account, let alone anything relating to social media. All they were able to find were the basics; a birth certificate, national insurance and NHS numbers, and a bank account, which after they had gained permission to take a closer look was found to be virtually empty. The address listed for that account was over five years old, and after further investigation they discovered it was now occupied by someone who had no knowledge of anyone by the name of Isaac. They couldn't even find him on the current electoral roll. The only physical location they had for him was his boat, which had been registered under his name with the Broads Authority, giving them reason to believe that it must have been his only residence.

It was Jenny who had the idea of trying to contact his book's publisher, to see if they knew anything more about him. But the publishing house had gone into administration a long time before. All they could find were the names of its editor, Margot Falkner, and its proofreader, Alan Birch. Fortunately they were easy enough to track down, helped largely by the fact that they'd become husband and wife at some point after the book was published, and were now listed as being the owners of an independent book shop, just down the road in the village of Coltishall.

Within ten minutes Tanner was pulling up outside the business address, in a quiet road just off the village high street.

'Not the best location for a shop,' he observed, as he stepped out of his car to glance up and down a road that was devoid of both traffic and people.

Crossing to the other side, he studied the shop, the outside of which had been painted black. On display behind a leaded bay window was a collection of weird and wonderful books, none of which looked even remotely like the latest best sellers.

The name was unassuming enough: *Coltishall Books*, which had been painted in elaborate gold lettering above the window, as well as on the door's glass panel.

As he pushed open the door, a small bell rang above his head with a tinkling sound, one that was in perfect keeping with the shop's Victorian frontage.

The inside was littered with all manner of old books, crammed into shelves and piled high on tables, from which there seemed to emanate a dry musty smell.

With nobody around, either behind the counter or anywhere else, Tanner was eventually forced to clear his throat and call out, 'Hello?'

A moment later they heard the distant sound of a man's voice, which echoed out from somewhere near the back of the shop to say, 'I'll be with you in just one minute!'

As they waited, they began browsing through the collection of ancient-looking piled-up books.

'Do you think they've got the latest Stephen King?' enquired Jenny, as she picked up one particularly hefty leather-bound volume from off of a table.

'I think they're probably more likely to stock Charles Dickens,' said Tanner with a wry look. 'They may even have his latest!'

They soon heard footsteps rattling down an ornate iron spiral staircase in the far corner of the shop, and it wasn't long before a sprightly old man with a thin frame, a quick step and a cheerful countenance appeared.

'Sorry to keep you waiting,' he said, skirting the half dozen or so display tables as he made his way over to join them. 'We've just had some new books come in.'

Whispering over to Jenny, Tanner said, 'Maybe they do have the latest Stephen King after all!'

As the man reached the counter, Jenny raised her hand to hide what she knew would have been a most inappropriate smirk.

Offering them each a warm smile, the man asked, 'Now, how may I help?'

Bringing their minds back to the task at hand, they

each pulled out their IDs.

'Detective Inspector Tanner and Detective Constable Evans, Norfolk Police. Are we speaking to Alan Birch?'

'You are, yes,' he answered, concern creasing his forehead. 'There's nothing wrong, I hope?'

Getting straight to the point, Tanner asked, 'Do you by any chance know a man called Martin Isaac?'

'I don't think so, no. Why?'

Tanner's eyebrows rose in surprise. 'Apparently, he's sometimes called *Reverend* Martin Isaac, if that helps?'

'Sorry, but I'm not sure I know any clergymen.'

'He's not a clergyman.'

'Well, that explains it then. Now, is there anything else I can help you with?'

'At least, not anymore,' Tanner went on, as though the man hadn't spoken. 'In fact, I don't think he's much of anything.'

With concern turning to confusion, the bookshop owner said, 'Sorry, I'm not with you.'

Changing tack, Tanner asked, 'Have you ever heard of a book called *Christianity in Purgatory?*'

Glancing around the shop as if looking for it, the man eventually said, 'I can't say it rings a bell, no.'

'That's funny,' said Tanner, 'since you're accredited as being its proofreader.'

'Then you must be looking for a different Alan Birch. I'm fairly sure I'm not the only one.'

'But your wife's accredited as the editor, under her maiden name, Margot Falkner.'

Birch continued to stare at him, but the cheerful smile had faded, leaving in its place a cold, blank expression.

'Margot *is* your wife's name, is it not?'

There was no reply.

Raising one of his solid dark eyebrows, Tanner persisted, 'It's just that Martin Isaac is the author, which is why I'm going to have to assume that you *do* know him, even if you say that you don't.'

'I'm sorry,' the man eventually said, 'but I'm afraid I can't help you.'

'Oh dear. That's a shame. It's just that this man you say you don't know - Martin Isaac - he was found this morning.'

The bookshop owner made no response.

'Lying within the ruins of St. Benet's Abbey.'

Still nothing.

'He was found dead, Mr Birch.'

Birch's eyes shifted between the two police officers. As his expression changed from resolute non-disclosure to confused concern, he eventually said, 'I'm sorry, Inspector, but you must be mistaken. It must be someone else you found.'

'So, you do know him then?'

'Very well, yes. I admit that I do know Martin Isaac, but the person you found at St Benet's can't be him.'

'And what makes you say that?'

'Because I was with him last night.'

'I see!' Tanner's interest was most definitely aroused. 'And whereabouts was that, may I ask?'

'Well, if you must know, we were attending a meeting at St. Benet's Abbey together. But afterwards, I walked with him back to his boat. And I watched him climb on board, so I'm sure he's fine.'

'Is he an old man with a gaunt face and no hair,

who'd have been wearing a black robe at the time?'

The bookshop owner fell silent again, the colour draining from his face.

'Does that sound like him?'

'But - it can't be!'

After giving him a moment to accept the news that someone he must have known fairly well, despite what he'd been saying earlier, was dead, Tanner asked, 'How did he seem, when you left him?'

'How'd you mean?'

'Did he seem depressed at all?'

'You - you don't think he killed himself, do you?'

Unwilling to comment, Tanner said, 'If you could just answer the question.'

'Then, no. I'd have to say he didn't seem depressed.'

'So, he was his normal cheerful self?'

'Well, I can't say I'd describe Martin as being cheerful, but I wouldn't say that he was depressed either. He's always been an extremely serious, focused sort of a chap.'

Glancing over at Jenny, Tanner said, 'Sounds like he was suffering from depression to me.'

Taking offence at the remark, Alan said, 'He was a deeply spiritual man!'

'So you don't think he'd have killed himself?'

'I see no reason why he should have done.'

Pleased to see Jenny had taken her notebook out, Tanner decided to move the conversation along. 'You said you walked down to his boat with him. Was anyone else with you at the time?'

'No. Just Martin and myself.'

'So you were the last to see him?'

'If it is really him you've found, then I suppose I must be, yes.'

'But you said there were other people with you?'

Birch hesitated. 'There were, but they'd all left by then.'

'Would you be able to tell us who they were?'

'The other people?'

'Uh-huh.'

'I'm sorry, but I'm afraid that would be quite impossible.'

'And why's that, may I ask?'

'Because I can't.'

'How about your wife. Was she there?'

'I'm afraid she's no longer with us. She passed away.'

After pausing for a brief moment, Tanner said, 'I'm sorry to hear that.'

'Don't worry. It was a long time ago.'

Tanner pushed on by saying, 'I'm afraid we're still going to need to know who else was with you last night.'

'And as I said, I'm unable to tell you.'

'Yes, but you haven't said why?'

'Because we're not allowed to divulge the names of other church members.'

It was evident from the stricken look on Birch's face that he'd said something he hadn't intended to.

'Which church is that, and why were you meeting within the ruins of St. Benet's Abbey in the middle of the night, and not inside a more normal church on a Sunday morning?'

'I'm afraid I can't say.'

'Perhaps you weren't there for spiritual purposes,

but were there to buy drugs instead?'

There was no response to that, forcing Tanner to provoke him further by saying, 'Or maybe it was the annual general meeting for the Broad's Paedophile Society?'

The colour surged back into his face, and with a furious snarl the bookshop owner said, 'How dare you! Of course it wasn't!'

'Then what was it about?'

'I'm sorry, but I just can't say.'

'OK, tell you what. How about we arrest you on suspicion of murder, and see how you feel about it then?'

'Murder!'

'That's what I said.'

'But I thought you said he killed himself?'

Glancing over at Jenny, Tanner asked, 'Did I say that?'

Referring to her notes, Jenny replied, 'No, sir. You only asked Mr Birch if Martin Isaac suffered from depression.'

'Which implies that he took his own life,' Birch insisted.

'Put it this way; he was found with his throat sliced open, which would suggest murder. However, a knife was resting in his hand, hence the reason for us thinking more along the lines of suicide. So it could probably go either way.'

Birch stared in wide-eyed horror at Tanner's face.

'Consequently, if we've been able to identify someone who was, say, at the exact same place where we believe Mr Isaac died, and at a very similar time, who at first denies having ever known the man, and who seems strangely reluctant to tell us what he was doing, wandering about the ruins of St. Benet's Abbey in the middle of the night, then that would give us sufficient grounds to arrest that man on suspicion of murder.'

'But - I - I didn't!'

'Then you'd better tell us what you were doing there, hadn't you?'

Despite the threat of being charged with murder, Birch still seemed reluctant to answer, and instead just stood there, exchanging panicked glances between the two detectives.

With a heavy sigh, Tanner said, 'Alan Birch, you are under arrest for the murder of Martin Isaacs. You do not have to say anything, but it may harm...'

'All right, all right!' he blurted out. 'I'll tell you!'

They waited in silence for him to begin, before Tanner felt it necessary to give him a prod. 'Sometime today, if you please; or would it help if we hand-cuffed you first?'

After a furtive glance out of the shop window he leaned forward, and with his voice kept low, eventually came out with, 'I'm a member of the Ecclesia Diaboli.'

'I see,' said Tanner, none the wiser. 'And what's that when it's at home?'

'It's a monastic order, a church if you will, of which Reverend Isaac was the founder.'

'I see, but that still doesn't explain what you were doing in the ruins of St. Benet's Abbey in the middle of the night, and not sitting on a pew on a Sunday morning like most normal church goers.'

'It's not that sort of a church.'

'You mean, it's not a church at all.'

'I suppose that depends on your definition of "church".'

'And what's yours?'

Birch paused for a moment, before eventually going on to say, 'Most people consider a church to describe a building, whereas its original meaning was simply a group of people. It's from the Greek *ekklesia*, which means to assemble or to be called out.'

'So you're basically saying that your church is more of a cult?'

Pulling his shoulders back, the bookshop owner fixed Tanner with an offended look and said, 'If you say so.'

'It's what *you* have to say that's of interest to me.'

There was a lull in the conversation, before Birch eventually relaxed his stance a little and began to speak more freely.

'We've always thought of ourselves as being a spiritual religion, just one that differs from a Christian one. Reverend Isaac helped us to understand that our existence isn't governed by either God or the Devil, but that they are two sides of the same coin; good and bad, positive and negative, male and female. The law of nature makes it impossible to have one without the other, and anyone who thinks they can is deluding themselves. The two are inextricably linked, and if you choose to embrace one whilst ignoring the other, your life will be in a permanent state of discord and imbalance.'

'And so, to redress the balance, you spend your lives standing around five-pointed stars in the middle of the night worshipping Satan?'

'And it's because of such ignorant, dogmatic

prejudice that our religion was forced into secrecy.'

'Well, fair enough. But am I correct in thinking that's what you were doing last night, in amongst the ruins of St Benet's Abbey?'

Silence followed, during which Birch seemed to be considering how much he should be telling the two detectives. Eventually he reached a conclusion. 'It was our Blood Moon Sacrifice. It's our most hallowed gathering, and the only time we offer a sacrificial gift.'

'But I assume Martin Isaacs wasn't the intended gift, or at least he wasn't supposed to be?'

Ignoring the question, Birch asked, 'Are you really sure it's him?'

'At this stage we're about as sure as we can be. We've found items belonging to him on board his boat, but we've yet to locate the whereabouts of any relatives to help us with a formal ID.'

'To be honest, I'm not sure he had any. I believe he was an only child, and never married. He used to be a parish priest.'

'Yes, we know,' said Tanner, glancing briefly over at Jenny.

Assuming that was an invitation for her to say something, she explained to the bookshop owner, 'I went to school at St. Andrew's, in Horning.'

'So, you'd have heard the stories then?'

'Only that he was the local priest and that he was accused of murdering one of the pupils from my school.'

'Claire Judson,' said Birch, as he stared off with a lost, haunted look.

Seeing his expression, she asked, 'Did you know her?'

'Me?' he asked, shaking his head clear of whatever thoughts had been crowding his mind. 'Not directly, at least not before she was attacked. I used to be a lawyer, in a former life, or so it feels now. I was a solicitor for the Church, and was on the defence team for Martin's trial. When he told me afterwards that he'd started to write a book, both I and my wife - fiancée at the time - became curious, and we ended up helping him to write it, my wife acting as the editor and me doing my best at the proofreading.'

'And then you left the practice of law to open a bookshop?'

'Something like that, although as you can see, we're hardly Waterstones.'

'And the accusation that he'd murdered the girl?'

'All nonsense, of course.'

'But someone did murder her?'

'Yes. Poor girl. She's actually buried within the church grounds where it all happened. But it had nothing to do with Martin.'

Having first heard about the story when she started school, out of personal as much as professional curiosity, Jenny asked, 'Did they ever find out who was responsible?'

'Not that I'm aware of. Martin was eventually cleared of all charges, but not before it had gone on to what became a lengthy and very public trial.'

From experience, Tanner knew that just because someone was acquitted didn't mean they hadn't done it. All it meant was that the law had been unable to prove beyond reasonable doubt that he had. 'The police of the day must have had grounds to think that he was guilty, else it wouldn't have made it to court.'

'Perhaps, but having known him for over forty years, I've never known a man to be so *un*interested in women.'

'You mean he was gay?'

Birch sent him a look of disgust. 'No! I meant that he's never been interested in anything of a carnal nature. He certainly wasn't the type to rape a fifteen year old school girl.'

'You may think that, Mr Birch,' said Tanner, 'but nobody can ever really know what goes on inside someone's head.'

'I know he wasn't because I never once saw him look at a girl; not in that way. He just wasn't the type. Up until the time he was accused of attacking Claire Judson, he was devoted to the Catholic Church. All he ever wanted in life was to be a parish priest. The fact that he was accused was bad enough, but when he was excommunicated by the Church after being cleared of all charges, that was a blow he very nearly didn't recover from.'

'*After* he was cleared?' queried Tanner, in some surprise.

'That was why he lost his faith, at least in what the Catholic Church preaches.'

'Don't you think the whole experience of having been let off a murder charge only to end up being excommunicated would have left him feeling suicidal?'

'I've no idea. He may have done, I suppose.'

'But you said earlier that he wasn't the type to take his own life?'

'Not now, no. But that was over forty years ago.'

As he carefully studied the bookshop owner's face, Tanner asked, 'What if he had something else in mind?'

'How do you mean?'

'We found a copy of his book on board his boat. It had been left open at a particular page in a chapter called *Ritual for Resurrection.*'

Birch hesitated for a moment. 'I believe he included that chapter more as a theoretical proposition than any sort of statement of fact.'

'That if someone were to sacrifice themselves to Satan, they could be born again, as his son, otherwise known as the Antichrist?'

'As I said, I'm sure he meant it to be more theoretical than practical.'

'That's as maybe, but do you think he believed it enough to have a go?'

'Well, I - I don't know. Having immersed himself in the subject for as long as he had, I suppose it's a possibility.'

'One more thing, Mr Birch. Can you think of anyone who'd wish Mr Isaac harm?'

'Nobody in particular, but there were plenty of people who didn't agree with his views.'

'Enough to want him dead?'

'Again, it's a possibility. I know he received a lot of hate mail when his book first came out.'

'Any death threats?'

'I've no idea, but it wouldn't surprise me. It was another reason why he decided to keep such a low public profile.'

- CHAPTER SEVEN -

A S THEY CROSSED the quiet road to Tanner's car, Jenny asked, 'What did you make of all that?'

'I think it's looking increasingly likely that Martin Isaac had become so deluded by his own cult religion thing - what was it called again?'

'The Ecclesia Diaboli,' she said, without needing to refer to her notes.

'Yes, that - that he decided to have a go at what he'd written about: a self-sacrifice. And who knows - maybe at this precise moment he's attempting to raise himself up from the dead to begin wandering the earth as Satan's son, all set to do his evil bidding.'

'If he is, then he'll need to get out of the morgue first. And it will certainly give Dr Johnstone quite a fright, especially as he's probably about to start cracking open his ribcage.'

'Quite!'

Reaching the car, deep in thought, Jenny said, 'Maybe he wanted to give his followers the impression that he'd sacrificed himself as a way to hide his real intention: to commit suicide out of depression. Or maybe he'd been diagnosed with some sort of a terminal illness, and didn't have long to live anyway.'

'If it's the latter, then Johnstone should be able to

tell us, but I still think it's an odd method of doing it. I mean, to cut one's throat, from ear to ear? My god!'

'Didn't the Japanese used to do something similar?'

Tanner shook his head. 'You're thinking of Seppuku - suicide by disembowelment, which sounds much worse.'

'But if it's possible for someone to disembowel themselves, then I suppose it's equally possible to cut your own throat.'

'But the question would be, why choose that particular method, when there are so many others that would have given him a far less painful way out?'

'What about the other alternative?'

'What - that Alan Birch, the bookshop owner, gave him a helping hand?'

'Why not? He certainly spent long enough trying to deny that he knew who Martin Isaac was.'

'I suspect that was more because he'd probably been sworn to secrecy about the Ecclesia Diaboli, and that he doesn't want people finding out that he spends every other evening attending midnight satanic rituals within the ruins of St. Benet's Abbey.'

'What about the others who he claims were there?'

'It comes down to motive, in both cases. If someone assisted him according to his own will, fair enough; but if not, they'd have to have had a very strong reason for wanting him dead. That level of violence isn't usual, and speaks of massive anger, or outright hatred. Unless Isaac had a secret hoard of cash stashed away somewhere, it's difficult at this point to see what other motive there could be.'

'I suppose it could have been a relative of Claire Judson's,' Jenny said. 'Someone who was convinced

Isaac was guilty of her murder, and was out for revenge.'

'If it was, then they certainly took long enough to do anything about it.'

As he said that, Tanner's phone began to ring.

'It's the boss,' said Tanner, having dug it out from his pocket. 'I'd better take it.'

A moment later, the familiar voice said, 'Tanner, it's Forrester. How'd you get on with that bookshop owner?'

'Well, we had an interesting chat, but there's nothing at this stage to suggest that he had anything to do with it. He only confirmed what we already suspected.'

'Forensics seem to be suggesting the same thing. The only prints found on the knife were his own, and the same goes for the book we found on his boat. We've also had an interim report back from the medical examiner. He's found no evidence to suggest foul play. He did discover something, though.'

'What's that, sir?'

'Isaac had severe atherosclerosis. All his major arteries were completely clogged up. Johnstone estimates that he probably only had a few months to live anyway. Six at most.'

'Does he think Isaac would have known about it?'

'Even if he wasn't diagnosed, he would have been suffering from severe chest pains, so he must have known something was up. It doesn't seem like much of a stretch to conclude that once he knew, he decided to take matters into his own hands. Anyway, we'll await the full medical examiner's report before going any further, but assuming nothing else comes to light, hopefully we'll be able to leave this one in the coroner's hands.'

- CHAPTER EIGHT -

'WHAT'S THE VERDICT?' asked Jenny, as Tanner put away his phone.

'Looks like you were right. According to Johnstone, he was a heart attack just waiting to happen, and there's no evidence of foul play.'

'And forensics?'

'The knife's clean of prints, apart from Isaac's. It's the same story with his boat.'

'So we're going with suicide?'

'Well, Forrester's going to have to hand it over to the coroner's office. If they think the ritual element plays a significant role, it may end up being classed as death by misadventure; but either way, it doesn't look like there's a criminal element to it, so as far as we're concerned, the investigation is over.'

As he placed his hand under the XJS's chrome door handle, he stopped, staring off into space.

Seeing the distant look on his face, Jenny said, 'Are you OK?'

'It's probably nothing,' he said, 'but didn't Birch say that they were at St. Benet's last night for what they called the Blood Moon Sacrifice?'

'He did, yes. Why?'

'The knife Isaacs allegedly used on himself - did you get to see it?'

'To be honest, I wasn't too keen.'

'I don't suppose you'd be able to pull up a picture of it from the database?'

'Only if they've loaded the pictures up,' she replied, retrieving her phone from out of her handbag. 'Any particular reason?'

'I'm not sure, but before we head off, I'd like to ask our bookshop owner one more thing.'

Back inside the shop, with no sign of the owner, Tanner called out, 'Mr Birch? It's Detective Inspector Tanner again.'

'Hold on!' came the familiar voice from towards the back.

While they waited, Tanner asked Jenny, 'Any luck?'

'It's here, yes.' She passed her phone over to him, just as Birch emerged from the rear of the shop holding a steaming mug.

'Sorry about that. I was making myself a coffee.'

'And I'm sorry to bother you again, but I have just one more question.'

'OK, fire away!'

'It concerns the ritual you said you were taking part in: the Blood Moon Sacrifice.'

'Yes? What about it?'

'Judging by its name, I assume you did actually sacrifice something?'

Birch hesitated for a moment, before saying, 'It was a chicken. It belonged to one of our members. But we've checked, and there's nothing illegal about doing so.'

Holding out the image on Jenny's phone, he said, 'May I ask if that's the knife you used?'

Placing his mug down on the counter, he put on a pair of reading glasses before leaning forward to take a closer look.

The picture Jenny had found was a close-up of the knife taken at the scene, when it was still resting on the fingers of Isaac's blood-splattered hand.

Seeing the image, Birch wrenched his face away from the screen, pulling his glasses off as he did.

'Is that the knife?' Tanner repeated.

'It is,' came the stilted response. 'But you could have warned me first!'

'Who would have used it, to make the sacrifice?'

'That would have been Martin. He always acted as our High Priest.'

'And nobody else would have touched it?'

'We'd have all held it, as part of the ritual, both before and afterwards. Doing so signifies that the sacrifice is made by all in attendance, not just the person doing it.'

'And is this the only one?'

'The only knife? I think so.'

'And who looks after it?'

'It's Martin's, as far as I know.'

Tanner studied Birch's face for some moments before handing the phone back to Jenny, saying, 'Anyway, I was just curious. Thanks again for your time. We'd better be on our way.'

As soon as they were back outside the shop, Jenny asked, 'What was all that about?'

'I just wanted to find out if anyone else had touched the knife that night.'

'And the fact that they all had...?'

'…means that it's odd that the only prints we found on it belonged to Isaac.'

'Doesn't that just suggest he must have cleaned it before using it on himself? To be honest, I think I'd have done the same thing. I mean, as mentally imbalanced as you'd have to be to want to cut open your own throat, you'd want to clean some poor chicken's blood off before doing so.'

'Off the blade, yes. But would you clean the handle as well?'

Jenny thought about that for a moment. It was a fair point. It certainly didn't sound like that was something someone would have done, not unless they had a good reason to.

'And there's something else as well,' said Tanner. 'Let me see that picture again?'

Jenny brought up the image, and held it out for them both to see.

'It struck me at the scene,' he said, pointing. 'You see the way it's resting in his hand?'

'What about it?'

'Wouldn't the knife have fallen out as he'd gone over backwards? Here it looks more like it's been placed there, after the fact.'

Again, Jenny found herself in agreement with him. 'I think you should mention this to Forrester.'

'I'm not sure there's much point,' he replied, heaving open the XJS's long heavy door. 'There's no physical evidence to suggest anything other than he'd done it himself. And as you said, he could have easily decided to clean the whole knife beforehand. Whether a knife would remain in someone's hand after they cut their own throat would be a question of speculative debate more than anything else.'

Climbing inside, as they each fastened their seatbelts, Jenny said, 'You're going to have to tell him anyway. It would be remarkably easy for someone to make it look like he'd cut his own throat, especially if they'd read his book, and knew where he'd be that night.'

'I'll give it some thought,' Tanner replied. 'But I suggest we head back to the station first, to see if there have been any more developments.'

- CHAPTER NINE -

STANDING OUTSIDE DCI Forrester's office, Tanner gave the door a rather hesitant knock.

Despite some niggling doubts concerning the nature of Martin Isaac's death, at that stage he knew that was all they were. On their own, they didn't amount to much, and it was unlikely that they'd warrant further investigation without some sort of physical evidence to back them up.

He also knew that had Jenny not asked him again to speak to Forrester about them as they drove into the station's car park, he would have probably put them to one side and quietly forgotten about them. If he was to be completely honest with himself, the only reason he'd agreed was not out of professionalism, but because of his personal feelings towards her. Put simply, he didn't want to say no to her. Their relationship was barely two months old, and was still at that delicate stage where even the slightest disagreement could have them heading in different directions.

There was another reason as well. He didn't want her to think he was afraid of expressing his opinions to Forrester. As pathetic as that may have been, coming from a forty-something year old man who should be too old to care what people thought about him, at the end of the day he was just a middle-aged divorcee attempting to maintain the affections of a woman who was not only half his age, but was attractive enough to catch the eye of just about every man she happened to walk past. He'd seen how men looked at her, some more obviously than others, and he knew he had his work cut out if he was going to be able to keep a hold of her. He'd already started to make the effort to shed a few pounds, and was becoming increasingly conscious of his grey hairs and the early signs of a receding hairline.

Hearing Forrester's voice inviting him to enter, he stepped inside. 'Just to let you know we're back from speaking with Alan Birch, the bookshop owner, sir.'

'Right, good, yes,' responded Forrester, seemingly more interested in the file he was reading.

Hoping to garner a little more of his attention, Tanner asked, 'I don't suppose there's been any more news from forensics?'

Forrester marked his place with one finger and looked up. 'You mean, about that suicide case?'

'The death of Mr Isaac. Yes, sir.'

'Nothing yet, no, but I was under the impression that we'd put that one to bed?'

'I thought we were going to wait until we had the final reports back from forensics and Dr Johnstone?'

'Yes, but I can't say that I was expecting anything more to come from them. So unless you've learnt something new...?'

'Well, sir, since we spoke on the phone, a couple of things have come to mind which I thought I should run by you.'

'And those are?'

'It's what forensics said about the knife, sir. That it only had one set of prints on it.'

'Which belonged to Mr Isaac. Yes, I remember. What of it?'

'Well, sir, Birch confirmed that the knife we found at the scene was the same one they used for their Blood Moon Sacrifice.'

'And…?'

'And that everyone who was there handled it at some point during the ceremony.'

'What of it?' questioned Forrester, looking back down at the report to turn the page over.

'It just seemed odd to me that he'd go to the trouble of cleaning the knife before using it on himself.'

'I suppose that depends on what they'd been doing with it beforehand, doesn't it?'

'Perhaps.'

'Do we know what that was?'

'They'd used it to sacrifice a chicken.'

'Charming!'

'Quite,' agreed Tanner. 'And I can certainly understand why he'd want to clean the blade, but to clean the handle as well? It just seemed like an odd thing to do.'

'To be honest, Tanner, if it was me, and I'd just used it to kill a chicken, I'd have scrubbed the thing in bleach before running it through the dishwasher!'

'But maybe not if you were suicidal, and were about to use it on yourself.'

'I think that's debateable. Now, was there anything else?'

With the sense that his concerns were being treated

with flippant disregard, Tanner persisted. 'And there's where the knife ended up as well, sir, after the incident.'

'What, you mean in Martin Isaac's hand?'

Tanner could clearly hear the barely disguised sarcastic undertone to the remark.

Feeling his resentment turn to anger, he stepped all the way into the office. 'I just feel, sir, that if you've gone and cut open your own throat, in the manner in which Isaac is thought to have done, you wouldn't still be holding on to the knife afterwards. It would have dropped out of your hand as you fell.'

Forrester gave it some thought, but eventually shook his head. 'Again, I think that would be open to interpretation, but even if we could find someone to agree with you, there's still no physical evidence to support the theory that someone else was involved. And please don't tell me you have a gut feeling about it. In my experience, a detective's intuition rarely stands up in court.'

'No, sir.'

'And it wouldn't do any harm for there to be some sort of motive as well. From what I understand, the guy's virtually penniless, he has no family, and the only thing he ever did that anyone may have reason to harbour a serious grudge against him for took place over forty years ago, and that was for something for which he was acquitted.'

Remembering what Jenny had said about that, Tanner pointed out, 'But that may be exactly why someone would want him dead, sir: because they thought he'd escaped the punishment he deserved.'

'And so they decided to wait forty-odd years before

doling out their own form of vigilante justice?'

'I know it's unlikely, sir, but it *is* possible.'

'So is winning the lottery, Tanner, but that doesn't mean it's going to happen, does it!'

'But the fact that it is possible should at least give us reason to investigate the matter further.'

'Tell you what. If you let me know what you've got in mind, I'll tell you if I think it's worth having a go.'

'Well, sir, I think it would be worthwhile trying to find out who was at that meeting with them last night.'

'Didn't you ask the bookshop owner?'

'We did, sir, yes, but he refused to tell us.'

'Well, that's his prerogative, I suppose. Unfortunately, we can't make him.'

'We could if we thought there was some sort of criminal involvement.'

'But when we spoke on the phone, you were of the opinion that he had nothing to do with it.'

'At the time I was, yes, sir.'

'So you're saying that you've changed your mind?'

'Well, not really, sir, no. But I think someone else who was there may have.'

'But based on what evidence? That for some extraordinary reason Isaac decided to give the knife a bit of a clean after he'd just used it to kill a chicken, or because he forgot to drop it having used it to slice open his own throat?'

Tanner paused, swallowing the urge to argue. 'I take it that that's a no, sir?' he said, unable to keep the resentment from out of his voice.

'Look, Tanner, I know you mean well, but I think we're just going to have to accept the fact that the guy had some serious issues. Not only was he about three months away from having a massive heart attack, he was also the founder of some weird cult religion who seemed to be of the opinion that if he sacrificed himself to the devil, he'd be resurrected from the grave as a way of saying thank you. Bearing all that in mind, I really don't think anyone would be too surprised to find him lying on his back having cut open his own throat. So as I said before, unless you can find some firm evidence to back up your suspicions, or at least some sort of a motive, then that's what will be in my report to the coroner's office.'

- CHAPTER TEN -

TANNER PULLED THE XJS off the country lane into St. Andrew's church car park, the same place they'd been only the day before in happier circumstances.

Nothing more had been heard from either forensics or the medical examiner, and the investigation into the death of Martin Isaac had been handed over to the coroner's office, allowing Tanner, Jenny and the rest of Wroxham station's CID team to leave work at a sensible hour.

Having time on their hands, but still too early to think about food, after leaving Jenny's car at her flat they decided to drop by her old church again.

With everything they'd learned about Martin Isaac; how he'd been acquitted of Claire Judson's rape and murder only to be excommunicated from the Church, when Jenny and Tanner found out that the victim had been buried within the very church grounds where her life had come to an untimely end, they were both keen to see her grave for themselves.

With the sun warming their backs, they split up to search through the hundred or so headstones, many of which were so old, they'd become almost impossible to read.

It was Jenny who found it, along with a single white

tulip resting in a thin glass vase set before the headstone on a marble plinth.

She waited for Tanner to join her before reading aloud the epitaph that had been carved on the stone.

'In loving memory of Claire Louise Judson. Our thoughts and prayers will be forever with you.'

They stood in silence for a moment, the peaceful serenity of the setting graced by the sublime song of a distant blackbird.

'Her parents would have been devastated,' Tanner eventually said.

Having lost his own daughter only eleven months before, he knew exactly how difficult it must have been for them.

Jenny tucked her arm around his and gave him a comforting squeeze. He'd told her what had happened a few weeks before, when explaining the reason for his move up to the Broads. Her heart had gone out to him then, as it did now. Before he told her, she'd sensed there was something he'd been keeping to himself; that had been obvious since their first meal together. But she'd made a point of not asking him about it, hoping he'd tell her when he thought the time was right. The moment had come one night on board his boat. They'd been wrapped in each other's arms, feeling the protective comfort of the soft warm bed covers as they'd listened to the rhythmic sound of water lapping up against the boat's hull. That was when Jenny realised that the emotional barriers she'd surrounded herself with for most of her adult life were melting away, like dew before the morning sun, and she could feel herself falling in love with him.

'Have you seen the flower?' she asked, gesturing

down at it.

When they'd first met, Tanner had told her he thought men had a blind spot for such items of natural beauty. He'd gone on to say that even if they were placed directly in front of them, the average man would be oblivious, hence the reason for her making sure that he was aware of it.

Suspecting her mind was harking back to that conversation, Tanner smiled. 'Surprisingly, I did. Even before you pointed at it.'

'It means that someone's been here recently.'

'And on a fairly regular basis, judging by how clean the vase is.'

They stood for a moment longer before Tanner stared up at the church. 'Do you feel brave enough to go inside yet?'

'Do you want to?'

'I wouldn't mind.'

'Come on then. I doubt if anyone's around at this time anyway, not on a Monday evening.'

With her arm still encircling his, she led the way past the rows of misaligned gravestones, following the narrow path that led up towards the church's entrance.

As they approached, they heard the sound of iron rattling against wood as the door began to open.

'I assume they're not expecting us?' queried Tanner.

A grey haired middle-aged man dressed in the familiar attire of a priest emerged from the church squinting at the brightness. Holding tight to Tanner's arm, Jenny wondered if it was too late for them to turn around and head back in the opposite direction.

It was. He'd already seen them.

'Good evening!' he called out, raising a hand to

shade his eyes from the sun.

'Hello!' replied Tanner, with a friendly wave, as Jenny tugged at his arm like a rider pulling a horse back by the reins.

Tilting his head towards her, Tanner whispered, 'Don't worry. He won't bite.'

'Are you sure about that?'

As they came closer, the priest gave them a welcoming smile. 'Are you looking for a wedding venue, by any chance?'

After a brief exchange of embarrassed glances, Tanner returned the smile. 'Actually, no. We just came to have a look around.'

'Well, you've certainly picked the perfect evening,' replied the priest, gazing at the surrounding trees, the tops of which swayed gently in the warm summer breeze.

Feeling brave, Jenny decided to ask, 'I don't suppose Father Jeffrey is still here?'

'Father Jeffrey?' he said, as if he'd not heard the name in years. 'I'm afraid he passed away some time ago. I take it you knew him?'

'He was my parish priest when I was growing up. You probably know my parents. Francis and Sarah Evans?'

'Yes, of course!' he exclaimed. 'Now that you mention it, the resemblance is rather obvious. You're the spitting image of your mother.'

'A little younger, I hope,' Jenny said, with a wry smile.

'Slightly,' replied the priest, displaying a mischievous grin all of his own.

Even though it was obvious that she had taken the

comment in the light-hearted manner in which it was intended, the priest scolded himself, saying, 'I do apologise. That was quite unforgiveable. For some unknown reason, God bestowed on me a rather odd sense of humour, which has proven to be a heavy burden over the years.'

'Don't worry,' said Jenny, taking an immediate liking to him. 'My mother does look young, but only because she wears so much makeup.'

The priest extended his hand. 'I'm Father Thomas. Very pleased to meet you.'

Taking his hand, Jenny returned the smile to say, 'I'm Jenny, and this here is John.'

'Jenny and John. That has a certain ring to it, don't you think?'

Jenny found herself blushing slightly. He must have realised that they weren't married, since neither of them were wearing wedding bands, and she suddenly felt consumed by guilt for standing side-by-side with a man she was sleeping with out of wedlock.

Keen to move the focus away from herself, and her relationship with the man nudged up against her, she said, 'We actually came to pay our respects to someone who's buried here. Claire Judson?'

The priest smiled back at her, but with no sign that he'd recognised the name.

'She was the victim of an unfortunate incident here,' continued Jenny, 'back in 1976.'

His smile fell away to be replaced by a look of sorrowful remembrance.

'Claire Judson, of course. Poor girl. To have passed away at such a young age, and in such an appalling manner.'

Jenny switched naturally into work mode. 'I don't suppose you know anything about what happened that day?'

'I'm afraid it was a little before my time. But I've heard the stories, of course.'

'There's a flower beside her grave. Do you have any idea who may have left it there?'

'Oh my! Aren't you the inquisitive one?'

'Sorry,' she apologised, a look of embarrassed guilt passing over her face. 'I'm afraid I've always been far too nosey.'

'I take it you're a reporter?'

'Worse, I'm afraid. I work for Norfolk Police. Actually, we both do.'

'Right!' stated the priest, standing to attention. 'I suppose I'd better tell you then, hadn't I!'

After they'd all exchanged mutually amused smiles, gazing over towards Claire Judson's grave, the priest continued by saying, 'Nobody I know, although I've often thought I've seen him somewhere before, but I've never been able to recollect from where.'

'But it is a man, though?'

'A fairly senior one, yes.'

'It could be one of her old friends,' Tanner said. 'They would all be in their late fifties by now.

'Or someone from her family?' suggested Jenny.

With his eyebrows knitting together, the priest replied, 'I'm not sure she had any.'

'Parents?'

'They passed away some years ago now, within a few months of each other, if memory serves. You'll see their headstones alongside their daughter's. But I was fortunate enough to get to know them, before they passed. They attended every Sunday. It was through my conversations with them that I was able to find out what had happened to her. They missed her terribly. Even after all that time, she was all they ever talked about.'

The three of them shared a moment of respectful silence.

As the priest's look of prayerful remembrance faded to be replaced by his former more cheerful countenance, he returned his attention to the couple standing before him. 'Now, if you'll excuse me, there are one or two things I must attend to. But do feel free to have a look around.'

'I don't suppose we'd be able to go to the top of the tower?' asked Tanner, as he leaned back a little to take it in.

'I'm afraid it's closed off to the public now. It has been since the incident. I suspect it was considered to be too dangerous. But the rest of the church is open.'

As he turned to leave, Jenny said, 'Thank you for your time, Father.'

'Maybe we'll see you in church one day?' he called out, over his shoulder.

Watching him ambling down the path that led around the side of the church, Jenny called out, 'I'm sure you will,' which was an answer she felt was ambiguous enough to make him think that he would, without actually agreeing to.

'He was pleasant enough,' observed Tanner, as they watched him wander away. 'How does he compare to your old priest?'

'Father Jeffrey? Oh, he was lovely, but then again, I think he had to be.'

'Why's that?'

'Because of who he had to replace.'

'Of course, yes. Martin Isaac. I'd almost forgotten he used to be the priest here.'

'My parents always said that they thought there was something odd about him.'

'They were coming here, when all that was going on?'

'They grew up here, like me.'

'Did they know Claire Judson?'

'Not that they've ever said.'

'It was interesting to hear what Father Thomas had to say about the man who he's seen attending her grave,' he said, looking back to where she was buried. 'And that he thought he knew him from somewhere.'

Following his gaze, Jenny said, 'It was, yes, but whoever it is, there's not a whole lot we can do about it now. Not with Forrester having handed the investigation over to the coroner's office.'

'I suppose not,' he said, and they turned to head back to the car, their conversation naturally moving on to where they were going to eat dinner that night.

- CHAPTER ELEVEN -

Saturday, 29th June

J ENNY NUZZLED UP to Tanner, seeking the comfort and warmth she always found from resting her head against one of his solid, well-developed arms.

After glancing briefly round at the hundred or so people chatting quietly together as they took their seats, confident that there was no one else from work there, Tanner placed one of his arms over her shoulders to draw her in towards him. The wooden pews were hard and cold, like the surrounding ornately decorated pillars and arches of the church, and in their light summer clothes they were both feeling the chill in the air.

It was Saturday, nearly two weeks since the body of Martin Isaac had been found in the ruins of St. Benet's Abbey. The coroner's inquest had concluded the Wednesday before, the verdict being death by misadventure, not suicide as Tanner had expected. Having read the report, he'd learnt that they'd reached that conclusion due to Isaac's strong belief in the occult, and although their investigation had discovered that he had indeed known about his advanced atherosclerosis, the report felt it was more likely he'd taken his life as part of his religious ideology than because he'd become depressed over his illness, or anything else.

When Tanner and Jenny heard the surprising news that his funeral was going to be a public affair held at Norfolk Cathedral, the cathedral church of St. Barnabas of all places, a vast gothic edifice that lay at the heart of the city, it was he who suggested that they go along. He used the excuse that it would be an opportunity for them to dress up and visit the city, and, more importantly, to see who, if anyone, would show up.

After glancing around again, Tanner leaned in towards Jenny, and in a voice barely loud enough for her to hear, said, 'Who on earth are all these people?'

'I've no idea,' she said, having a look herself. 'Judging by what some of them are wearing, they must be members of his religious cult.'

As many of the people in attendance looked as if they'd just stepped off the set of some sort of gothic horror film, Tanner agreed.

His wandering attention focused on the interlinking beams of wood that made up the ceiling, some two hundred feet above their heads. 'What I'd really like to know is what Isaac is doing having his funeral in this place? I thought he'd been excommunicated?'

'I think anyone living within the cathedral's diocese is permitted to have a funeral here,' she told him, glancing down at the order of service they'd been given on the way in.

'But doesn't this sort of thing cost money?'

'He may have been saving up - preparing for the event.'

'Not using his bank account, he wasn't.'

'Maybe he had a trust fund.'

'If he did, how come we didn't find it?'

Their conversation faded into silence, as Tanner once again looked around at the faces of some of those in attendance.

A moment later, Jenny gave him a prod with her elbow, leaning in to whisper, 'Have you seen who's giving the service?'

Looking down at the Order of Service in her hand, Tanner read out, 'The Bishop of Norfolk. Isaac must have been more popular than I thought.'

'Maybe he presides over all the cathedral's services?'

'Doesn't it seem a little odd to you, though?' continued Tanner. 'That a man who was excommunicated by the Church, and who went on to found a satanic cult of all things, is being given an almost regal send-off by none other than the Bishop of Norfolk?'

'As I said before, it's anyone's right to have their funeral here, anyone from within the diocese.'

'Hold on. Doesn't the Catholic Church think that anyone who commits suicide goes straight to hell, and subsequently isn't allowed a Christian burial?'

'I think the rules for that changed a few years ago.'

'So they don't go to hell anymore?'

Choosing to ignore the comment which was about as sarcastic as it was agnostic, Jenny said, 'Suicide is still considered to be a sin, but I suppose the Church had a change of heart about them being allowed a Christian funeral.'

'Well, anyway, I'd certainly be very interested in speaking to the bishop afterwards.'

'If you mean about hiring the venue, you haven't even proposed to me yet,' she said with a smirk.

'I was thinking more along the lines of asking him about Martin Isaac.'

Pulling back with a look of absolute horror, she said, 'Please, tell me you're not being serious?'

'Why not?'

'Well, for a start, he's the Bishop of Norfolk!'

'He's still a human being, though, right?'

'Only just!'

'And what was the other reason?'

'Same as the last one.'

'That he's the Bishop of Norfolk?'

'Uh-huh.'

'I'm not sure you can use the same reason twice.'

'I think in this instance I definitely can.'

'I really don't see the problem,' continued Tanner, looking away casually. 'I'd only like to ask if he knew Isaac.'

'But the case is officially closed.'

'I know, but I still can't help think there's something odd about the whole thing.'

'So what are you proposing to do - go up to him, shake him by the hand and say, "Sorry to bother you, Mr Bishop, but I don't suppose you know anything about the death of the guy whose funeral you just presided over?"'

Tanner thought about it for a moment, before saying, 'You're right. It would probably be better if I formally introduced myself first.'

She looked at him in amazement. 'If Forrester finds out that you've shown up at Martin Isaac's funeral in order to formally question the Bishop of Norfolk, for a case that doesn't even exist, he'll have you kicked off the Force!'

'I doubt it, and anyway, who's going to tell him?'

'The Bishop of Norfolk, for a start!'

'Why would he do that?'

'But what if he does?'

As the sound of uplifting organ music began filling up the church, and with muted conversations being brought to rapid conclusions, Tanner said, 'Don't worry. I'll be the soul of discretion. I promise.'

- CHAPTER TWELVE -

WHEN THE SERVICE came to an end they remained seated, while the bulk of the congregation shuffled towards the exit at the back of the Cathedral. There they could see the bishop taking people's hands, presumably thanking them for coming.

Tanner watched everyone as they filed slowly past, wondering if they'd all known Martin Isaac through his cult, or through some other connection, either business or social.

When he felt confident they'd be the last to leave, he stood up and led Jenny over to the central aisle, tagging on to the back of the queue.

After a few minutes, as they drew ever nearer to the bishop, Jenny pulled at Tanner's arm, and in a low whisper, asked, 'Are you still intending to speak to him?' with the clear hope that he'd changed his mind.

'If I can, I'd like to try.'

'OK, but if you do, remember, you *must* be discreet!'

With only one couple remaining ahead of them, Tanner began to have second thoughts; after all, he'd never met a bishop before, and he didn't strictly speaking have the authority to approach him. He reminded himself that underneath all the robes and the ceremonial hat was just a man like any other, the only difference being that this one was supposed to be more spiritually-minded.

He studied the bishop's face, trying to get the measure of the man. Although heavily lined, his skin was bone white, without so much as a hint of a tan, and he was grossly overweight. Watching the way he was interacting with the departing congregation, his smile seemed to come naturally, and his pale blue eyes sparkled with cheerful warmth, leaving Tanner with the impression that he was pleasant enough, and that he wouldn't mind being asked a couple of quick questions.

Jenny was first to take hold of his outstretched hand to say, 'Thank you, your Grace. It was a lovely service.'

'Wasn't it?' agreed the bishop, as his benign gaze met hers.

Standing beside her, Tanner contributed to the sentiment. 'And it was good to have so many people in attendance.'

Regarding them both, the bishop said, 'Martin was a good person, one who will be sorely missed.'

'May I ask, your Grace,' continued Tanner, 'if you knew him personally?'

'Are you a friend, or a relative?'

'Neither. My name's John Tanner. I work for Norfolk Police.'

The moment he said that, Tanner could feel Jenny's eyes boring a hole into the side of his face.

Raising a grey unkempt eyebrow, and standing just a little taller, the bishop said, 'I must admit to having heard about the unfortunate manner of Martin's passing, but I wasn't aware that there were any criminal proceedings surrounding it.'

'The coroner reported a verdict of death by misadventure,' Tanner said, 'but there still remain a few unanswered questions.'

'I see! Well, no doubt the answers will be made clear in due course.' With that, he turned to look outside, where a group of priests could be seen waiting for him.

Before he was ushered away, Tanner decided to have another go at his original question. 'Excuse me, your Grace, but did you say that you *did* know Mr Isaac?'

'Hardly at all, I'm afraid.'

'Was that when he was the parish priest at St. Andrew's?'

'It was probably around that time,' he replied, glancing back towards the waiting priests.

'I don't suppose you know anything about why he was excommunicated from the Church, after he'd been exonerated for the crimes of which he'd originally been accused?'

'Sadly, no.'

'So you weren't included in that decision?'

Returning his attention to Tanner, with an amused smile the bishop said, 'At the time I was nothing more than a humble altar boy. I doubt I was included in *any* decision, let alone one of such magnitude. But let's not forget that ultimately all decisions belong to God. In Martin's case, I was pleased to see that he was eventually led towards his own path. Despite it not being one that the Catholic Church could have ever condoned, his teachings were at least spiritual in nature. And judging by how many people attended his funeral today, he had evidently touched a number of lives, hopefully helping to elevate them beyond the material shackles which so often seem to bind us to this mortal existence of ours.'

'Indeed. But thinking back to when he was acquitted, can you remember if there was anyone in particular within the community who may have perhaps been more upset than others over the court's decision?'

'Nobody that I can think of. To be honest, I think most people were relieved that he'd been found innocent. He was, after all, a parish priest. I suspect many more questions would have been asked if he *had* been found guilty, especially with the church's ties with St. Andrew's school.'

Tanner nodded, before going on to ask, 'After the trial, do you know if anyone else was accused?'

'Not to my knowledge.'

'Were there any rumours as to who else may have been responsible?'

'I'm sorry, Mr Tanner, but I make a point of never listening to idle gossip, and I'd advise you not to either. Now, you must excuse me, I'm afraid.'

'Just one more question. Can you tell me who paid for his funeral?'

Losing all pretence of patience, the bishop said, 'I've no idea. Now, I have people waiting for me.'

Without offering either of them a smile, he left them to step outside to join the group of priests.

As soon as he was far enough away not to be able to hear, Jenny stared up at Tanner, and in a low, harsh whisper, said, 'For Christ sake, John, what the hell did you think you were doing?'

Surprised to see the look of anger in her eyes, Tanner said, 'Sorry, but…how do you mean?'

'I thought I told you to be discreet!' she added, darting a look over towards where the bishop had joined his colleagues.

'But nobody overheard us, did they?'

'I meant discreet as in what you were going to ask him. You may as well have read him his rights and asked if he wanted to see a lawyer.'

'Oh, come on, Jen…'

'*And* you told him you were from Norfolk Police.'

'Well, yes, but only in passing.'

'But would he have known that? I mean, you were talking to him as if he was a suspect in a murder investigation - and there isn't even a murder investigation for him to be a suspect in!'

'Honestly, Jen, I really think you're over-reacting.'

The moment he'd said it, he knew it was a mistake.

'You think *I'm* over-reacting? My god! Just wait till you hear what DCI Forrester will have to say about this!'

'Are you going to tell him?'

'Of course I'm not going to bloody tell him! How could you even think that?'

'OK, so who will?'

'Who do you think?'

'The bishop? I hardly think he's going to be calling Head Office to make a complaint about having some off-duty policeman asking him a couple of questions.'

'But it was hardly a couple of questions, though, was it?'

'I was trying to find out what he knew about Martin

Isaac.'

'You even asked him if it was his idea for him to be excommunicated!'

'I asked him if he'd been involved in the decision.'

'And then if he knew who paid for the funeral!'

'Well, yes, but it could be important.'

'He's the Bishop of Norfolk! He deserves to be spoken to with more respect.'

'Why? Because he's wasted his entire life believing in something that doesn't exist?'

A dark, ominous shadow fell over Jenny's face. Fixing him with a furious glare, she snarled, 'Are you suggesting that *I've* wasted my entire life believing in something that doesn't exist?'

'Well…no, but you're hardly a devout follower, are you?'

Stunned as much by his attitude as by what he'd said, Jenny stared at him open-mouthed. But it didn't take her more than a moment before she came charging back with, 'And why's that? Because I'm having sex outside of marriage with some middle-aged divorcee?'

Tanner was about to reply, when he saw the tears threatening the corners of her eyes.

'You may as well call me a slut!' she said, her voice breaking with emotion.

Tanner realised just how stupid he'd been. By insulting her religion, he'd inadvertently managed to insult her as well, which was the last thing he'd wanted to do.

'I'm sorry Jen. I didn't mean…'

'You didn't mean what? To say that I'm stupid for believing in God, or to tell me that I'm too much of a slut to be a Catholic?'

'No, of course I didn't...'

'Well, *fuck you!*' she spat, tears spilling out over her eyelids to begin tumbling down her face.

Shrugging away from him, keeping her head down so nobody would be able to see just how upset she was, she stormed out of the church, pushing and shoving her way past the dozens of people who'd assembled outside.

'Shit!' cursed Tanner, watching helplessly as she stormed off. He couldn't even call after her, not with so many people standing around.

The moment she drifted out of sight, he realised that he was going to have to chase after her. After all, he'd driven her there, and he had no idea how she'd get back without him. But by the time he'd side-stepped his way through the crowd, apologising profusely as he did, Jenny was nowhere to be seen.

With worry now adding to his deep sense of guilt, he began working his way around the cathedral, desperately trying to find her. Having reached the far end, there was still no sign.

Berating himself for having been so insensitive, not only to her religion, but to how difficult it must have been for her to have entered into a relationship with him at all, let alone knowing that he'd been married before, sick with worry he pulled out his phone and dialled her number.

It rang through to answerphone.

He tried again, but the same thing happened.

Deciding to leave a message, on hearing the beep, he said urgently, 'Jen, I'm sorry. It was incredibly stupid of me to have said those things. I didn't mean any of it. And you were right. I should have treated the bishop with more respect. I certainly shouldn't have asked him all those stupid questions. I don't even know why I did. Probably just a force of habit. Anyway, please call me, and I'll take you home. OK. Bye for now.'

Ending the call, he cursed again.

'Bye for now?' he repeated. What sort of a stupid way to end the call was that? For a second he thought he should have told her that he loved her, but he hadn't even told her as much face-to-face.

Out loud, he asked himself, 'What the hell am I going to do now? Drive back without her?

'Shit,' he cursed again. There was nothing for it. He'd no idea how, but he had no choice. He was going to have to try and find her.

- CHAPTER THIRTEEN -

TANNER SPENT THE next two hours wandering around Norwich town centre, desperately hoping to catch a glimpse of Jenny, occasionally stopping to check his phone for missed calls. After leaving her a few more messages, each one more desperate than the last, finally, at just after four o'clock, he received a text message from her. It said, simply, 'Gone home by train.'

Relieved to hear that she was safe, he responded, thanking her for letting him know and apologising once again, before making his way back to his car.

About forty minutes later he arrived back at Ranworth Marina's car park, only to find that her Golf had gone from where she'd left it on Friday evening. Assuming that one of her friends must have given her a lift over to pick it up, his heart sank. He'd been hoping that she'd be waiting there for him, even if it was to spend an hour yelling at him. Anything would have been better than her not being there.

He hurried over to his boat.

'Jen?' he called out, placing his foot on the side.

Unsurprisingly, there was no reply.

Leaving the canvas awning where it was, he undid the two elastic ties which secured the entrance to scramble on board.

Checking inside the cabin only served to confirm his fears.

Her clothes, magazines, makeup - everything had gone.

He forced his lips together. He wanted to cry, but wouldn't allow himself. He knew then that he was in love with her; but it had taken for her to leave for him to realise it.

Pulling out his phone, he was about to dial her number again when he stopped himself. He must have called her more times during that one afternoon than he had since they'd met. To do so again would only come over as immature desperation. He knew she was safe. For now, that would have to be enough.

Slumping down on one of the bench seats in the cockpit, he buried his head in his hands and started going over the argument once again in his head, in the exact same way he'd been doing since she'd stormed off. Cursing himself once more for not realising just how hurtful his remarks would have been, he stood up with the intention of driving over to her flat to speak to her in person. A second later he realised how suicidal that idea was. Turning up at her place, unannounced and uninvited, was probably worse than leaving her half a dozen answerphone messages. He was the one who was at fault, and he couldn't push her. He was just going to have to wait for her to call him. Hopefully she would, and preferably before they had to see each other on Monday.

- CHAPTER FOURTEEN -

Monday, 1st July

TANNER WAS LATE heading in to work. He hadn't overslept. Quite the opposite; he'd woken up long before his alarm had gone off, but he'd been slow to get out of bed. When he did eventually manage to claw his way out, he'd completely lost track of time; his normal weekday routine being interrupted by bouts of doing nothing but staring at either his phone, or the space just beyond it.

It didn't help that he found himself in no particular rush to get to work, as doing so would mean having to face the person who he'd treated with such irreverent insensitivity on Saturday afternoon.

Apart from the text message she'd sent to him saying that she'd taken the train home, he hadn't heard from her. Subsequently they'd yet to speak. It was therefore looking increasingly likely that a frosty reception awaited him, Jenny probably doing her best to ignore him, while he looked for ways to make amends. Despite that, he found himself desperate to see her, hoping she'd allow him to make a proper apology, face to face.

As he crossed the car park, heading for the entrance to Wroxham Police Station, he was unusually nervous.

He had no idea what she was going to say to him, if anything. Nor had he the slightest clue what he was going to say to her.

Pushing open the heavy main door and giving his customary nod to the duty sergeant, he began flirting with the idea that maybe she wouldn't be in, and had decided to call in sick instead.

The moment the thought crossed his mind he fumed at himself for being such a pathetic coward. The argument had been his fault, and his alone. It was therefore only right that he should face whatever punishment was forthcoming, whether that was in the form of a wall of silence or being told what an arse he was in front of the entire department.

As he approached the office doors, he stopped to peek through the circular glass windows.

She was there, sitting at her desk, exactly where she should be.

Checking his watch, he realised that he was nearly half an hour late. So without delaying things any longer, he took a deep breath and pushed open the door to slink his way inside.

Reaching his desk, he glanced over to where she sat glaring at her monitor, occasionally stabbing an accusatory finger at a wholly innocent keyboard.

As he draped his coat over the back of his chair, still without a single idea as to what he was going to say, but knowing he had to come up with something, he eventually plumped for what he hoped would be a safe, albeit rather lame, bet.

'Morning, Jen.'

She didn't look up. Instead, in a flat monotone voice, she said, 'Forrester's looking for you.'

Pleased that at least they'd started talking again, sort of, Tanner made a point of glancing at his watch. 'I am a little late. I don't suppose he said what it was about?'

'Not really. Although I did hear him mention something about how Head Office had been on the phone, after receiving a call from the Bishop of Norfolk, although I can't imagine why he'd have been calling them.' Finally looking up, she glared at him to ask, 'Can you?'

'Look, Jen, I'm really sorry about what I said on Saturday.'

'I think you should be more worried about what Forrester's going to say to you today,' she said, before turning back to her monitor, muttering, *'you insensitive prick.'*

'You're right. I am an insensitive prick.'

When no further response was forthcoming, he added, 'Is there anything I can do to help make it up to you?'

'Apart from stepping under a bus, nothing springs to mind, no.'

'Right.'

'But before you do that, you'd probably better see what Forrester wants.'

Tanner looked over towards his superior's office with a distinct lack of enthusiasm.

'Oh, and good luck!' she added, sending him a sour grin that overflowed with sarcastic insincerity.

Without feeling the need to respond, he stood up and began making his way over to Forrester's office.

Having knocked on the door, he poked his head around the corner to say, 'You wanted to see me, sir?'

'Ah, good morning, Detective Inspector Tanner, or

should I say, good afternoon.'

'Yes, sorry I'm a little late, sir. Traffic over Wroxham Bridge.'

'Is that so?' replied Forrester, with a look of unabashed contempt.

Given that half the people working there probably had to cross the same bridge to get to work, including DCI Forrester, and that Tanner was apparently the only person who'd arrived quite so late, he made a mental note not to use that as an excuse again.

'As you've already had such a busy morning, I suppose you'd better sit down and take the weight off your feet.'

Tanner hated to be talked to in such a patronising manner, but anticipating what was to follow, he thought it was probably best to simply do as he was told, making sure to keep his mouth shut.

Staring at his computer screen, in a conversational tone, Forrester said, 'I hear you went to church at the weekend.'

'Er, that's right, sir.'

'Not just any church either, but none other than Norfolk Cathedral!'

'It was Martin Isaac's funeral, sir.'

'I'd no idea you knew him personally.'

'I didn't, sir.'

Turning to glare over at him, Forrester asked, 'Then what the hell were you doing there?'

'I was interested to see who would show up.'

'But for what possible reason?'

'Curiosity, I suppose,' he shrugged.

'I see. And your decision to interrogate the Bishop of Norfolk afterwards was what - because you wanted to know what that would be like as well?'

'I hardly interrogated him, sir.'

'But you did ask him a series of questions relating to the death of Martin Isaac, did you not?'

'Well…'

'Even though you knew full well that we weren't pursuing it as a criminal investigation?'

'Yes, but…'

'And that the coroner's office had concluded that it was nothing more sinister than death by misadventure?'

Tanner elected to remain silent. At the time it had seemed harmless enough, but with hindsight, he knew that it had been a mistake. Jenny's reaction had been enough for him to know that.

Still glowering, Forrester asked, 'Just what in god's name were you thinking?'

'I'm sorry, sir,' he said. 'We started talking to him after the service, and I suppose I got carried away.'

'We?' questioned Forrester. 'Who's *we?*'

'Er, Jenny and myself, sir.'

The second he'd said it, he wished he hadn't.

'You mean Jenny, as in DC Evans?'

'Yes, sir.'

'What the hell was she doing there?'

'I invited her to come with me.'

'My god! I suppose I should be grateful that you didn't invite the whole of the Norfolk Constabulary.'

'No, sir. Just Jenny…that is, DC Evans, sir.'

Hearing her first name being mentioned again, Forrester realised what that must have meant. Spreading his hands out over the surface of his desk, in an imploring tone he said, 'Please don't tell me that you two are seeing each other.'

'Er, no, sir,' said Tanner, muttering under his breath, 'At least, not anymore.'

'Well, that's something, I suppose. I simply won't tolerate inter-personnel relationships.'

'Yes, sir.' He'd never known the DCI to express his opinion on the subject before, but it didn't come as much of a surprise.

'I've seen enough of them in my time,' continued Forrester, 'and they never end well, believe you me!'

Tanner was tempted to agree with him, but refrained.

'Anyway, suffice it to say that you've been suspended, until further notice.'

It took a full moment for Tanner to realise what Forrester had just said. The second it had, wide-eyed in shock, Tanner raised his voice to ask, '*What?*'

'I'm sorry, Tanner, but I don't have any choice. Superintendent Whitaker was on the phone to me even before I got in. To say that he was furious would be an understatement, and I could fully understand why. A complaint of police harassment from the Catholic Church? I mean, it's unprecedented!'

'*Harassment?*' Tanner's face flushed with humiliated anger.

'You interrogated the Bishop of Norfolk, Tanner, in the middle of Norfolk Cathedral, in front of an entire congregation! Furthermore, you failed to formally identify yourself, your questions were relating to the very guy he'd only just presided a funeral over, and if all that wasn't bad enough, there wasn't even an investigation for him to be questioned over! I mean, what the *hell* were you expecting, the Queen's Medal for distinguished service?'

Tanner's mind spun as he struggled to find something to say. He'd never been suspended before, not once in his entire career.

'Aren't you at least going to apologise?'

'It was a mistake, sir. I realise that now. And yes, I'm sorry. But to have me suspended?'

'Anyway, it's too late for all that now. You need to clear your desk, and make sure that you brief DI Cooper on anything you're currently working on before you leave.'

'*DI* Cooper? Don't you mean, *DS* Cooper?'

'He applied for a promotion when I first took over, which I've decided to approve.'

'But…he's not ready, sir.'

'I wasn't aware anyone asked for your opinion, Tanner, especially in light of the fact that you've just been suspended.'

'No sir, but don't you think he's too young?'

'It's not about age, it's about experience.'

'Which he's also lacking.'

'Unfortunately, Tanner, your actions over the weekend have left me with little choice. I need at least *one* DI working here, and I've had bugger-all luck in finding a replacement for DI Burgess.'

An awkward silence fell over the office, with Tanner just sitting there, desperately hoping that his boss would change his mind.

Eventually Forrester leaned forward in his chair to say, 'Look, I'm sorry Tanner, but it's only a suspension. You're not facing disciplinary charges, or anything. And it's not as if there's all that much going on at the moment.'

'It's fine, sir,' Tanner replied, pushing his chair away from him as he stood up. 'No doubt I deserve it.'

With the sense that nothing more needed to be said, he turned and walked out, closing the door behind him.

Heading back over to where Jenny was still sitting, he saw her eyes flick up towards him before returning to stare back at her monitor.

'Enjoy that, did you?' she asked.

'Not very much, no,' he replied, pulling his coat from the back of his chair.

'And where are you off to?' she asked, her curiosity piqued.

'I've been suspended.'

'Suspended?' she repeated, staring up at him, clearly shocked by the news.

'You were right. The bishop did make an official complaint: one of police harassment.'

'But - suspended for how long?'

'I've no idea. He just said until further notice.'

'Jesus, John. I thought they'd give you a slap on the wrist. I never seriously thought they'd suspend you.'

'Don't worry. It was my fault, as was the way I spoke to you. Anyway, I've got to brief DI Cooper on my case files, and then I'd better be off.'

'*DI* Cooper?' she repeated, in much the same way as he had done a few minutes earlier.

'Forrester's promoted him.'

'But…he doesn't have the experience, surely?'

'I'd have to agree with you. Apparently, he put in for a promotion shortly after we lost DI Burgess, and with me being suspended, I'm not sure Forrester had much of a choice.'

With that, Tanner set off for the far end of the office, where Cooper sat opposite Burgess's empty desk which stood as a stark reminder as to what had happened two months before.

- CHAPTER FIFTEEN -

Tuesday, 2nd July

HANNAH BEAL COULD hear the faint sound of the number 23 bus growling its way up the hill behind her. She was never going to make it, even if she ran, which she knew she wouldn't. Apart from the fact that her pride would never allow it, she probably wasn't fit enough to make it all the way to the top. Besides, the shoes she had on made it impossible.

A heavy blob of rain smacked into the top of her head.

She'd been expecting that. The sky had been growing increasingly dark since she'd left work. She had neither a coat nor an umbrella, but why on earth should she have had? A blue sky had greeted her when she'd left the house that morning, and the forecast the night before had said nothing about rain.

A sudden chilly breeze pinched at her ears, bringing with it another drop of water.

Picking up her pace, she glanced over her shoulder.

The bus was coming up fast.

It was no use. She was never going to make it. She was just going to have to wait for the next one. But wait where? The bus stop at the top of the hill didn't have a shelter, and there wasn't a single tree anywhere along the road to duck under.

The rain began slamming into the pavement around her.

She was going to get soaked!

Staring around, she searched for shelter.

Up ahead, she saw the footpath that led into St. Peter's Cemetery. It was hardly her first choice, but she knew there'd be somewhere in there for her to hide, at least until the rain had passed.

A flash of lightning lit the sky, followed a few seconds later by the ominous rumble of thunder.

As if on cue, the skies opened.

There was nothing for it. With her leather handbag held over her head, as fast as her heels would allow she tottered through the cemetery's entrance and swung right.

Following the narrow footpath, with gravestones watching her from either side, she glanced up to see a stone mausoleum standing in grim solitude at the end. Seeing the entrance had a pillared alcove, she headed straight for it, doing her best to ignore the water that had begun to trickle down her arms, plummeting the depths of her sleeves.

By the time she reached it, she was running full pelt, despite her shoes. Unable to stop, her body slammed into the mausoleum's heavy wooden door, loud enough to wake whoever had been laid to rest inside.

Ditching her handbag on the ground, she leant on her knees, gasping for air, a drop of rain hanging precariously from the tip of her nose. Wiping it away, she shook the water off her hands to stare down at her boot-cut trousers. She'd only bought them that weekend, and she had a sneaking suspicion that they were supposed to be dry-clean only.

She was completely soaked. The idea of using her handbag as some sort of makeshift umbrella had done nothing to protect her from the elements.

Glancing back towards the road, over the top of the cemetery wall she saw the roof of another bus beginning a gradual ascent of the hill she'd been walking up only about a minute before.

'Fuck it!' she exclaimed. She may as well have kept going to the stop and waited there. It would have made no difference. She'd have been just as wet, but at least she would have had a bus to climb on to.

Lightning tore through the sky, followed immediately by a sudden crash of thunder so loud, she felt the ground shake beneath her feet.

As quickly as it had started, the rain stopped.

In the eerie silence that followed, she waited a moment before daring to poke her head out and cast her eyes up at the sky.

Then it really began to come down, with even more fury than it had done before.

She pushed herself back up against the mausoleum's door. The alcove wasn't nearly as deep as she'd first thought, and water was being splattered up over her shoes.

She stared out, following the bus's roof as it continued up the hill. Eventually it came to a halt at the very stop where she could have been waiting, if only she'd had the good sense to have kept going.

Seeing it pull away, she cursed again, knowing that she could have been on it now, watching the rain through a window, instead of from the alcove of some god-forsaken tomb.

After a few minutes, as she watched a torrent of water run over the path in front of her, it was becoming increasingly obvious that the storm wasn't going to stop. If anything, it was getting worse.

Realising that she was just going to have to wait it out, she retrieved her handbag from off the ground and searched its contents for her phone.

The moment she touched it, the surrounding air was ripped apart by a blast of burning white heat.

The next thing she knew, she was lying face down on the soaking wet path, rain cascading over the length of her body while a constant whining noise seemed to be drilling its way through her head.

Blinking away the rain, she tried to work out where she was, and what had happened. One of her arms was wedged under her body, the other lay beside her head. She moved the fingers of both. They felt OK, but the moment she tried to move her legs, a wave of pain surged up through them, burying itself into the base of her spine. She had a go at lifting her head, but she couldn't, not without amplifying the pain in her back.

Moving only her eyes, she tried to look down the length of her body to where she could feel something pressing down on her legs. It looked like a broken slab of stone.

Glancing over to one side, she could see one of the two pillars which had been supporting the arch she'd been sheltering under. The mausoleum beyond, what was left of it, was nothing more than a crumpled ruin, from which a plume of dust and smoke rose steadily up through the still falling rain. What was pinning her legs to the ground must be the concrete arch itself.

Using her free hand she scrabbled for her phone. She remembered she'd been holding it just before the explosion, which she could only assume to have been a bolt of lightning striking the mausoleum; but she couldn't find it.

As the whining noise inside her head began to subside, she heard what sounded like lumps of concrete being moved from within what was left of the mausoleum, as if someone was searching through the rubble. She tried moving her head to see better, but the same pain as before tore its way down her spine.

Holding on to the hope that it was someone looking for her, she tried calling for help, but her mouth was filled with the taste of chalk, and her throat felt as dry as paper. Forcing herself to swallow, she did her best to call, but it was nothing more than a whimper. Breathing in through her nose, she tried again.

'Help me! Someone!'

The sound of movement stopped.

The person, whoever it was, must have heard her.

Without moving her head, she could see a shadow climbing over boulders of concrete, heading towards where she lay.

As it grew closer, she tried to see its face, but its head was covered by a hood, leaving nothing but a gaping black hole.

She watched as the figure approached.

As it grew nearer, from the angle at which she lay she was only able to see its feet, which were bare, clad in a pair of open-toed leather sandals.

As the figure knelt down beside her, she was finally

able to penetrate the darkness of the hood, to where the face of a man stared silently back.

'My legs,' she croaked. 'I...I can't seem to move them.'

Without saying anything, the man shifted his gaze to look down at them, where indeed a slab of concrete lay.

Standing up, he carefully manoeuvred his way around to her feet. There, he squatted down to take a firm hold of either side of the broken piece of masonry. Grunting as he did, he heaved it off her legs, and stood upright.

Still unable to move her head, she croaked out a quiet, 'Thank you!'

Grinning at her, he began lugging the huge stone up the length of her body, stepping either side of her shattered legs as he went.

Hannah watched as the lump of stone rocked first one way, then the other, as the man carried it towards her head, all the while trying to work out what he was doing.

Reaching her chest, the figure stopped to gaze up into the sky. With rain streaming down his face, he called out, 'Lord, your power brings us to birth, your providence guides us through life. It is by your command that we return to dust.'

Holding her hand up so that it rested against the base of the stone, Hannah stuttered, 'I - I don't understand.'

'Into your hands I commit this spirit,' the man continued.

'What - what are you doing?'

'Into your arms I commit this life.'

'No, please, wait!'

Positioning the stone slab so that it hung directly above Hannah's head, he looked down at her and said, 'Your sins are forgiven. Go in peace.'

After offering her a warm smile of graceful benevolence, he let go, leaving her skull to be crushed to a pulp underneath.

- CHAPTER SIXTEEN -

Wednesday, 3rd July

JUST AFTER TEN o'clock the following morning, bleary-eyed and wearing nothing more than a pair of jeans and an old polo shirt, John Tanner emerged from his cabin.

He'd hardly slept a wink the night before, despite having polished off a bottle of rum he normally kept for weekends. The storm that had battered the Broads throughout the night had seen to that. Usually he didn't mind the patter of rain falling onto the yacht's canvas awning. Like the rhythmic lap of waves against the hull, he found it helped him to sleep. But last night's deluge was unlike anything he'd experienced before, especially as it felt like he was sleeping out in it. While the drumming of the torrential rain prevented him from drifting off, the thunder and lightning had him staring wide-eyed up at the sloping low ceiling, hoping to god that his boat's mast wouldn't be struck. He knew the storm had passed directly overhead, as most of the flashes of lightning were followed almost immediately by the almighty crashes of thunder. At one point he'd become so concerned that his boat would be hit, he'd considered fleeing to seek shelter somewhere on land, but the only places he could think of were the marina building, the shop, or the pub, all of which would be locked. Besides, he'd be soaked in the process, and knowing his luck, would have been struck by the very lightning he'd been so keen to escape.

At some point though, he must have fallen asleep, as he'd woken that morning as if being dragged out of a coma.

Having remembered that he'd been suspended, and that there was no particular reason for him to get up, he'd lain there for another hour or so, drifting in and out of sleep, until his bladder had finally forced him up.

The morning's air felt as if it had been washed clean by the storm, as had his canvas awning. He noticed that the boat was sitting higher against the bank, and that his mooring lines were far too tight. Realising that the water level must have risen during the night, he stepped down to slacken off the lines. Had he known it was going to rain so much he'd have loosened them the night before, but with neither a TV nor Wi-Fi, he hadn't had a chance to check the weather forecast.

Once he'd done that, he gave the boat a quick once over, but nothing else seemed out of place. Even the flag at the top of the mast was still where it was supposed to be, fluttering merrily away.

Avoiding the water-logged grass, he walked over to the shop to pick up a few morning essentials.

Behind the counter, the plump middle-aged lady who seemed to be permanently stationed there glanced up at him from over the top of her thick-rimmed glasses.

'Good morning, Mr Tanner,' she said. 'I see you

managed to survive the storm.'

'Just about,' he replied, 'although I can't say I got much sleep.'

'I'm not surprised. Cats and dogs, it was!'

As he made his way towards the back of the shop, he heard her call out, 'Is that why you're not working today, *again?*'

Feeling a prickle of embarrassment, hoping there wasn't a customer listening from behind another aisle, Tanner raised his voice slightly to say, 'Not really.' He'd worked out a long time before that there wasn't much that escaped her attention. And keen for her not to find out that he'd been suspended from duty, just in case she put a notice up in the window announcing the fact, and as she'd already asked him something similar the previous morning, Tanner thought he'd better come up with some sort of a plausible explanation.

'I've taken a couple of weeks holiday,' he announced, pulling a litre bottle of milk from the fridge cabinet.

'I'm surprised they could spare you,' she called back, as he made his way around to where they kept the bread.

'Why's that?' he asked, with casual indifference.

'Haven't you heard?'

With both items in hand, he returned to the counter.

Seeing her heaving a pile of that day's issue of the local free newspaper, the Norfolk Herald, onto the counter, he asked, 'Sorry, but haven't I heard about what?'

'What happened last night,' she said, handing him a paper. 'It's all over the news.'

Placing the milk and bread down, he took hold of the Herald to see a picture of what looked like a half-demolished building, underneath which the headline read, 'Dead Monk Kills Girl.'

Tanner raised an eyebrow at the cashier. 'Seriously?' He'd read some farcical headlines in his day, but that one really took the biscuit.

'It was on TV as well,' she proclaimed, as if that proved it to be true. 'OK, not the part about the dead monk,' she conceded, 'but a girl *was* murdered last night, in St. Peter's cemetery, right next to where that cult leader was buried at the weekend. Apparently, his mausoleum was struck by lightning, his body's missing *and* there's a witness who saw a hooded black monk rise up from the ashes to murder a girl who was standing next to the tomb.'

Tanner had little time for sensationalist newspapers, as the Norfolk Herald was proving to be; however, the headline had done its job, and curious to read the story, at least the Herald's version of it, he tucked it under his arm and said, 'Well, I guess that just proves that you can't believe everything you read in the papers, or what you see on the news, for that matter.'

Looking a little put-out, as she scanned in his items, she said, 'Well, maybe not, but the police *are* asking for witnesses, and they did say that they're not ruling out murder.'

Digging out some loose change from his pocket, Tanner placed it on the counter to say, 'Yes, but that doesn't mean they're ruling it in, either. I don't mean any disrespect to the Norfolk Herald, or the local news, but I'd have thought that if a girl was unfortunate enough to find herself standing next to a building when it was struck by lightning, I suspect there's a slightly more obvious explanation as to how she died, other than being murdered by a black monk rising up from the ashes. No doubt such a story would help to sell a lot of newspapers, but honestly!'

The lady gave Tanner a look of irritated condescension. It was clear that she'd not taken at all kindly to his reproachful remarks. 'Anyway, I'm still surprised you've not been told about it,' she continued. 'You *are* still working for the police, I take it?'

Tanner paused. To the best of his knowledge he'd never told her what he did for a living.

His surprise only lasted a moment. He already knew what a small community the Broads was, and juicy titbits like a local detective living on board a boat of all things, who'd just been suspended for having upset the Bishop of Norfolk, would no doubt be just the sort of story to set tongues wagging. For all he knew, both stories had been featured in the local news. The latter may have even made it into that day's edition of the Norfolk Herald.

Checking to make sure it was still tucked under his arm, he said, 'Which is why I doubt there's anything more to the girl's death than a tragic act of God, but I'll certainly let you know if I hear otherwise.'

With a forced smile, he took the bag she was offering and headed for the door.

The moment he stepped outside, he realised he should have bought some paracetamol. The conversation had left his head thumping, and he'd used his last two pills the morning before.

He kicked himself for having been quite so judgemental towards the woman and her laughable news story; after all, it was only a headline from a local newspaper. He knew their job was to entertain more than inform, and her life was probably so dull that she needed such stories in her life, just to give her a reason to get up in the morning. His comments also meant that he wouldn't be able to turn around and go back inside; his pride wouldn't allow him to. He'd just have to put up with the pounding in his head. It was his fault, after all. The conversation may have brought it on, but it had been the volume he'd drunk the night before which had been the cause.

Once back on board *Seascape*, he put the kettle on, poured out a bowl of cereal and sat down to read through the Herald's front page news.

He concluded that a good part of the story was probably true, which meant that the lady behind the counter was at least half right. He'd suspected as much when she'd said that the police were calling for witnesses. They wouldn't have bothered had her death been a so-called act of God. However, the second part of the story was pure fiction, based on what an eye witness had said he'd seen, someone who in Tanner's opinion must have been on drugs; either that or he'd been watching too many horror films. The hooded black monk he claimed to have seen rise up from what was left of the mausoleum beside which the girl was found was more likely to have been someone simply wearing a waterproof coat. The fact that the person had their hood up was hardly a surprise, given the intensity of the storm. Had they been seen using an umbrella, instead of a hood, the witness would have probably said it was an evil Mary Poppins, or the return of Penguin, from the Batman comic book, such was the quality of the reporting.

Assuming the girl had been murdered, one thing he did know was how much pressure DCI Forrester would be under. With Tanner on suspension, Forrester's most senior staff member was young Cooper, who'd been a detective inspector for all of three days; two if you didn't count the current one.

He pulled out his phone to check to see if he'd missed either a call or a text, asking him to come in.

There was nothing.

The last message he'd had was from Jenny, on Saturday afternoon. His phone had been idle since then. If Forrester wasn't going to bring him back after someone had been found murdered, when would he?

A wave of depression drifted over him. He checked the time, wondering if it would be too early to start drinking again. Then he realised he'd run out of that as well.

He momentarily entertained the idea of going back to the shop to buy a fresh bottle of rum, along with some coke to go with it, and some paracetamol. But he could already see the look of disdain the lady would give him as he placed the items on the counter. There was nothing for it. He was going to have to make the effort to climb into his car and drive around to find a shop where there'd be zero chance of anyone recognising him.

- CHAPTER SEVENTEEN -

Thursday, 4th July

TANNER WAS ENTANGLED inside a dark incoherent dream when he heard a distant phone begin to ring. Attempting to answer it, he turned towards the sound, but found himself trapped underwater, unable to breathe.

His mind focused on the familiar call of his phone. He knew that was real. Everything else wasn't.

By sheer force of will, he pushed himself towards a fractured light shining above his head. Bursting through the surface of an endless blue ocean, he gasped for air to find himself awake, his face buried deep within his pillow.

Lifting his head, he sucked air into his lungs to begin scrabbling around for the phone. Eventually finding that it had somehow slipped underneath his bedsheets, he reached inside to grab hold of it, but the moment he did, it rang off.

'Shit!' he said, falling back onto the bed.

Flipping over onto his back, he lifted the phone above his head to check the time. It was nearly ten o'clock.

He was about to look to see who'd been trying to call him, when it rang again, making him jump.

It was DCI Forrester.

Before answering, he swung his legs off the bed and sat there for a moment, rubbing the web of sleep from his eyes. Blinking them open, he swallowed, and then took the call.

'Tanner, it's Forrester!'

'Good morning, sir,' he replied, doing his best not to sound like he'd just woken up. 'Sorry I missed your call earlier.'

'Don't worry. How are you doing?'

Surprised to have been asked, Tanner answered, 'Er…OK, thank you, sir.'

'That's good, because I need you back at work.'

'Oh, right,' he said, a relieved smile creeping over his face.

'Are you able to come in today?'

'What time?' he asked, feeling the three days' worth of stubble that he'd allowed to grow over his chin.

'As soon as you can.'

Knowing he'd need time to make himself presentable, and to down at least two cups of coffee, he replied, 'I can be there in an hour, sir.'

'I suppose that will have to do.'

'Is it the girl at the cemetery, sir?' asked Tanner, keen to show that he'd been keeping up with the news.

'No. I've got DI Cooper working on that.'

With begrudging ambivalence that Cooper had been given the investigation instead of him, Tanner asked, 'Then may I ask what I'm to be working on?'

'It's something far more serious. We've got a dead priest on our hands, and the manner in which he's been killed is, well, it's disturbing, to say the least.'

Tanner allowed a moment of silence to fall, before

asking, 'Where do you want me?'

'St Mary's Church, in a town called Acle. It's about a twenty minute drive from Wroxham, so probably only about ten minutes from where you are.'

Sensing the urgency, Tanner said, 'I'll aim to be there within half an hour, sir.'

'OK, good. I'll have Jenny text you the address.'

- CHAPTER EIGHTEEN -

ABOUT FORTY MINUTES later, Tanner was turning his XJS off the road that led from Ranworth to Acle and into an unkempt gravel car park. Up ahead was what Tanner considered to be a typical English village church, perhaps older than most, with crumbling moss-lined walls and a short, rounded tower, encircled by a jumble of ancient dilapidated gravestones.

Judging by the number of vehicles parked there, it was clear that he was somewhat late to the party. Out of all of them, there were two he recognised instantly; DCI Forrester's black BMW, and of more interest, Jenny's silver VW Golf.

Since he'd been told to report for duty, he'd been wondering if she'd be assigned to the same investigation. When Forrester had said that Jenny would be texting him over the directions, he'd assumed she would have been. Seeing her car parked there only served to confirm it. It also made him realise that he was having mixed feelings about having to work alongside her again.

Over the past few days it had felt like their relationship was about as dead as the people buried underneath all the gravestones. He'd even found himself resenting her for not having bothered to call him since his suspension, which he honestly thought she should have done, even if it was only to ask if he was OK. After all, she must have known how difficult such a reprimand must have been for him; but then again, maybe she didn't? Maybe she thought he was the type who got suspended all the time, and had come to accept it as part of the job, or at least the way he went about doing it? Worse, maybe she just didn't care. At that stage, he'd no idea, and not being able to talk to her meant that it was going to be difficult for him to find out.

As he climbed out of the car, he could see two uniformed police officers guarding the entrance to the church.

Making his way towards them, he couldn't help but wonder if Jenny still had feelings for him, or if she'd already moved on. He wouldn't have been surprised if she had. There must have been a long line of men waiting to take his place; no doubt all considerably younger than he was as well.

Just the idea that she may have already started to see someone else began to upset him, and he made a mental effort to push such negative thoughts to the back of his mind. In their place, he forced himself to consider the case in hand, in particular, what could have happened to the priest inside that had given Forrester reason to use the word *disturbing* to describe it.

Recognising both police constables, he nodded at each as he approached.

'Morning, sir,' they replied.

Tanner wasn't sure, but hiding behind their eyes seemed to be the merest hint of a smirk. If there was, it was hardly surprising. No doubt they knew about his suspension, along with the reason behind it. They'd probably also found out about the argument he'd had with Jenny, leading them to discover their relationship. If they did know, they weren't making it obvious, which was something for him to be grateful for.

The inside of the church was much like any other, with rows of pews lined up on either side of a central aisle, flanked by large arched windows that would have been graced with brightly coloured glass when the church had first been built, but which were now just dull and lifeless, their jagged lead frames making them look like the barren branches of decomposing trees.

The only sound other than his own footsteps came from the far end of the church, where a large white plastic sheet hung down from the rafters. He watched as it lifted and moved in an unfelt breeze, like a ghostly apparition, waiting to fall on an unsuspecting congregation with a deadly embrace.

To the right of the sheet he could see DCI Forrester, deep in conversation with someone, but he couldn't see who, as they were hidden behind the plastic.

As he began heading down the aisle, Forrester glanced up to beckon him over.

Rounding the front right-hand pew, he saw the two people with whom Forrester was speaking: the Medical Examiner, Dr Johnstone, and Detective Constable Jenny Evans, who he couldn't help but notice was looking paler than normal.

'Welcome back, DI Tanner,' said Forrester, with a grim smile.

'Sir,' said Tanner, in acknowledgment, nodding

from Dr Johnstone to Jenny, who looked away the moment he caught her eye.

Inside his head, Tanner shrugged. Her reaction made it obvious that she was still upset with him, which was fair enough.

Knowing that there was nothing he'd be able to do about it, at least not then, he turned to face Forrester to ask, 'What have we got, sir?'

'Nothing good, I'm afraid,' Forrester replied, before guiding Tanner's eyes upwards.

Seeing what he was being led to look up at, Tanner stopped, the blood fast draining from his face.

Against the church's far wall stood a large wooden cross, and nailed up to it was the body of a man, stripped of all clothing, gaffer tape flattened over his mouth.

'Jesus!' exclaimed Tanner.

'Actually, we think it's Father Richard Illingworth,' responded Dr Johnstone, the unintended irony of Tanner's remark having not being lost on him. 'He's the parish priest, or at least he was.'

They stood transfixed by the macabre but iconic scene, all apart from Jenny, who began flicking through the pages of her notepad instead.

'Whoever did it certainly knew what they were doing,' continued Johnstone. 'They drove the nails in through his wrists, not the palms of his hands, as is the popular misconception.'

'What difference would that have made?' questioned Tanner, still staring.

'It's unlikely that the full weight of a man could be supported by a single nail driven through each of the palms, especially as whoever did this gave the victim nothing to use to help support his weight.'

As Tanner gazed into the man's face, where a pair of dark brown eyes stared vacantly back at him, he asked, 'How would he have died?'

'An interesting question. Assuming his heart held out, respiratory failure is believed to be the most common cause. It takes a surprising amount of effort for the body to be able to inflate its chest when held in such a position. As the victim's strength ebbs away, it's thought that they eventually die through lack of oxygen. It's basically a very slow and painful form of asphyxiation.'

'How long would it have taken?'

'Not that long, I wouldn't have thought. According to historical accounts, they used to provide a platform for the victim to stand on, which is thought to have extended the time it would have taken by up to three or four days. At that point, if they felt it had gone on long enough, out of kindness they'd break their legs. However, in this case, with his legs hanging suspended as they are, I'd say that he'd have lasted no more than a few hours.'

'Any idea of a time of death?'

'Not a clue. Sorry. And I won't until the body's been taken down.'

'Do you at least know if he was killed by having been nailed up there? He wasn't dead beforehand?

'Judging by the amount of blood he's lost from his wrists, I'd say he was alive at the time.'

Tearing his eyes away, Tanner glanced around the otherwise empty church to ask, 'Does anyone know who found the body?'

Entering the conversation, Forrester replied, 'It was

a lady who helps out with the flowers.'

'Is she still here?'

'No, she was given a sedative and taken home. Understandably, she was very upset, but she was at least able to give a brief statement before she left.'

'Which was?'

'That when she couldn't find the priest at his home, she came up here, looking for him.'

'Do we have forensics over there?'

'We do. They've found what they believe may be traces of trichloromethane on his bedding, and there's evidence to suggest that the place had been broken into. So at the moment it looks like the priest was drugged when he was asleep, stripped, and then dragged over here and...'

Instead of finishing the sentence, Forrester gestured up at the horrific scene hanging over them.

The conversation came to a standstill, until Forrester broke the silence by saying, 'Admittedly, there's not a lot to go on at this stage, but hopefully forensics will come up with something. Anyway, Tanner, I'd like you to work with DC Evans on this one. I trust that's OK with the both of you?'

'OK by me,' muttered Jenny, under her breath, as she continued to stare down at her notepad.

'I'm sure that will be fine, sir,' replied Tanner, with a little more professionalism.

After giving each of them a look of stern reproach, Forrester said, 'I'll leave it with you two then.'

As he turned to head out, Tanner asked, 'What about the other body?'

'You mean, the girl?' he replied, looking back at Tanner.

'Yes, sir. May I ask what happened to her?'

'It would appear that someone decided to drop a large slab of masonry on top of her head.'

'Any idea why?'

'Not yet, no.'

'The newspaper said that there was an eye witness?'

'Just some spaced-out junkie, I'm afraid. Nobody we were able to take seriously.'

'And was it true that she'd been taking shelter under Martin Isaac's tomb at the time?'

Scowling over at him, Forrester said, 'I'm not sure where you're going with this, Tanner.'

'I was just wondering if a link has been established between what has happened here, and what happened to the girl.'

'No, and I don't see why there should be.'

But Tanner considered the fact that two people had been murdered in almost as many days, three if he was allowed to include Martin Isaac, was more than enough. And given how one had been killed directly outside Isaac's tomb, someone who used to be a priest, as was the man nailed to a cross behind them, he honestly thought that a five year old would have been able to see the connection.

However, being all too aware that he'd only just been brought off suspension, as tactfully as he knew how, he said, 'Just the religious aspect, sir.'

Narrowing his eyes at Tanner, with his jaw set, Forrester said, 'I sincerely hope that you're not going to attempt to drag the Church into this, *again?*'

'Not at all, sir, at least not intentionally. But we are standing in the middle of a church, with a crucified priest staring down at us.'

'And what the hell has that got to do with a girl who had her head smashed in by a lump of concrete?'

'I suppose just the fact that Martin Isaac used to be a priest as well, sir.'

'Forty-three years ago!'

Tanner didn't answer that.

'As far as I can see, there's *nothing* that connects the two!' stated Forrester, with some impatience. 'The death of the girl looks likely to be nothing more than a random act of unhinged brutality, probably involving one of her less stable ex-boyfriends, whereas this one looks as if it's been in the planning for months. That's why we're giving this one priority, and why, I may add, I've been so good as to forgive that little stunt of yours, so enabling you to take over as the SIO for this investigation. Now, please, Tanner, tell me I've done the right thing?'

'No sir, I mean - you have, sir, yes,' replied Tanner, before Forrester elected to suspend him again.

'I'm pleased to hear it. Now, I'm going to head back to the station to see how Cooper and Gilbert are getting on. No doubt Jenny here will be able to fill you in on anything else you need to know.'

With that, he spun around and marched out, past the plastic sheeting and down the central aisle.

With Forrester gone, Jenny gave Tanner a condescending glare to ask, 'What now, *sir*?' with about as much disrespectful over-emphasis on the last word as it was possible.

Clearing his throat, Johnstone said, 'I suppose I'd better leave you two to it,' and slunk away to chat with one of his overalled colleagues.

As Tanner began to get the feeling that the entire

Norfolk Constabulary had found out about the argument he'd had with Jenny, along with the relationship that had preceded it, he matched her disparaging look with one of his own. 'Well, Detective Constable Evans, Forrester is correct in saying that whoever did this had been planning it for a while. But for them to have gone to quite so much trouble, I don't think this was just a murder. To me, this looks more like a public execution. And that means someone felt a strong sense that an injustice had been done. They also wanted to make a statement, aimed directly at those they thought would see it.'

'You mean us?'

'Possibly. But as I said to Forrester, there's clearly a religious angle to this. I also suspect that what happened to Martin Isaac, and the girl at the cemetery, are linked somehow.'

'DCI Forrester didn't seem to share that opinion.'

'Well, at this stage he's probably more concerned with not upsetting the Church again.'

'I thought it was *you* who upset the Church?'

Keeping his voice low, looking deep into her eyes, he said, 'Now listen, Jenny, I've apologised numerous times for my behaviour that day. I've openly admitted to both Forrester and you that I was wrong. I wish more than anything that I'd kept my mouth shut, especially with regards to the comments I made to you. I think you're the most thoughtful, intelligent, caring woman I've met in a very long time. The last thing I wanted to do was to offend you *or* your beliefs. But as much as I'd like to, I can't turn back the clock. What's done is done. Now, if I am correct, and the three cases are linked somehow, then we may well have a psychotic serial killer on our hands. That could mean that this is just the start of it. It also means that I have work to do in order to stop whoever's been doing this. My preference would be to do that with you working alongside me, but if you don't feel that's possible, then you need to tell Forrester, and preferably sooner rather than later.'

There was a reprimand there. Jenny knew it. She'd allowed her anger at Tanner to spill out into her work, something which lacked both maturity and professionalism. There'd also been what felt like a genuine, heart-felt apology.

With a brief hesitation, she offered him a sheepish smile to say, 'You had me at psychotic serial killer.'

Tanner let out the breath he didn't know he'd been holding. 'OK, good.' Taking advantage of the positive momentum, he went on, 'I'd like to take a quick look at where he lived before we get back to the station. We need to find out everything we possibly can about him, especially about his past; how long he'd been a priest, what influenced him to become one, who he knows, who knows him, who may have been holding a grudge against him, and most importantly, if there is anything that links what's happened here with Martin Isaac, and that girl at the cemetery.'

Nodding in agreement, Jenny said, 'Before we go, there's something that Forrester neglected to mention which, if you're right about everything being connected, may be important.'

'What's that?'

'It's something that we deliberately kept out of the papers.'

'Go on.'

'It concerns Martin Isaac. When forensics were going over what was left of the mausoleum where he'd been buried, they couldn't find him.'

Confused, Tanner said, 'Sorry, I'm not with you.'

'His body,' continued Jenny. 'They couldn't find it.'

- CHAPTER NINETEEN -

'I THINK I'VE got something,' said Jenny, as Tanner stepped back into the office carrying two coffees and a couple of sandwiches.

'Something useful, I hope?' he said, dumping everything down on the desk to hand her one of the cups.

They'd been trawling through Father Richard Illingworth's life for nearly four hours but had yet to find anything of even the vaguest interest. All they'd discovered was that the priest of St Mary's church had been a veritable saint for the entirety of his adult life. He'd been Acle's priest since he was ordained. He had neither a passport nor a driver's license, and when they'd called various members of his congregation, whose letters and cards they'd found back at his house, they all seemed to have nothing but the highest praise for him.

'There's a reference to him having been involved in the trial of Martin Isaac.'

'Really?' Intrigued to learn more, he leaned over Jenny's shoulder to get a closer look at what was displayed on her monitor.

On her screen was the scanned-in image of a page from an old newspaper, the headline reading, 'Church rallies in defence of Isaac.'

'How on earth did you find that?' he asked, with genuine surprise.

'I ran a search for his name through the British Newspaper Archive. According to this, he was a key defence witness at the trial.'

'You mean, a character witness?'

'It says here that he provided an alibi.'

'What? Halfway through a trial?'

'That's what it says.'

'That must have come as a bit of a surprise, for both sides.'

'According to the article, it's because of the evidence that he and another priest gave that Isaac was acquitted.'

'Who was the other one?' questioned Tanner, doing his best to scan through what had been written.

'The other priest?'

'Uh-huh.'

'It doesn't say. Why?'

'Because if that story's true, then someone may have come to the rather belated conclusion that Martin Isaac was guilty all along, and is seeking retribution for him having been let off the hook.'

'But why now?'

'Maybe they unearthed some new evidence? Who knows? But if that is what has happened, and whoever killed Father Richard knows the name of that other priest, then he could well be next.'

At that moment they heard Forrester call for them from his office doorway.

'Perfect timing,' said Tanner, and pushed himself up to go and find out what he wanted.

Sitting back behind his desk, Forrester glanced up

at Tanner and Jenny as they entered, before returning to frown at his monitor. 'We've had interim reports from Dr Johnstone and forensics concerning our murdered priest.'

Tanner asked, 'Anything of interest?'

'He died in the early hours of the morning, sometime between 3am and 6am, from asphyxiation, as was predicted.'

'And forensics?'

'That's where things begin to go slightly awry. I think someone may have been incompetent enough to have contaminated the crime scene, or maybe they've mixed up the samples. Either that, or someone's deliberately trying to make it look like someone else did it.'

As they pulled out a couple of chairs, Tanner said, 'Well, it would hardly be the first time someone has tried to frame someone else for a murder, sir.'

Forrester looked over at them to say, 'I think it would be in this instance.'

'How do you mean?'

'The person they seem intent on trying to frame is dead.'

'Dead?'

Looking from one to the other, Forrester explained, 'Your Martin Isaac. His DNA's been found all over the crime scene.'

Understandably a little confused, Jenny said, 'I don't follow, sir.'

'I'm not sure I do either,' replied Forrester. Turning to Tanner, he asked, 'Did you hear that his body had been taken from his tomb?'

'I did, sir, yes.'

Catching Forrester's eye, Jenny asked, 'But why would someone try to make it look like a dead man killed the priest? Surely, if shifting the blame was the intention, they'd have at least chosen someone who was alive?'

Sitting forward in his chair, addressing them both, Tanner said, 'Not if you're a member of his cult, and you *wanted* people to believe that Isaac had managed to raise himself from the dead, in order to seek retribution on those who'd maligned him in life.'

'But Father Richard was one of the witnesses who helped him get off the murder charge,' Jenny said. 'He was on Isaac's side.'

Forrester looked perplexed. 'Sorry, I don't follow?'

Taking over, Tanner said, 'Just before you called us in, Jenny discovered that the priest we found over at Acle this morning was a key defence witness at Isaac's murder trial. It was thanks to his evidence, and that of another priest, that he was acquitted. Before you told us about his DNA being found at the crime scene, to be honest, sir, I was assuming that the priest was murdered by someone who believed Martin Isaac was guilty, and it was retribution for Father Richard having helped him get off the murder charge. I was going to suggest that maybe we should try to figure out who the other priest is who gave evidence at Isaac's trial, just in case he's an intended target.'

Sitting back in his chair, Forrester brought his index fingers together to rest against his mouth. As he stared off into space, deep in thought, he eventually said, 'The press will have an absolute field day if they think the deceased Martin Isaac is our prime suspect!'

Focusing his attention back on Tanner, he

continued by saying, 'I don't suppose you've found out anything else about the victim, Father Richard?'

'Only that he was a much-loved member of the community, someone who'd led a solitary life, didn't seem to have been involved in any scandals, doesn't appear to have had any enemies, and according to those who knew him, wouldn't have hurt a fly.'

'So, what you're saying,' continued Forrester, now tapping his index fingers against his chin, 'is that we've either got someone who's decided that after having thought about it for forty-three years, has finally decided to start seeking vengeance for the murder of a girl, way back in 1976; or, alternatively, that there's some psychotic member of Isaac's cult who's attempting to make everyone believe that he's risen from the grave and has set about his dark lord's work, by dropping a rock on top of some poor girl's head, before randomly popping over to Acle to drug the local vicar, drag him out of bed and nail him up to a cross?'

'Of the two, I'd have said the former does seem to be the most likely, sir.'

'Neither seems very likely, Tanner!'

'Well, no, sir. But assuming it is the first, and that someone is seeking vengeance for the death of Claire Judson, then I'd like to suggest that we find the person who was the second witness at Isaac's trial, and warn them, sir.'

'Do we know who that person is?'

'Not yet, no; but I know someone who should.'

'Who's that?'

'Alan Birch. The owner of the bookshop in Coltishall. He was part of the legal defence team at

Isaac's trial.'

'Yes, of course. OK, you'd better head off then, and make sure you let me know how you get on.'

'Yes, sir.'

As they stood to leave, Tanner said, 'May I ask how DI Cooper's getting on with the murder at the cemetery?'

Returning to stare at his monitor, Forrester said, 'I know what you're thinking, Tanner. That the two cases are linked, and that you should be leading both.'

'Well, I do think the cases are linked, sir, yes, but I wasn't pushing to take over Cooper's investigation.'

'That's good, because you're not!' he replied, glaring over at him. 'After that stunt you pulled with the Bishop of Norfolk, you're lucky to be here at all.'

'I appreciate that, sir, but that doesn't mean the cases aren't linked.'

'I'm fully aware of that, thank you. But as far as I can make out, the only way the two could be is if someone is attempting to frame Martin Isaac, who happens to be dead. I'm sorry, but that's the most ridiculous theory I've ever heard in my entire life. So until there's a more sensible link established, I want Cooper and Gilbert to stay on the girl, and the two of you to focus on who killed the priest. But before you do that, find out who that other witness was at Isaac's trial, and let him know what's been going on. If he's still local, then it may be prudent for us to post a couple of PCs outside his front door.'

'Yes, sir,' replied Tanner, turning to lead the way out.

- CHAPTER TWENTY -

AFTER A SHORT drive up the road to Coltishall, Tanner pushed open the door of Alan Birch's Victorian bookshop, setting the bell ringing as he did.

As on the previous occasion, there wasn't a single customer in sight, and the owner was nowhere to be seen.

'How on earth does he make any money?' whispered Jenny, staring around at all the books.

'I've got no idea,' said Tanner, picking one up from a nearby display table. 'But judging by how much he's asking for them, he probably wouldn't need to sell that many to get by.'

'I won't be a minute!' called a voice from the back.

Hurried footsteps rattled down the spiral staircase, and it wasn't long before Alan Birch came into view.

The moment he saw who it was, the expectant cheerful expression fell from his face to be replaced by a smile which lacked both warmth and sincerity.

'Sorry to bother you again, Mr Birch,' began Tanner, 'but we were wondering if you'd be able to help us with something?'

Taking up his position behind the counter, he replied, 'Of course. Anything for the police.'

'You mentioned when we were last here that you

were a part of the legal defence team at Martin Isaac's trial.'

'That's right.'

'Since then we've discovered that there were two key witnesses at the trial, both priests, and both of whom were able to provide Isaac with a somewhat belated alibi.'

'Father Michael Minshall,' stated Birch, in a matter-of-fact tone of voice.

Confused, Tanner said, 'I'm sorry?'

'The name of the second witness. It was Father Michael Minshall. I assume that's what you came to find out?'

'Well, yes, but how could you have possibly known that?'

'Because there was a reporter here from the Norfolk Herald about half an hour ago, asking the exact same thing.'

The two detectives exchanged intrigued glances; then Tanner turned back to ask, 'I don't suppose that person gave their name, by any chance?'

'I can do better than that,' Birch replied, picking up a business card from the counter to pass to him. 'He left me this.'

Deliberately not touching it, Tanner leaned over to read out what it said.

'Kevin Griffiths, Investigative Journalist.'

'That's the one.'

Motioning for Jenny to bag the business card as possible evidence, Tanner continued by asking, 'And he was looking to find out who the defence witnesses were at Martin Isaac's trial?'

'He was asking who the second one was, yes.'

'I assume you didn't tell him?'

'Why shouldn't I have told him?'

'You mean you did?' asked Tanner, with a look of incredulity.

'Well, yes, of course.'

'You did hear what happened to the other witness, Father Richard Illingworth, over at Acle?'

'It was on the news this morning,' acknowledged Birch. 'To think that someone could have done such a thing. Quite horrific!'

'And yet, despite knowing that one of the key witnesses at a trial where you served on the defence team was executed, as you quite rightly said, in such a horrific manner, you decided to freely tell some bloke who just happens to wander in off the street who the other witness was?'

'Yes, but I didn't think the two were connected.'

Tanner stared at him in astonishment.

In a defensive tone, Birch added, 'Besides, he was a journalist.'

'I see. And you knew that for a fact, did you?'

'Well, that's what it said on his card.'

'Do you have any idea how easy it is to get a business card printed up these days?'

Birch didn't answer, but hung his head with a particularly glum expression.

'I suppose if he'd said he was looking for blood donors, you'd have given him a pint of the stuff?'

'Of course not!'

'Then why the hell did you tell him the name of the second witness?'

With a guilty shrug, he said, 'Well, he asked me, so I told him.'

Shaking his head in disbelief, Tanner asked, 'I suppose you told him where he lived as well, and maybe suggested a few alternative ways he'd be able to break in without being overheard?'

'As I told the reporter, I've got no idea where he lives. For all I know, he could have died years ago.'

Tanner stared at him for a moment, before asking, 'Can you at least describe what this so-called reporter looked like?'

After gazing up at the ceiling, the bookshop owner eventually came back with, 'Well, he was young, probably in his late twenties, a bit taller than me, thin, scruffy, short hair.'

'What colour?'

'Light brown.'

'Anything else?'

'He had one of those goatee beard-type things.'

Turning to Jenny, Tanner said, 'Give the Norfolk Herald a call and ask them if they have a Kevin Griffiths matching that description working for them.'

Nodding, Jenny left to step outside the shop, leaving Tanner to focus his attention on the bookshop owner.

'When was the last time you saw the second witness; Marshall, wasn't it?'

'Minshall,' corrected Birch. 'Not since shortly after he'd testified.'

'You mean, back in the Seventies?'

'Not since then, no.'

'And yet you were able to remember his name?'

'Well, yes, but I've always been good with names, and Michael Minshall was an easy one to remember.'

'And you're sure you don't know where he is?'

'Not a clue, sorry.'

'What about Martin Isaac?'

'What about him?'

'Did you hear what happened, at the cemetery where he was buried?'

'I heard that his mausoleum was struck by lightning.'

'And that a girl was murdered, just beside it.'

'That too, I'm afraid.'

'How about the story of the hooded monk seen rising from his grave?'

'I have the Norfolk Herald pushed through the door just like everyone else, so yes, I did.'

'And what did you think of the story?'

'The one about the hooded monk?'

'That one, yes.'

'Well, I suppose I thought Martin would have enjoyed it.'

'And how about the other members of your cult? What do you think they'd have thought about it?'

'I'm sure they thought exactly as I did, that Martin would have seen the funny side.'

'But you must have been pleased, though?'

'*Pleased?*' Birch questioned, looking confused.

'That people are being led to believe that he's managed to cheat death?'

'Why would that please me?'

'Because it's what your cult would want people to think, isn't it?'

'If there was an element of truth to it, then maybe, but unfortunately the Norfolk Herald hardly has the best reputation for factual reporting.'

'So, where's his body then?'

'Sorry, I'm not with you.'

'What have you and your satanic chums done with his body?'

'Why would you think we've done anything?'

'Because, as I suspect you already know, it's been removed from what most people would have considered to have been his final resting place.'

As he spoke, Tanner studied the bookshop owner's face for his reaction to the news. He was expecting to see a hint of wry amusement, or maybe even a sign of knowing guilt. But what he actually saw surprised him. It was fear hiding behind his eyes: pure, unadulterated fear.

'But - that can't be,' he spluttered. 'There was nothing about it in the news.'

'It was deliberately kept out. So, anyway, Mr Birch, where's his body being hidden?'

'How the hell should I know?'

'Because you and your cult friends are making the rather sad attempt to make it look like he's risen from the grave, as he said he would in his book.'

As blood began draining from his face, Birch leaned over the counter, and in a muted tone, asked, 'Haven't you considered the other alternative?'

'What other alternative?'

'That the story is true?'

A mocking smile spread over Tanner's face. 'Surprisingly, that's not one of the lines of enquiry we're currently pursuing.'

'Don't you think it should be?'

He was sorely tempted to tell him not to be so stupid, but swallowed the words. 'For now, we've decided to focus on the human angle, which leads nicely into my next question.'

'And what's that?'

'Where were you last night and in the early hours of this morning?'

'I was here - upstairs, in my flat.'

'Can anyone vouch for that?'

'Nobody, no.'

'And your satanic cult worshipping chums?'

'I've got no idea what they were all doing.'

'So you don't meet up every night to bite the heads off chickens?'

Taking offence, Alan blurted out, 'As I've already told you, we only sacrifice animals on very special occasions.'

'Hardly special for the animal, though, is it?'

'Do you have any idea how many millions of animals are butchered every single day in order to feed the planet's population?'

'Not really no, but at least they're being killed for a reason, and as humanely as possible.'

Alan collected himself for a moment, before speaking in a calm, more deliberate fashion. 'Forgive me, detective, but assuming you didn't come all the way over here to give me a lecture about animal sacrifice, are we done?'

Tanner said nothing, but continued to stare at the man.

Behind him, Jenny came back into the shop.

She hurried over towards the counter, and in a voice easily loud enough for both Tanner and the bookshop owner to hear, said, 'I was able to speak to someone at the Norfolk Herald. They've never heard of Kevin Griffiths.'

Glaring over at the bookshop owner, Tanner said, 'Nicely done. You've successfully managed to provide a possible serial killer with his next victim.'

With a look of panicked desperation, Birch said, 'But - he said he was doing a story for them!'

'Evidently not. Anyway, you can begin to make amends by coming with us to the station to give us a statement. You'll then be able to spend a few happy hours with us putting together a facial composite of this so-called reporter.'

- CHAPTER TWENTY ONE -

ONCE ALAN BIRCH had squeezed himself into the cramped rear seat of the XJS, Tanner drove him the short distance back to Wroxham Police Station and left him with the duty sergeant.

Heading into the main office, Jenny was tasked with the job of tracking down Father Minshall, while Tanner made his way over to DCI Forrester's office to give him a quick update.

'The bookshop owner gave us the name of the second defence witness from Martin Isaac's trial, sir. It's another priest, Father Michael Minshall. Jenny's trying to track him down now.'

'Well that's something, I suppose.'

'Yes, sir, although…'

Looking up at him, Forrester asked, 'Although…what?'

'By the time we'd got there, he'd already told someone else the same thing, someone who said they were a reporter, and that they were doing a story for the Norfolk Herald.'

'And that's a problem, because?'

'When we checked with the newspaper, they'd never heard of him.'

Leaning back in his chair, Forrester thought for a

moment, before saying, 'OK, I'd have to agree that that doesn't sound so good. What name did he give?'

'Kevin Griffiths, but we're not holding out much hope that it was his real name. We've brought Birch in to give a statement, and to help us put together a facial composite of this so-called journalist.'

'Is there anything else to go on?'

'The reporter left a business card. We've bagged it, and I'm about to have it sent over to forensics.'

There was a knock at the still open door, through which Jenny's head appeared.

'Sorry to bother you, sir,' she said, looking from DCI Forrester to Tanner. 'I've got an address for Father Michael Minshall. He was in the phone book. He's the parish priest for St. Patrick's Church, over in Martham.'

Sitting forward in his chair, Forrester leaned over his desk to say, 'OK, I want you two to get straight over there. And you'd better give him a call on the way. Tell him to stay inside, and whatever he does, not to open the door to anyone, especially if that person is saying that he's a bloody reporter!'

- CHAPTER TWENTY TWO -

JENNY DIRECTED TANNER for the short drive through Horning, Ludham and Potter Heigham and onto Repps Road, heading for the village of Martham.

Shortly after the red-ringed speed limit sign of 30mph, flat green fields gave way to an eclectic mix of houses and a series of triangular village greens.

'His house should be just up here on the left,' advised Jenny, as they rounded a gradual bend in the road.

Slowing down accordingly, she guided Tanner into a short driveway at the front of a two-storey red brick house under a tired thatched roof. From there they could see St. Patrick's church looming up above a clump of trees, its angular stone tower rising into an oppressive grey sky.

Pulling up next to an old Skoda, Tanner turned off the engine to say, 'Let's hope he's in.'

'And let's hope nobody's beaten us to it,' added Jenny, as they each climbed out.

Reaching the front door, Tanner pressed the bell to listen to it chime out from inside.

Having waited in silence for a few moments, he tried again, before standing back to stare up at the windows, searching for signs of life.

Hearing footsteps on the drive behind them, they spun around to see an elderly lady approach carrying a plastic shopping bag.

'Are you looking for Father Michael?' she asked.

'We are, yes,' replied Tanner. 'Have you seen him?'

'Not since Sunday. He tends to keep himself to himself these days.'

'Any idea if he's in?'

'Well, his car's here, so he should be. But his hearing isn't as good as it used to be, a bit like mine really. Try using the knocker instead.'

Doing as she suggested, Tanner lifted the cast iron knocker to bash down twice.

When that brought no response, the old lady shrugged. 'He's probably up at the church, preparing Sunday's sermon. The path at the side will take you up to it. Do please excuse me, but I must get on,' and she turned to head back towards the road.

Seeing the path she was referring to, Tanner and Jenny thanked the lady for her time and headed over towards it. As they followed it up, they stared at the church ahead, taking in its vast square tower, and the angled ridges that ran all the way to the top.

Realising that this was the fourth church he'd visited in nearly as many days, Tanner asked, 'Just how many churches does Norfolk have, anyway?'

'Quite a few,' she replied, climbing the path behind him. 'Apparently we have the highest concentration of medieval churches anywhere in the world; at least that's what I was told at school.'

'And how many's that?'

'Around six hundred.'

'Six hundred churches? In Norfolk?'

'It used to be over a thousand!'

As they approached the ancient wooden door that had been fortified with a gridwork of wrought iron, Tanner said, 'I'm assuming they're not all still in use?'

'Most aren't, no. But this one is, and look. It appears to have a visitor!'

Tanner followed her gaze towards the main church car park, where someone had left a grubby black Audi A3.

Turning his attention back to the door, Tanner wrapped his hand around a large circular handle to first pull, and then push at it; but it didn't budge.

'I assume churches don't have lock-ins?' he asked, as he tried heaving at the handle again.

'Not that I'm aware of. They normally leave their doors open during the day.'

Giving up, he said, 'Maybe he's around the back?' and crossed to where the path curved around the side.

He was about to round the corner, when the sound of rapidly approaching footsteps forced him to stop.

The moment he did, a man came charging around the side to plough straight into him, sending him spinning away, smashing his face against the wall's sharp stone cladding.

With Jenny stumbling backwards, the man sprinted on, heading for the church carpark.

Pushing himself off the wall, with a hand held up to the side of his face, Tanner screamed out, 'OI, YOU! STOP!'

But apart from a quick glance over his shoulder, the fleeing man did nothing of the sort.

Jenny was about to set off after him, when she noticed the blood running freely down Tanner's cheek.

'Are you OK?' she asked.

Seeing the concerned look on her face, with male stubbornness he insisted, 'I'm fine,' and took a faltering step, intending to give chase; but instead of running forwards, he staggered sideways, only avoiding the wall by putting out an unsteady hand.

Realising that he was unable to stand up straight, Jenny said, 'You're very obviously *not* fine, John!'

Looking back, she saw the man had already reached the car park, and was making a beeline for the Audi they'd seen earlier.

'You're not going after him,' stated Tanner, bending to rest a supportive hand on his knee, while keeping the other pressed against a cut above his eye. 'Not without me, you're not.'

'It's too late now anyway,' she replied. 'He's already at the car, and you're hardly in a fit state to drive.'

Pulling out her notebook, she continued by saying, 'Let me take down his number plate. I'm sure someone will be able to pick him up.'

As they watched him jump into his car, start it up and spin the wheels on the gravel to leave nothing but a cloud of dust hanging in the air, Tanner said, 'You do know who that was, don't you?'

'Our mysterious journalist, yes. But I think the more intriguing question is, what was he so desperate to get away from? There's no way he could have known who we are. But first things first. We need to get you cleaned up.'

Looking at the blood on his hand, he was forced to agree. 'Fair enough, but let's have a look around the back while we're here, shall we?'

Pushing himself up from his knee, after a few

faltering steps, together they continued around the side of the church, with Jenny providing a steadying hand on Tanner's shoulder.

But the view around the corner provided nothing more than row upon row of barren slate-grey headstones, each marking the site where a body lay buried, six feet under.

It was the call of a crow that alerted Tanner to the possibility of there being something up ahead, hidden from view. With cautious steps, he continued to follow the path towards the back of the church.

As they rounded the corner at the far end, they stopped dead, neither of them able to speak.

Amidst the gravestones ahead of them stood a thin bald-headed old man. He was wearing the black suit of a priest, but there the resemblance ended. His face was torn and twisted, his head hung over to one side, and from his neck rose a sharpened wooden post, the top of which glistened with blood.

Daring to follow the post down, Tanner saw it continued into the grass, where the man's feet hung suspended, just above the ground.

Movement near the priest's head caused him to glance back up. There he saw a crow, as black as the night, perched on the figure's shoulder, jabbing its blackened beak into a bulging eye.

Jenny tore her gaze away, gagging as she did, leaving Tanner to continue to watch as the crow lifted itself into the air to clatter off towards the nearest tree, an eyeball held fast in its half-open beak.

- CHAPTER TWENTY THREE -

D CI FORRESTER ARRIVED at St. Patrick's carpark about twenty minutes later to find DC Evans and their forensic medical examiner, Dr Johnstone, huddled around DI Tanner, sitting on the back of an ambulance.

Catching Tanner's eye, Forrester called out, 'Is it the priest?'

After waiting for Forrester to come a little closer, Tanner eventually said, 'Unfortunately, we think so, yes.'

Seeing the cut above Tanner's eye, and a paramedic in the process of treating it, Forrester asked, 'Are you alright?'

'Nothing to worry about, sir,' he replied. 'DC Evans and I were shoved out the way by that so-called journalist as he did a runner, and I scraped my face against the church wall. But it did mean that we weren't able to stop him.'

With a rare smile, Forrester said, 'Don't worry. We've already picked him up. He came off the road in Potter Heigham. Drove straight into a bollard. Nearly ran over a couple of tourists in the process. I've told traffic to take him back to the station under caution for dangerous driving, for now at least.'

Observing the length and depth of the cut that was

being treated, he continued, 'Do you think you'll be up to having a chat with him a little later?'

'Definitely!' stated Tanner, wincing in pain as the paramedic dabbed at the cut which eclipsed his right eye.

'I hate to be the bearer of bad news,' said the paramedic, glancing over at Forrester, 'but he'll need to go to hospital. This cut will need stitches.'

To Tanner, Forrester said, 'Don't worry. DC Evans and I can interview him.'

Fixing one of his eyes on him, Tanner said, 'No offence, sir, but sod that!'

With Forrester raising a surprised eyebrow, Tanner turned to look up at the paramedic to ask, 'Can't you just sew it up now?'

'Well, I can, but it's going to hurt. And you'll still need to be checked over for concussion.'

'I'm fine!' Tanner stated, once again. 'And I'm certainly not prepared to spend half my life sitting around some insipid hospital, waiting for a doctor to tell me I am, so I suggest you get on with it.'

With a shrug, the paramedic said, 'Your choice,' and left Tanner holding a surgical pad up to the still bleeding cut to climb back inside the ambulance to dig out the necessary equipment.

Engaging Dr Johnstone's eye, Forrester asked, 'What sort of state is the victim in?'

'Not a good one, I'm afraid.'

'He's not been nailed to a cross again?'

'I'd say it's probably worse.'

'Worse?'

'Unfortunately, yes. It looks as if he's been impaled.'

'You mean, as in…?'

'As in - someone inserted a stake into his rectum, and drove it through the length of his body until it came out of his neck.'

Turning a visible shade of green, Jenny took herself around the side of the ambulance, leaving Forrester to ask, 'But - how is that even possible?'

'There are rope burns around his wrists and ankles. At a guess, I'd say that someone must have tied him spread-eagled to the surrounding headstones and driven the stake through him using a sledgehammer, or something similar.'

Hearing an act of depraved cruelty described in such a dispassionate medical manner left even Tanner and Forrester feeling nauseous.

Looking considerably paler than he'd done before, Forrester forced himself to ask, 'Time?'

'Ah, now, that's going to be a little harder to say.'

'And why's that?'

'It depends on how long it took him to die.'

'My God! You mean being impaled wouldn't have killed him?'

'Not immediately, no. If whoever drove the stake through him was able to miss all the vital organs, then he could have been up there for hours, if not days.'

A sombre silence fell over them as they all considered what that must have meant for the priest.

As the paramedic returned, Tanner said, 'It couldn't have been days. He'd have been found before then, surely?'

'Hopefully not, no. Given the victim's age, I think it's more likely that his heart would have given way during the process. I'll have a better idea when I get him back to the lab.'

'Would it have been possible for one man to have done it?' asked Forrester.

'The act of impalement, yes, but I'd have thought it would have been more of a challenge to insert the stake into the ground once he had been.'

'So, maybe more than one person?'

'I'm sorry, I'm a medical examiner, not a mechanical engineer.'

'No, of course,' replied Forrester, by way of an apology.

As the paramedic hovered, needle and thread at the ready, Tanner held up a hand to delay the start of having his face sewn back up in order to say, 'From what I saw, a hole had been dug large enough to slide the stake into before pushing it up, and there was a block of wood wedged in behind it. So I think it would have been possible for one person to have done it, although they'd need to be in pretty good shape.'

Brushing Tanner's hand away, the paramedic said, 'Now hold still. It will hurt a lot more if this needle goes into your eye.'

'No kidding,' he said, and winced with pain as the point was inserted into the first section of skin.

'Anyway,' said Dr Johnstone, who'd no particular interest in watching a living human being sewn up, 'if you'll excuse me, I need to see to the body being taken down.'

With Johnstone gone, doing his best to avoid having to look at the surgical process that was now in full swing, Forrester said to Tanner, 'If this so-called reporter only found out who the second priest was just before you did, it doesn't seem likely that he'd have had the time to both find him and then do what the doctor so eloquently described.'

Happy for the distraction, Tanner replied, 'I must admit that it does seem less likely, sir, although it's equally possible that he'd asked the bookshop owner for the priest's name *after* he'd impaled him, to make us think exactly that.'

'Could be,' agreed Forrester. 'Are you sure you're going to be OK to interview him?'

'Not a problem, sir,' replied Tanner, grimacing in pain, 'but I may need a couple of aspirin first.'

- CHAPTER TWENTY FOUR -

'GOOD AFTERNOON,' TANNER said, entering through the door to the first of two interview rooms at Wroxham Police Station. 'Remember us?'

Kevin Griffiths looked up from where he'd been sitting, staring at the table. Seeing the two people he'd almost knocked over earlier, he rolled his eyes in frustration. 'Don't tell me you're the police?'

'Correct! Well done! Have a shiny gold star!'

Griffiths squirmed in his seat, evidently not sharing the humour. 'Look, what have you got me in here for, anyway?'

'You mean apart from reckless driving, damaging council property and almost killing a couple of tourists?'

'Some idiot nearly drove straight into me. I had no choice but to swerve to avoid them.'

As he and Jenny each pulled out a chair opposite the supposed journalist, Tanner said, 'According to the couple you nearly ran over, you were driving well above the speed limit.'

'I was doing thirty! It was the other guy who was going too fast.'

'Is that so?'

'Yes, it is so!'

'Well, we can revisit that later. It's not what we're here to talk to you about.'

Tanner reached over to start the digital recorder, and after completing the formalities necessary to begin the interview, kicked off the proceedings by asking, 'Are you absolutely sure that you don't want a lawyer?'

'What would I need a lawyer for?'

'It's your choice, of course, but I'd strongly recommend that you have one.'

'Apart from driving into a bollard, which wasn't even my fault, I can't see what I've done wrong; so I don't see why I would.'

'As I said, it's your choice. So anyway, shall we push on?'

Without waiting for a response, Tanner continued by asking, 'What we'd really like to know is what exactly you were doing at St. Mary's church in Martham earlier today?'

'I've already made a full statement about that.'

'Yes, of course,' said Tanner, with an insincere smile. 'I actually have it here.'

Sliding a single sheet of A4 paper from the case file he'd brought in with him, he read out, '"I was looking to conduct an interview with Father Michael Minshall in connection with a story I'm currently working on."'

'That's right.'

Tanner allowed a moment of silence to hang over the room, before asking, 'Where were you last night, between the hours of nine and twelve o'clock?'

'I was at home, with my girlfriend.'

'And the night before?'

'The same. You're welcome to ask her, if you want.'

'We will, thank you. Coming back to today, I'm

curious to know why you were in such a hurry to leave the church, after you'd knocked us both over.'

'Why do you think?'

'Because you'd just finished impaling the parish priest, and you weren't too keen to be caught having done so?'

'You can't possibly think that I did - that I did - *that?*'

Tanner didn't answer. Instead, he continued to glare over at Griffiths, before looking down at his file to ask, 'I don't suppose you've ever heard of something called the Ecclesia Diaboli?'

'What's that got to do with anything?'

'Does that mean that you have?' questioned Tanner, staring back up at him.

'Yes, but so what?'

'I don't suppose you're one of its weirdo satanic worshipers?'

'Of course not!'

'Then how do you know who they are?'

'Well, I don't know, but it's probably got something to do with the fact that I'm an investigative journalist, and that their cult lies at the centre of the story I'm writing.'

'Ah yes, that's right. You work for the Norfolk Herald.'

'I submit stories to them, if that's what you mean.'

'Then may I ask why it is that they've never heard of you?'

Shifting uncomfortably in his seat, Griffiths replied simply by saying, 'Because.'

'Because...what?'

'If you must know, they haven't published anything

I've sent to them, at least not yet. But they're going to, and when they do, they've promised to put me on their official books.'

'So, between now and then, you just go around telling everyone that you're working for them, when you're not?'

'I've never told anyone I work for the Norfolk Herald.'

'That's not what the owner of Coltishall Bookshop says.'

'I told him I was doing a story for them; I never said that they employed me.'

'So they've commissioned a story from you, have they?'

'No, but they will when they see it.'

'I see. I suppose it's another fascinating factual account of how Martin Isaac has risen from the grave to become the devil incarnate, in order to set about randomly murdering aged local priests?'

'Not randomly, no.'

'But it is going to be centred around Martin Isaac?'

Griffiths gave a dismissive shrug.

'Don't you think the story would be a little more believable if he actually had a motive for killing the priests?'

'Who says he doesn't?'

'I assume you at least know who the two priests were - that they were defence witnesses at Martin Isaac's murder trial?'

'Of course.'

'And that their testimonies helped him get off the murder charge.'

'Uh-huh.'

'I see. So you're saying that your story's going to be about how he was so looking forward to spending the rest of his life in prison, and was so furious to have been denied the opportunity, that he decided to let off a bit of steam by hanging about for forty-three years before sacrificing himself to the Devil and raising himself up from the dead, in order to seek vengeance on the very two priests who'd risked perjury in order to have him acquitted?'

With a particularly smug expression, the journalist said, 'Something like that, yes.'

'Well, good luck with that!'

'That's very kind of you. Thanks! Can I go home now, to finish my story?'

Tanner said nothing, but just stared back at him, his blood pressure steadily rising. He'd reached the unfortunate conclusion that the man was telling the truth. Kevin Griffiths was far from being the kind of demented serial killer who'd be able to crucify one priest and impale another. He was exactly as he claimed, nothing more than a wannabe investigative journalist, desperate to do whatever it took to get his first story published. And that meant Tanner wasn't a single step closer to identifying who the real killer was, despite having not one, but two brutally murdered priests on his hands.

As his head began to pound behind the cut above his eye, and a wave of discontented exhaustion swept over him, he leaned forward to say, 'You may, but we have your DNA and fingerprints on file now. If we find one single shred of evidence that says you've so much as touched the bodies of either Father Richard or Father Michael, you'll be back here facing a conspiracy to murder charge, if not murder itself!'

- CHAPTER TWENTY FIVE -

'DO YOU THINK it's him?' asked Jenny, as soon as they were back out in the corridor.

'I doubt it,' said Tanner, pressing the palm of his hand gently against his forehead.

'But he looked pretty shaken up.'

'Aren't we all? I think he's what he says he is: a freelance journalist looking for his first commission, which means I'm now going to have to tell Forrester that we're back to square one again, without having a single suspect in sight.'

'What about Birch, the bookshop owner? He doesn't have much in the way of an alibi.'

'He doesn't have much of the way of a motive either. And that's the whole problem, right there. Nobody seems to have much reason to have killed anyone: the two priests, the girl at the cemetery, Martin Isaac, any of them!'

'Do you still think Isaac was murdered?'

'To be honest, I'm not sure what to think anymore. All I know is that my head hurts like hell, and I can hardly walk straight.'

Watching him with concern, Jenny said, 'I really think you need to get yourself checked over. I can drive you to the medical centre, if you like?'

'That's kind of you, Jen, thanks, but I expect it's

more down to being over-tired and the fact that I've hardly had any food all day.'

'Then how about we go out for something to eat?'

Reaching the double door that led out into the main office, Tanner stopped to look at her. 'Does that mean…?'

'That means we're both hungry, and could probably do with some food. Nothing more!'

From the fierce look she shot back into his eyes, it was crystal clear that that was all she meant. Besides, even if she was suggesting something else, Tanner knew he wasn't up to it.

'I would, Jenny, thank you, but I doubt I'd be much company at the moment. It's probably better if I just tell Forrester the bad news and head straight back to my boat.'

With a flicker of disappointment in her eyes, Jenny said, 'You're probably right. No doubt we could both do with an early night.'

- CHAPTER TWENTY SIX -

Friday, 5th July

THE BRIEFING WITH DCI Forrester had been short and uneventful, with Tanner telling him that although they'd need to check his alibi, he thought it was unlikely that Kevin Griffiths had either the motive or the mental capacity to have executed the two priests in such a horrific manner. He'd gone on to suggest that he'd probably fled the scene of the most recent murder from terror at what he'd discovered, rather than for fear of being caught having committed such an atrocity.

The meeting had ended with them pinning their hopes on forensics - that they'd be able to come up with something tangible for them, but until then, there wasn't a huge amount they could do.

Afterwards, Tanner had driven back to his boat, only stopping to pick up something to eat on the way. And having taken another couple of aspirin, he'd lain awake for an hour before eventually drifting off to sleep.

Rising early, after chasing away what was left of his headache with more pills and some coffee, Tanner was back behind his desk at just after eight o'clock, before Jenny, Forrester and the rest of the team had arrived.

Lying in bed the night before, he'd found his thoughts turning to the one event that seemed to connect everything together: the murder of the girl at the top of St. Andrew's church tower, back in 1976. It had occurred to him that if Martin Isaac was innocent, and that he hadn't simply been able to escape a life behind bars thanks to the dubious last minute alibis provided by the church defence team, then of course that meant that the person who *had* committed the crime had never been found. It was therefore a real possibility that they could have also murdered the priests; maybe even Martin Isaac as well, along with the girl at the cemetery. At least someone who was capable of raping a fifteen year old girl and throwing her from the top of a church tower would have the psychological capability for torturing to death the more recent victims.

Before asking DCI Forrester for permission to re-open the old investigation, a request that could easily be declined, especially with so much going on already, he decided to see what he could find out on his own, without anyone looking over his shoulder as he did so. That meant gaining access to the Norfolk Police Intranet when nobody else was around, hence his earlier than usual arrival.

In the end, attempting to search out the old case files proved to be a waste of time. They simply weren't there. Tanner wasn't sure why he thought they would be, given that the events had taken place a good ten years before the British police fully embraced computer technology, but he'd hoped that some of the old papers would have been scanned in.

Next to arrive was Jenny, carrying a coffee and that

morning's copy of The Norfolk Herald, which she dropped down on top of Tanner's desk with a thud, saying, 'I think you're going to want to read that!'

The headline screamed, 'Dead Monk Kills Again.'

Raising an eyebrow, with a pained look he said, 'Do I have to?'

'I know what you mean,' she replied, 'but look who's written it.'

Noting the name, Tanner said, 'Looks like our Kevin Griffiths has finally had the break he was looking for.'

'From what he writes there, he withheld information from us which might have a direct bearing on our investigation.'

Intrigued, Tanner returned to the article, but after reading the first sentence, he gave up and said, 'How about you give me the edited highlights?'

'Take a look at the next page. It says they've managed to unearth a letter dating back to just after the trial.' As he turned the page, she went on, 'It was sent to the then Cardinal, recommending that Martin Isaac be excommunicated from the Church.'

'Yes, but we already knew that he'd been excommunicated.'

'But look who the article says made the recommendation.'

'Father Michael Minshall, Father Richard Illingworth, and Alan Birch!'

'It goes on to suggest that that's why Martin Isaac resurrected himself from the dead - to take revenge on the two priests for having had him kicked out of the Church.'

'Even though it's more likely that some deranged

lunatic has been acting in Isaac's name.'

After a quick scan through of the article, Tanner continued by saying, 'Somehow we've got to find out who the other members of his cult are. I can almost guarantee that one of them is behind all this.'

'What about the bookshop owner?'

'No, I still don't think it was him.'

'I meant, shouldn't we warn him that he's been publicly named as being one of those behind Isaac's excommunication?'

'We can do better than that. Let's have him in for questioning under caution. That way he'll have no choice but to tell us who the other members of his cult are. We also need to find out if this article is true - if the letter they mention actually exists, or if it's just the figment of Kevin Griffith's overly developed imagination.'

'Maybe we should bring him in as well,' suggested Jenny. 'If it is true, he deliberately withheld information from us about the letter, and by making its contents public, he may have put Birch's life in danger.'

'OK. Birch has probably already seen the article, but in case he hasn't, give him a call and warn him that his name has been mentioned.'

'Should I ask him to come in?'

'No. We're going to need Forrester's permission to do that, and he's not even in yet. It's probably better if Birch remains where he is for now, until we can get down there and pick him up. But I'd certainly be keen to bring Griffiths back in. I'm very curious to know why he didn't think to mention the letter to us, and who the kind soul was who gave it to him.'

- CHAPTER TWENTY SEVEN -

EARING THE MAIN office door open behind them, they turned to see DCI Forester marching in, his face a mask of dark foreboding. As he passed their desks, he glowered over at them and said, 'You two, my office, now!'

The moment he'd passed, Tanner whispered over to Jenny, 'Any ideas?'

'I think that's just his way of saying good morning.'

Following him, that day's edition of the Norfolk Herald in Tanner's hand, they entered his office and waited as Forrester took his seat, switched on his computer, looked up at them and said, 'The forensics report's come in on Father Michael Minshall. I assume you've already seen it?'

'I'm sorry, sir,' Tanner said, 'I've yet to check my email.'

With a look of stern rebuke, as Forrester waited for his computer to boot up, he pulled out his phone, woke it up and handed it over to Tanner. 'Guess whose DNA they found all over the crime scene?'

As Tanner took the phone, Forrester answered the question himself.

'Martin bloody Isaac!'

With Tanner scrolling through the email, Forrester continued by saying, 'I've told you before, Tanner, I can't have some dead guy as our prime suspect.'

'No, sir,' Tanner replied, still trying to read through the report.

'What's worse,' continued the DCI, with his elbows planted firmly on his desk, 'is that he's our *only* bloody suspect! If this gets out, we'll be the laughing stock of the entire police force. Now please, tell me you've got something more to go on, other than that the murderer is some old dead guy?'

Returning his phone, Tanner said, 'There has been a development, sir.'

'Well? Go on!'

Tanner handed him the copy of the Norfolk Herald. 'Jenny brought this in this morning.'

Glancing down at the headline, Forrester said, 'Not this satanic crap again?'

'It is, sir, yes, but what's of interest is who wrote the article, and what he says that he's found.'

'And what's that?'

'Kevin Griffiths claims to have unearthed a letter that was written to the Cardinal, shortly after Martin Isaac's murder trial, recommending Isaac be excommunicated from the Church, despite having been found not guilty.'

'Yes, and...? We already knew that.'

'We did, sir, yes; but it's who made the recommendation that's of particular interest.'

When Forrester reached the relevant part, he looked up. 'Have you warned Birch yet?'

'We were about to when you called us in,' said Tanner, before nodding at Jenny. 'You'd better do that now.'

She excused herself and left the room, leaving

Tanner standing in silence, whilst Forrester finished skimming through the article.

When it looked as if he was coming to the end, Tanner said, 'I'd like permission to bring Alan Birch in for questioning, sir.'

'For what purpose?'

'He needs to tell us who the other members of his cult are. The last time I asked him, he refused, but I'm confident that it's one of them who thinks Martin Isaac was guilty and is out for revenge, whilst at the same time attempting to make it look as if the murderer is Isaac himself, risen from the grave.'

After a momentary pause, Forrester eventually said, 'OK, you'd better bring him in.'

'I'd also like to bring Kevin Griffiths in as well, sir. We need to know if this letter actually exists, and more importantly, who gave it to him.'

'Can't you just ask him?'

'I doubt he'll be too keen to tell us.'

'You won't know until you try.'

'There's also the fact that he withheld information from us, sir, when we were interviewing him yesterday.'

'Did you ask him about the letter during the interview?'

'Well, no sir, but only because we didn't know about it.'

'Then you can't say that he withheld information from you; at least that's what a court would say. You can't withhold something that you haven't been asked for.'

'Fair enough, but by publishing the letter's contents, he may have placed Alan Birch's life in danger.'

'Possibly, but isn't that what journalists do? Besides, if the priests were murdered for their involvement in having had Isaac excommunicated, whoever did it must have known about them a long time before this article was published. And if they knew about the priests, then they'd no doubt know about Alan Birch as well. It could be that the murderer was the one who gave the letter to Griffiths. So, for now, I suggest you call him up and ask him who gave it to him. If he says he's not prepared to reveal his source, then feel free to bring him in under caution.'

'Yes, sir.'

Turning to leave, he was about to step out when he turned back to face his DCI.

'Was there something else?' questioned Forrester.

'There is, sir, yes. I'd like permission to re-open the investigation into the death of Claire Judson.'

'Claire who?'

'The girl Martin Isaac was accused of murdering, sir, back in 1976.'

'Please tell me you're not being serious?'

'I am, sir, yes.'

'Aren't the murders of the two priests enough for you?'

'It's just that it seems to be what links everything together, sir, especially if Isaac was innocent, as the court found, and the priests wanted him kicked out of the Church because his character had been tarnished by the accusations made against him, not because he was guilty.'

'Sorry, I'm not with you.'

'If he was innocent, that means Claire Judson's murderer was never found. It could be him who's doing all this.'

'But for what reason?'

'Maybe someone told him that Isaac had found out who'd raped and murdered the girl. Maybe the priests had found out as well. He threw her from the top of the church tower, sir. If he was capable of such an attack upon a fifteen year old schoolgirl, then he'd certainly fit the psychological profile of someone who could commit murder with the sort of extreme sadism that we've been witness to.'

'That's as may be, but do you have any idea how difficult it would be to investigate a case that's over forty years old?'

'It will be challenging, of course, sir, but if it leads us to who murdered the priests...'

'Even if you were able to somehow unearth new evidence, I still think it's more likely that whoever killed the priests did so because they believed Martin Isaac was guilty, and they'd helped him escape the murder charge. But let's just say that your other theory is correct - that Isaac was innocent, and that the person responsible is still at large. If Isaac had somehow found out who killed her, and had for some obscure reason gone and told the priests as well, why would that person perform what are nothing less than public executions? Surely he'd have just bashed them on the head?'

'Maybe he did so to make it look like it was someone who was seeking revenge for allowing Isaac to skip the murder charge?'

'I'm sorry, Tanner, but you're way over-thinking this. I suggest you stick with the matter at hand, and leave the forty year old murder case well alone.'

'But sir…!'

'No! You need to focus on the here and now, not something that happened back in the Seventies. However, if it makes you feel any better, I do agree with you on one thing.'

'What's that?'

'That there is enough of a link between the girl who was killed at the cemetery, and the murders of the two priests. I'm therefore making you the SIO for both cases, and will have DI Cooper and DS Gilbert report to you. Happy?'

'Well, it's a start, I suppose.'

'I'll take that as a yes. I'll tell them to brief you as to where they are with that one. Meanwhile, call Kevin Griffiths. Ask him about that letter, and find out who gave it to him. If you have to bring him in under caution, so be it. If the story's true, then we need Alan Birch to give us the list of names of all known cult members, along with their contact details.'

As Tanner turned to leave, Forrester added, 'And I assume you're OK to work the weekend?'

Realising that it was Friday already, Tanner nodded. 'Yes, of course, sir. No problem.'

- CHAPTER TWENTY EIGHT -

TANNER EMERGED FROM the meeting feeling both frustrated and depressed. He'd never much liked being told what to do, which was one of the reasons why joining the police had probably been a poor career choice for him. He'd also never been much of a fan for having to work through the weekends, something which was expected of everyone; particularly when they were in the middle of a murder investigation.

Reminding himself that it wasn't entirely his fault that he had joined the police, and that a large part of the reason had been due to the expectations of his late father, he ambled over to his desk.

'How'd it go?' asked Jenny, noting the resigned look on his face.

'Well, at least he's had the good sense to bring the murder of the girl at the cemetery under the same investigation.'

'With you as the Senior Investigating Officer?'

'Uh-huh.'

'That's good, isn't it?'

'It is, but I'd hoped he'd allow us to get to what I can't help think lies at the heart of all of this.'

'What's that?'

'The murder of Claire Judson.'

'You mean, you asked him for permission to re-open a forty-three year old murder investigation, and he said no?'

Her exaggerated tone of surprise told him that she was being sarcastic.

'You're forgetting that if Martin Isaac was innocent, then the case of her murder remains unsolved.'

'But if he was guilty, and managed to get off simply because of a couple of dubious alibis, then the case died with him.'

'Which still leaves us with a serial killer living in the here and now, someone who must have had some sort of a connection with Claire Judson in order to be seeking vengeance on those who helped Isaac get off.'

'Not unless it's some deranged member of his cult, attempting to make it look like he's risen from the dead.'

At that reminder, Tanner asked, 'Were you able to get hold of Alan Birch?'

'I did, yes. I told him to sit tight, and suggested that it may be in his interest to close his shop for the time being.'

'How'd he sound?'

'I'd say somewhere between slightly concerned and completely terrified. But as he'd already read the article, he'd taken the precaution of closing his shop.'

'OK, let me give our favourite freelance journalist a quick call. Hopefully he'll be willing to show us a copy of that letter he says he has, and to tell us how he came by it. Then we'd better bring Birch in for questioning. Somehow, I don't think he's going to mind being held under lock and key, in the current circumstances. After that, I suggest we have a quick catch up with Cooper, to see how he's been getting on with that murdered cemetery girl.'

- CHAPTER TWENTY NINE -

'FANCY SOMETHING TO eat?' asked Tanner, holding the door for Jenny as they left Wroxham Police Station at the end of the day.

Having been forced to turn down her invitation the evening before, he knew she was unlikely to ask him again, leaving it for him to make what he hoped would be the first move in re-establishing their former relationship.

'As long as you're buying,' she replied, but without her normal mischievous smile.

'No problem,' said Tanner, noting that her response was far from enthusiastic. He was, however, relieved that she'd accepted. It would have been easy enough for her to have said no.

'Where'd you like to go?' he asked, as they came to a standstill in the middle of the car park, his car on one side, hers on the other.

'I don't mind,' she replied, suppressing a yawn, 'but I'd prefer if it was somewhere close to my flat. I don't want to be up late. Not when we have to work the weekend.'

Although the day had been beneficial, it had also been tediously long, leaving them both feeling tired and drained.

As expected, Alan Birch had been more than happy to accompany them for questioning. When he'd been cautioned, and had been asked if he wanted a lawyer, he'd become surprisingly communicative, providing them with a list of everyone he knew who was an active member of the Ecclesia Diaboli. It wasn't an exhaustive list, as he said he didn't know all the members by name, but it provided more than enough for them to be getting on with.

Kevin Griffiths had also been willing to oblige them with the letter they'd requested, which he'd brought into the station by hand. At first he'd been reluctant to let them know how he'd come by it, but when Tanner had pressed him on the matter, he'd told them that it had been sent to his home address via an anonymous source. That person had made contact with him through a website called TheJournalistsDirectory.com, where he'd registered himself as being a specialist feature writer within the field of Religion. He'd checked the boxes for every specialist area, from Politics to Pornography, but the tip-off had come through the Religion thread.

After making a note of the envelope's Norwich postmark, Jenny had sent both it and the letter off to forensics, to see if they could extract anything useful from it.

At the end of the day, they finally found time to sit down with Cooper and Gilbert, to see how they'd progressed with the girl murdered at the graveyard, which hadn't been far, leaving Tanner wondering what they'd been doing for the past three days.

With a plan for the evening agreed, they stopped by Jenny's flat to drop off her car, allowing her to have a couple of drinks when they were out. As she climbed into the XJS, Tanner said, 'I've managed to book a table at the Swan Inn, but it's not for another forty-five minutes.'

'We could sit by the river for a while.'

'I was actually wondering if we could stop by your old church again.'

Jenny eyed him suspiciously. 'Are you thinking about Claire Judson, by any chance?'

'I must admit that I am.'

'I do hope you're not considering re-opening her murder investigation, when Forrester's told you not to, especially as you're only just back off suspension.'

'I was just wondering if the priest we met there would be able to tell us any more about the man he'd seen visiting her grave, and maybe he'd be prepared to help us put together a facial composite.'

'Funny, but that sounds very much like re-opening the investigation to me.'

'Yes, well, it may sound like it, but it isn't, at least not officially.'

'You weren't *officially* interrogating the Bishop of Norfolk either, but you still managed to get yourself suspended for it.'

'Which is why I thought you'd be able to ask the priest on my behalf?'

'Are you trying to get *me* suspended?' she asked, raising her eyebrows at him.

'Don't worry. Forrester only said that *I* couldn't re-open the investigation. He didn't say anything about you.'

'Er…I'm fairly sure Forrester isn't going to see it that way, especially as I report to you.'

'Then I'd say that it was my fault.'

'And you'd be suspended again.'

'Possibly, but I doubt it. For a start, the priest at St. Andrew's is hardly a bishop, and secondly, with three murders on his hands, Forrester's short staffed as it is.'

'All right,' agreed Jenny, as she clipped on her seatbelt, 'but if we end up being late for our table, I'm not going to be happy. I'm hungry enough as it is.'

- CHAPTER THIRTY -

TANNER PULLED HIS car into the gravel layby outside the black wooden arch which marked the entrance to St. Andrew's church.

Stepping out, seeing the long shadows cast by the evening sun, Jenny said, 'I doubt he'll be in. Not this late.'

As he hurried around the car's long sweeping bonnet, Tanner asked, 'What was his name again?'

'Father Thomas.'

'If he's not here, do you know where his house is?'

'Next door, if I remember correctly.'

'OK, well, let's just have a quick look to see if he's around. We can always come back another time.'

'Or, alternatively, we could give it a miss altogether,' Jenny replied, still thinking he was making a mistake about them being there at all.

As they strode up towards the church entrance, seeing a thick shadow dividing the two doors, Tanner said, 'It's still open.'

Under her breath, Jenny muttered, 'Unlike the restaurant,' whilst making a point of checking her watch.

'It's only eight o'clock. We've got bags of time.'

As his words came out, so did Father Thomas, a large set of keys held jangling in his hand.

Seeing the two detectives suddenly loom up in front of him, the priest jumped with a start.

'Goodness!' he yelped, clutching at his chest. 'You scared the life out of me!'

'Sorry, Father,' Tanner said. 'We were just hoping to catch you before you left for the day.'

Smiling at them both, Father Thomas said, 'You know, I was just thinking about the two of you.'

'You were?' asked Tanner, desperately hoping that he wasn't going to say anything about them getting married again, especially as they'd barely got back together.

'It may come as a surprise to you,' the priest said, 'but I am allowed to think about more than just our Lord God on high all day.'

'Yes, of course.'

'I'm just ribbing you, Inspector,' said the priest, seeing the embarrassed look on Tanner's face. 'Naturally, I *do* spend all day thinking about God.'

Unable to see the slightest hint of amusement in the priest's face, Tanner was unsure whether he was joking or not, but remembering the humour he'd displayed the last time they'd met, he was about to come back with, 'At least, that's what you tell the Cardinal!' when thankfully fortune intervened, and the priest turned to Jenny to say, 'I found something at home that I thought might be of interest to you. I was going to drive it over to Wroxham Police Station later on this evening, but as you're here… Hold on, let me just pop back inside and get it.'

As he disappeared, Tanner turned to raise an eyebrow at Jenny.

'It's probably a bible,' she whispered over to him.

'One each, do you think?'

'Maybe a grown-up one for me, and a children's version for you.'

'As long as it has pictures, I'll be happy.'

'No pictures, I'm afraid,' said the priest, re-appearing through the gap in the door.

With both Tanner and Jenny hoping to god that he'd not overheard their entire conversation, Father Thomas handed Jenny a hefty looking A3 sized book.

'It belonged to my predecessor, Father Jeffrey,' he explained. 'When he passed away, with no family, all his belongings remained with the parish. I found this in amongst his personal effects a few years back. At the time, I can't say I gave it much thought, but what you were asking about when you were last here reminded me of it. I thought it might help with your enquiries.'

As Jenny opened it to the first page, she said, 'It's a scrapbook!'

'That's right. When he took over from Martin Isaac, he must have developed an interest into what had happened to that girl who was so sadly killed here. Judging by the contents, he clearly spent some considerable time cutting out all the relevant articles.'

Motioning for Tanner to take a look, Jenny said, 'This is really useful.'

'I think he may have even been trying to figure out who really murdered the girl.'

'What makes you say that?' asked Jenny, as she began turning over the many pages, each one thick with yellowing newspaper cuttings.

'He seems to have underlined some of the names, and has made a few notes in the margins. And one of the articles has a big circle around it, with a large note to the side.'

'I think I've found it,' said Jenny, staring down at the highlighted article. 'It's a bit of a scrawl, but I think it says, *Who was Claire going to meet?*'

'That's the one. According to one of the articles, her friends said that she'd gone to the top of the tower to meet a boy, one who was a lot older than her. But none of them knew who he was, and despite the police making a public appeal for the person to come forward, he never did.'

'I can't say I'm surprised,' said Tanner. 'If she *was* up there to meet a man, even if he had nothing to do with what happened to her, it's unlikely he'd have stepped forward, not when she was only fifteen.'

'There's more,' said the priest. 'Take a look at the last page.'

There they found another cutting, but judging by the crisp white colour of the paper, it had been glued in far more recently.

'It doesn't seem to have anything to do with Martin Isaac, or the murder trial,' noted Jenny, as she began speedreading her way through it.

'Which is interesting, don't you think?'

Struggling to read the text from where he was, Tanner eventually asked, 'What's it about?'

'Just some local property developer, trying to get permission to knock down a pub in order to build a block of flats.'

'And that's him, is it?' asked Tanner, squinting at the picture of a man standing in front of a pub, his hands held aloft as if he was trying to placate the group of placard-carrying protestors before him.

'Gary Mitchell, yes.'

'After you'd been here,' Father Thomas explained, 'asking about Claire Judson, and who it was who'd been tending to her grave, it dawned on me where I'd seen him before.'

'You mean, that's him?' questioned Jenny, pointing down at the picture. 'Gary Mitchell?'

'An older version, but I believe it is, yes. My predecessor must have somehow worked out who he was, or possibly was told in the sanctity of confession, and as he would have been unable to tell anyone, he must have pasted the article into the scrapbook as a sort of a clue.'

Catching his eye, Tanner asked, 'Have you shown this to anyone else?'

'Not a soul, no.'

'And when was the last time you saw him - the man tending to her grave?'

'It was just before your previous visit.'

'Not since then?'

'Not that I've seen, no, but I suppose he may have done. I've certainly seen him often enough. He probably comes about once a week, and he's been doing that since I first took over the parish.'

Carefully closing the book, Jenny asked, 'May we borrow this?'

'Of course,' replied the priest. 'Although I'd like to have it back at some stage.'

'I'm sure that won't be a problem. We only need to scan the newspaper articles, then I can return it to you.'

'That would be appreciated.'

With a grateful smile, and the book in both hands,

Jenny said, 'Thank you again, Father.'

'No problem at all.'

As they turned to leave, as if remembering something, the priest called after them, 'You know, I've seen the newspapers, about what's happened to Father Richard and Father Michael.'

Turning back to face him, Tanner said, 'It's all most unfortunate, I know.'

'It's just that...' began the priest, colouring a little. 'I was thinking...I mean, obviously the stories about monks rising from the grave are stuff and nonsense, but I was wondering if - well - if you thought that whoever's responsible...' He stopped and stared down at the scrapbook. 'Do you think he's deliberately targeting parish priests?'

It was evident that the man was concerned for his life, and with the possibility that he might have just identified the murderer, Tanner realised that he could have good reason to be.

Taking a step towards him, Tanner asked in a low voice, 'Are you sure you've not shown that book to anyone else?'

'Well, no, but...'

'But what?'

'I think someone may have been inside my house last night.'

'May have?'

'Well, I'm fairly sure someone was.'

'Did you report it?'

'I couldn't see any reason to. Nothing was taken, and besides, it was my fault. I forgot to lock the patio doors when I went to bed.'

'So, if nothing was taken, what made you think

someone had been inside?'

'Because I left the scrapbook on the kitchen table before I turned in for the night, as a reminder for me to bring it in for you today.'

'And it wasn't there when you woke up?'

'I found it at the end of my bed, open to the last page.'

A cold silence fell over them, before Tanner eventually said, 'Are you sure you didn't leave it there when you were going to bed?'

'No. I definitely left it on the kitchen table. I'd even placed another book on top of it, to hide it from view.'

Thumbing through it, Jenny said, 'But if someone broke into your house, looking for this, then why didn't they just take it, instead of leaving it on the end of your bed?'

'I've no idea.'

'I do,' said Tanner. 'At least, I think I do.'

Looking first at Jenny, then back at the priest, he continued by saying, 'Father, I think it may be sensible if we were to put you up in a safe house, at least until this matter is resolved.'

'You think he left it there as a warning, don't you?'

That was exactly what he was thinking, but as he'd no wish to alarm the priest any more than was necessary, he said, 'I think Jenny might be right. The logical thing to have done would have been to have taken it.'

Letting out a sigh of fateful acceptance, Father Thomas said, 'Well, anyway, it's too late. I've given it to you now.'

'We can put you up in a hotel,' Tanner said.

'Somewhere secure. It won't be a problem.'

The priest took a moment to take in his surroundings, drawing the summer evening's cool fresh country air deep into his lungs. As he did, he muttered softly to himself, 'I sought the Lord, and he answered me; he delivered me from all my fears.'

Turning back to see the questioning looks in the faces of the two detectives, by way of explanation, he said, 'It's from the 34th Psalm.'

Returning his gaze to the horizon, he added, 'I appreciate the offer, but this is my home. I can't spend my days hiding away in some hotel room, cowering in fear. Besides, I have to believe that God will protect me, as he has always done.'

Unable to stop himself, Tanner said, 'You mean, in the same way he protected Father Richard and Father Michael?'

The priest smiled. 'When you know perfect Love, you'll neither fear this life, nor the next.'

'Sorry, Father, I didn't mean anything by that. I'm just concerned for your safety.'

'Well, there's no need to be. I have all the protection I could ever ask for.'

'Can you at least allow us to post a police car outside your house, just to keep an eye out for you?'

Father Thomas thought about that for a moment. 'I suppose that would be sensible. Thank you.'

'And let me give you one of my cards,' Tanner added, pulling out his wallet and sliding one out.

Handing it over to him, he said, 'If you change your mind about staying here, or if you see Gary Mitchell again, please call me on my mobile.'

Taking the card, the priest gave him a warm smile.

'Thank you, Inspector. And if I see him again, I promise I'll call.'

- CHAPTER THIRTY ONE -

AN OPPRESSIVE SILENCE followed as they made their way back to the car.

He knew from Jenny's pursed lips and flushed cheeks that she was upset with him.

He also had a good idea as to why.

Desperate to avoid any further animosity developing between them, he blurted out, 'I'm sorry about what I said to Father Thomas earlier; about how God hadn't been much help to the other priests.'

'It's fine,' she responded, but in a way that made it clear that it wasn't.

'I only said it because I'm worried about him, and I was frustrated that he turned down the offer of the safe house.'

Stopping to glare up at him, Jenny said, 'Why do I get the feeling that you've got something against Catholicism?'

'I haven't,' he replied. 'I just wasn't brought up believing in it, that's all. To be honest, I'm not sure I was brought up to believe in much of anything. My father wasn't exactly the spiritual type. Spending half his life working for the Met probably didn't help.'

'How about your mother? What did she do?'

'Science teacher, I'm afraid.'

'Well, fair enough, I suppose, but it wouldn't do

you any harm to start showing a little more respect for the beliefs of others.'

'I know. Sorry.'

After holding his gaze for another moment, Jenny turned away to resume her march towards the car, forcing Tanner to hurry after her.

As he caught up, he said, 'I must admit that I'd have been far happier if he'd taken us up on our offer.'

'I know what you mean,' Jenny conceded. 'If what he'd described had happened to me, that someone crept into my house in the middle of the night to leave a book open at the end of my bed, I'd have been on the phone to the police, ambulance, fire service, and anyone else I had a number for. I'd have probably even called the AA, just in case one of their vans was nearby.'

Relieved to hear her sounding more like her normal self, Tanner said, 'I'm not sure the Automobile Association would have been much help.'

'Well, they call themselves the fourth emergency service; and waking up to find that some complete stranger had been staring at me while I slept would have definitely counted as an emergency to me.'

Stopping beside the car, she asked, 'So, what's next?'

'I think we're going to have to postpone our dinner engagement. I need to get that scrapbook back to the station to sign it in as evidence, and to let Forrester know about it. I also have to arrange for a couple of PCs to keep an eye on Father Thomas's house.'

'So you think Gary Mitchell is our man?'

'Well, if he's been visiting Clare Judson's grave every week for the last few years, like Father Thomas says he has, then the chances are that he must have been very much in love with her. I can only assume that somehow he must have found out about that letter sent to the Cardinal, asking for Martin Isaac to be excommunicated. He must have thought like we did; that it meant Isaac had been guilty after all, and that the Church had stepped in to cover it up.'

'So he killed Martin Isaac for what he'd done to Claire Judson, and the two priests because they helped him to be acquitted?'

'It would seem like the most plausible explanation.'

'OK, but why would he go to all the trouble of taking Isaac's body from his tomb and planting his DNA on the priests, all to make it look like he'd raised himself from the dead in order to execute them?'

'Probably in an effort to divert suspicion.'

'And the girl, at the cemetery?'

'I suspect she simply found herself in the wrong place at the wrong time. She probably saw his face. Anyway, whatever his motivation, we have to find him as a matter of urgency.'

As they heaved open the Jag's heavy doors, Jenny said, 'I think I'd better come back to the station with you.'

Tanner checked his watch. It was gone half eight, and they still hadn't eaten.

'Tell you what,' he began. 'How about we grab something to eat on the way?'

'You're still paying, I assume?'

'Of course.'

'Well, OK, but don't think that means you've wriggled your way out of taking me to an actual restaurant.'

- CHAPTER THIRTY TWO -

IT WASN'T UNTIL gone twelve o'clock on Friday night that Tanner was finally able to roll himself into his cramped but cosy cabin bed; but despite being both mentally and physically exhausted, he had a real struggle getting off to sleep.

After Father Thomas had given them the scrapbook, they'd sped back to the station, stopping only at a garage to pick up some sandwiches. Once there, Jenny had signed the book into the secure evidence room, leaving Tanner to update DCI Forrester with the new information they'd uncovered. At the same time he'd asked permission to have a squad car parked outside Father Thomas's house, just until they were able to locate the person Tanner now believed to be their prime suspect, the man Claire Judson had been planning on meeting that fateful day at the top of St. Andrew's church: Gary Mitchell.

Joining Jenny back in the main office, with the squad car arranged, it had soon become clear that tracking Mitchell down wasn't going to be as straightforward as they'd hoped. There were over twenty listed as living in the Norfolk area, and that was working on the assumption that he still lived there, and wasn't driving in from somewhere else to tend to his old girlfriend's grave. Once they'd removed those who were either too old or too young, their only means of identifying the right one was physically, by comparing each with the black and white photograph that had been published in the Norfolk Herald in 2006.

Reaching the reluctant conclusion that it was going to take longer than a few hours, Tanner had briefed a couple more constables on night shift to keep sifting through the names, and to call him if they had a result. After checking that Alan Birch was still happy to remain in a holding cell, he'd decided to call it a night.

Having dropped Jenny off at her flat where she'd left her car earlier that evening, before driving back to his boat, he'd made a slight detour via Father Thomas's house. He'd wanted to check that the car he'd requested had positioned itself where he'd asked, directly outside. Whilst there, he'd had a chat with the two constables, making sure they were both fully awake and understood their orders; to keep a close eye on the house at all times, and to make regular but discreet patrols of the property's boundaries.

Only when he himself had picked his way around the exterior, noting the most likely points of entry and relaying that information back to the PCs, did he allow himself to finally head for home. However, despite having done all that, it didn't stop him from worrying. If Gary Mitchell was someone who was psychologically imbalanced enough to nail one priest up to a cross and impale another, he couldn't help but worry what he might do to Father Thomas, were he to find out that he'd told the police what he'd learned, despite the warning that had been left for him.

At some stage he must have fallen asleep, because the alarm on his phone woke him from some unremembered dream.

As it was Saturday, he allowed himself the luxury of lying in bed for an extra ten minutes. Eventually, with his eyes half-closed, he dragged himself out of bed to begin his normal routine of getting ready for work.

He was showered, dressed and sitting down to enjoy his freshly made filtered coffee when his phone rang.

Pleased to see that it was Jenny calling, he answered, 'Hi Jen, what's up?' before taking a gulp from his cup.

'What the hell have you done?' came Jenny's voice, almost shouting at him down the phone.

Nearly choking, Tanner sat up straight to say, 'I'm sorry, I'm not with you?'

'You've been speaking to that reporter again, haven't you?'

'Which reporter?'

'You know damned well which reporter. Kevin Griffiths!'

'Not since we interviewed him, I haven't.'

'Then how come the Norfolk Herald has just published an article, written by him, in which he's quoted *you* as saying we've found out that Gary Mitchell was the man Claire Judson had been having an affair with, and who she was waiting for at the top of St. Andrew's church the day she was murdered? They've even published that photograph we have of him!'

'But why would I have told him that?'

'I presume to force Mitchell out into the open, or

to at least see if anyone is able to recognise him.'

'There are ways and means, Jenny, and that's not one of them, at least not one I'd ever use.'

'Well, somebody has. It's the front page story!'

'Does it mention anything about Father Thomas?'

After a moment's pause, Jenny said, 'Not that I can see, no.'

'Well, that's something.'

'So, if it wasn't you, then who was it?'

'Whoever broke into Father Thomas's house?'

'But - wasn't that Gary Mitchell?'

'I think we'd assumed it was, but we must have thought wrong. It could have been someone who'd already found out that Mitchell was Claire Judson's boyfriend, and thought they'd make some money on the side by leaking the story to the press. Either way, I'd better head over to make sure Father Thomas is OK.'

'Shall I meet you there? It's on my way.'

'Thanks Jen, but no. I need you back at the station. We *have* to find Gary Mitchell, especially now that he's been publicly named and shamed as being the person who was not only having sexual relations with an underage girl, but who may also have been responsible for killing the two priests.'

'Shall I tell Forrester where you're going?'

'If you could. You'd better show him that article as well, but do me a favour. Tell him it wasn't me who leaked the story. Also, can you let everyone know that I intend to hold a station-wide briefing when I get back? I'm sure Forrester will agree that we're going to need all hands on deck from this point forward.'

'OK. Will do.'

With the conversation over, Tanner downed his coffee, and was about to get up to leave when his phone rang again.

Not recognising the number, he answered it by saying, 'Tanner speaking.'

Over the line came the deep muffled whisper of a man's voice.

'Detective Tanner, it's Father Thomas.'

'Father! I was just on my way to see you. Are you all right?'

'I am, yes, but I'm, well… I just wanted to let you know that I think…'

'You think…what?' prompted Tanner.

'I think someone followed me up to the church when I left my house.'

'Oh, OK. I shouldn't worry about them. We posted a couple of police constables outside last night. I assume you saw their squad car?'

'I did, yes, but it's not them. This person's not wearing a uniform. I think - well, I think it might be Gary Mitchell.'

Tanner's heart thumped hard in his chest. 'Where are you?'

'I'm inside the church.'

'Have you locked the door?'

'I have, yes.'

'OK, now I want you to find somewhere to hide, and then whatever you do, don't move! I'll get a message through to the PCs outside your house to come up and find you, and I'll be there myself in ten minutes.'

Ending the call, Tanner grabbed his keys and wallet, launched himself from his boat, and sprinted over to his car.

- CHAPTER THIRTY THREE -

SCREECHING TO A halt behind the squad car still parked outside where Father Thomas lived, Tanner leapt out, slammed the door shut and began sprinting up towards the church.

Passing the house, something caught his eye.

Turning, he saw one of the uniformed constables come running out from around the back.

'Did you find Father Thomas?' asked Tanner, stopping where he was.

'No, sir,' came the PC's breathless reply. 'He's not in the house.'

'How about the church?'

'We've not looked up there yet.'

'What do you mean? I told Control he was hiding inside the church, not in his bloody house!'

'Sorry, sir. Nobody said anything about the church.'

'For fuck's sake!' spat Tanner, and raced on, the police constable at his heels.

Stumbling into the church alcove, Tanner noticed that one of the doors had been left open.

'Shit!' he cursed, under his breath.

As the police constable joined him, Tanner pressed a finger to his mouth, pointing down at the open door.

'Where's your colleague?' he whispered.

Leaning on his knees, the young PC glanced behind

him to say, 'He must still be searching the house.'

'That's just great,' replied Tanner, thick with sarcasm.

After thinking for a moment, he said, 'OK, we're going to have to go in. Stay close behind me, and keep your eyes peeled. Understood?'

The young PC nodded back, gulping as he did.

Returning his attention to the door, Tanner took hold of the black wrought iron handle and began easing it open, just enough to be able to peer inside.

As his eyes adjusted to the church's cool dark interior, movement caught his attention from the far end. There, hanging from the bottom of the ornately carved wooden pulpit, he saw a shadow, twisting and flapping, like a black bin liner caught in the wind.

It took him no more than a second to work out what it was: Father Thomas, hanging by the neck, eyes bulging, feet kicking, hands clawing at a noose pulling tight against his throat.

Grabbing the constable's arm, Tanner dragged him forward, hurtling down between the rows of pews.

'You take his feet! I'll untie him!'

As Tanner launched himself up the pulpit steps, the young constable took hold of the priest's legs to try to lift his body, desperate to ease the weight from the rope encircling his neck.

Reaching the railing where the rope had been tied, Tanner leaned over and grabbed hold of the priest's jacket to heave his body up.

With the noose slack, using his free hand he began tugging at the knot.

Within a matter of seconds it was untied.

Together, they lowered Father Thomas to the floor,

gasping and sucking at the air.

By the time Tanner had run down the steps, the priest was on his knees, rocking back and forth, his hands clawing at his dog collar, desperate to pull it away from his neck.

Turning to the young constable, Tanner said, 'Call an ambulance, then backup!' He then fell to his knees beside the priest to ask, 'Are you OK?'

But the priest could say nothing but nod his head in response.

'Did you see who did this to you?'

Swallowing hard, through purple lips he eventually managed to rasp out, 'Mitchell. It was Gary Mitchell. He had a black hood on, but it was him.'

Glancing up to see the second of the two police constables come running into the church, Tanner called out, 'Did you see anyone going out?'

'Nobody! No!'

'OK, have a look around for someone dressed up as a monk. Maybe try down by the car park. But if you see him, whatever you do, *don't* approach him! Not on your own. Is that clear?'

Nodding, the young man left the way he'd come in, just as the other constable returned to report that an ambulance was on its way.

'Good. Now, go find your friend. The guy who did this couldn't have made it far.'

- CHAPTER THIRTY FOUR -

TANNER WAITED IN prayerful silence with Father Thomas until the paramedics arrived. After offering him reassurance that he was going to be OK, he left him in their capable hands to step outside. There he glanced around, trying to work out what had happened to the two constables.

Eventually spying them down by the roadside, he called out, 'Anything?'

'Nothing, sir, no,' replied the nearest.

'Seriously?' asked Tanner, as he headed down to join them.

'We looked all over, sir. We even checked inside his house again.'

'How about the car park? Did you see anyone driving off?'

'There weren't any cars there, sir. We'd been keeping an eye on the whole road all night. Hardly any cars have driven past; none have stopped.'

'Then he must have parked up nearby somewhere and made his way by foot.'

The distant sound of approaching sirens reminded Tanner that the church was now the scene of an attempted murder. Forced to accept the fact that Gary Mitchell had somehow managed to slip past them, he instructed one of the PCs to begin cordoning off the church and the surrounding area, whilst the other was to begin knocking on doors, to see if any of the neighbours had seen or heard anything unusual.

Leaving them to it, he headed over to the small church car park, to help guide in the approaching vehicles.

After two squad cars came screaming in, lights flashing, sirens blazing, Jenny arrived in her silver Golf, closely followed by DI Cooper in his Mondeo, with DS Gilbert in the passenger seat.

Jumping out of her car, her voice tight with anxiety, Jenny asked, 'Is he all right?'

'He should be, but it was close. Another couple of minutes, and it may have been a different story.'

Cooper stepped out to join them, leaving Gilbert talking on the phone. 'Any idea who did it?'

'Gary Mitchell,' replied Tanner.

'Are you sure?' asked Jenny.

'No doubt about it. Father Thomas recognised him.'

'But there was no sign of him?'

'Nothing, no, although he must have been close. Father Thomas could have only been left hanging there for a minute, maybe less. Mitchell must have been hiding inside when we came in, and then slipped out the main door when we were busy taking him down. I had the two constables take a good look around for him, but they couldn't find a single trace.'

'No car?' asked Cooper.

'None that they saw, no. He most likely saw the squad car when he drove up and decided to park down the road somewhere. I've told them to start asking the neighbours if they saw anything, maybe an unfamiliar vehicle parked nearby. Hopefully we'll get a break.'

'I think we've just got one!' announced DS Vicky Gilbert, as she strode towards them, phone still in hand. 'We've had someone call in after seeing that newspaper article. They recognised Mitchell's picture from the photograph. They say he's their neighbour, and he just pulled into his drive.'

'You've got an address?'

'Yes. He's not far. Just outside Salhouse.'

'Right, I suggest we move in and arrest him, before he does a runner.'

'Forrester's on his way,' said Cooper. 'We'd better wait for his authorisation first.'

Ignoring him, Tanner barged straight past, saying to Jenny, 'You're with me,' leaving her stranded in the middle of the car park, exchanging anxious glances between Cooper and Gilbert.

As they turned to watch him stomp over to his car, Cooper called out, 'But he could be armed!'

Crossing the road, almost to himself Tanner replied, 'I doubt it.'

Realising that he wasn't going to change his mind, Jenny said, 'I'd better go,' and broke into a run to catch up to him.

'I'm not going without Forrester's permission!' cried Cooper.

Over her shoulder, Jenny called back, 'I think you're forgetting who the SIO is now.'

After a moment's pause, DS Gilbert fixed her steel blue eyes on to Cooper's. 'Well, I'm going, even if you're not.'

Seeing Tanner and Jenny already climbing into the Jag, Cooper reluctantly said, 'Shit! Come on then,' and hurried back to his car, with Gilbert close behind.

- CHAPTER THIRTY FIVE -

GILBERT PHONED THE address through to Jenny, and within less than fifteen minutes Tanner was turning his XJS into the sweeping concrete drive of a large detached house, set back from a quiet tree-lined avenue.

As the car's over-sized v12 engine pinged and ticked as its piston head cooled, he stepped out to glance up at the windows, checking for a twitching curtain, or any other signs that someone may have been keeping a look out.

Seeing Jenny open her door, he waved her back. 'You'd better stay here,' he said, and set off up the drive towards the house.

Despite having been told otherwise, Jenny climbed out to ask, 'Shouldn't we wait for back-up?'

'No time,' she heard him say, and watched helplessly as he stepped up to the door.

Becoming increasingly concerned with what was about to take place, she called out, 'John, wait, please!'

He rang the bell, waited for the briefest of moments, and then began banging his fist on the panels, shouting, 'Gary Mitchell! Norfolk Police! Open up!'

Wondering what was taking Cooper and Gilbert so long, Jenny ran to the edge of the drive. Relieved to see them indicating to pull in, she waved at them to hurry, before turning to sprint up to join Tanner.

She arrived just in time to see the door being opened by an older heavy-set man with greying cropped hair.

'What the hell do you want?' the man demanded, glaring out at Tanner.

'Gary Mitchell?'

'Yes, what of it?'

Pulling out his ID, Tanner said, 'Detective Inspector Tanner, Norfolk Police. You're under arrest for the...'

'Why don't you lot leave me alone!' he shouted back, and tried slamming the door shut. But Tanner's head was already half inside, and the door caught the exact place where his stitches were.

Blinded by pain, with his temper boiling over, Tanner took hold of the edge of the door and shoved it back with all his strength, the force of which sent Mitchell stumbling backwards, knocking into a side table before falling hard on the floor, bringing a lamp crashing down on top of him.

Flying into the hallway from the back of the house came a furious-looking woman with a tangled mop of jet-black hair.

'Just what the hell is going on?' she demanded, her eyes darting between the man on the floor and Tanner standing in the doorway.

With one hand held flat against his now bleeding eye, Tanner stepped into the property. Bearing down on the man still lying sprawled on the carpet, he said, 'Gary Mitchell, I'm arresting you for the murder of Father Richard and Father Michael, and for the attempted murder of Father Thomas.'

'You what?'

'You do not have to say anything, but it may harm your defence if you do not mention when questioned something which you later rely on in court.'

'What the hell are you talking about?'

'Anything you do say may be given in evidence,' finished Tanner, and stooped down to grab hold of the man's arm, only for it to be snatched away.

'You're welcome to add resisting arrest if you like.'

'I've got no bloody idea what you're going on about!'

Removing his hand from his eye to take a look at the blood running down it, Tanner added, 'And judging by the damage you've done to my face, I could probably add assaulting a police officer as well. That's twelve months in prison, right there!'

'All right! All right! I'll come. But the moment you realise you've got the wrong guy, I'll be suing you for wrongful arrest, entering my property without due cause, *and* the use of unnecessary violence.'

Allowing Tanner to pull him to his feet, handing the now broken lamp to his wife, he said, 'And you can pay for a new bloody light as well!'

- CHAPTER THIRTY SIX -

'COMMENCING THE INTERVIEW of Gary Mitchell of 45, Hambleton Avenue, Salhouse. The time is 11:33 on Saturday, 6th July. In the room we have the suspect's legal representative, Clive Percival, as well as Detective Inspector Cooper and Detective Inspector Tanner.'

Positioning a blue plastic folder between himself and DI Cooper, Tanner said, 'Mr Mitchell, do you understand the charges that are being brought against you?'

'Which are utter bollocks, of course.'

'Sorry, was that a yes or a no?'

After glancing over at his solicitor, with obvious reluctance he glared back at Tanner and hissed out a venomous, '*Yes!*

'And you understand your rights under caution?'

'Is there any chance we can just get on with it? You've already had me locked up here for over two hours.'

'And you'll be here a lot longer if you're unwilling to answer the questions being asked of you.'

'All right. *Yes!*

With the legal formalities over, Tanner sat back in his chair to consider the man before him.

Staring straight back at him, Mitchell eventually

said, 'Was that it? Can I go now?'

'Not *quite* yet, no.'

'Well?'

'The first thing I'm curious to know, Mr Mitchell, is why you were so reluctant to open the door to me, despite knowing that I was from the police.'

'Because, as you no doubt already know, I've been harassed by you lot before.'

'By harassed, I assume you mean arrested for drunken assault.'

'But never charged.'

'No. Well. There's a first time for everything. Anyway...'

Returning to the folder, Tanner opened it enough to retrieve a single sheet of A4 paper which he positioned squarely in front of the suspect.

'According to your statement, for every evening we asked you to account for your whereabouts you said that you were, and I quote, "At home, with my wife."'

'Yes, and...?'

'Don't you ever go out, or is it that you don't have any friends?'

'Of course I've got friends, I just don't feel the need to spend every waking hour with them, that's all.'

'Not even at the weekends?'

'Presuming you didn't drag me all the way in here to talk about my social life, is there any chance we can move this along?'

'Of course. So, for the evenings in which you've said you were at home with your wife, is there anyone else who'd be able to vouch for you?'

'Yes, my wife, given that she was there with me.'

'Apart from her?'

'Well, you can ask the cat if you like, but I'm not sure she'll be of much use.'

'Apart from your wife and your cat?'

'Who else is supposed to be there?'

'Someone other than a close relative?'

'Sorry, no, but had I known I was going to need someone to verify where I was on the nights in question, I'd have invited a homeless person in for a cup of tea.'

Tanner gave Mitchell a thin smile, paused for a moment, and then asked, 'Have you seen today's issue of the Norfolk Herald?'

'No, why? I suppose it has an article in it about a talking cat?'

'Remarkably, no, it doesn't,' said Tanner, feigning surprise.

Opening the case file, he pulled out a photocopy of that day's front page. After glancing down at it himself, he turned it around and laid it on top of the statement for the suspect to see.

'I believe that's a photograph of you?' he asked, pointing at the black and white image.

As Mitchell stared down at it, his heavily lined suntanned face visibly drained of colour.

'I - I've not seen this,' he said, as he began scanning through the article.

'So you said. Do you confirm that the man pictured is you, albeit a younger version?'

'It is, yes, but...'

'Does the name Claire Judson ring a bell?'

Glancing up, Mitchell said, 'Who?'

'Claire Judson? She was a schoolgirl who was brutally raped and murdered back in 1976.'

'I've never heard of her.'

'So why have you been placing flowers by her grave every week, possibly since the time she was killed?'

'I haven't!'

'We have a very reliable eye-witness who says that you have.'

'Well, whoever it is, they're lying.'

'And what possible reason would they have for doing that, I wonder?'

'I've no idea. Maybe you should ask them?'

'So you're saying that you've never heard of Claire Judson, and you've never attended her grave before?'

'No!'

'Not once?'

Mitchell hesitated for just a fraction of a second, before repeating, 'Never, no!'

'So you won't mind taking part in a line-up to see if our witness can point you out?'

Mitchell's eyes dropped to his hands, which were clasped so tightly together on top of the table that the whites of his knuckles were showing.

Sitting back in his chair, Tanner gave Cooper a discreet nod as a signal for him to take over.

Leaning forward, with his elbows on the table, Cooper said, 'Whilst you've been waiting here so patiently, we've been having a little look around your house.'

'I bet my wife appreciated that,' mused Mitchell, half to himself.

Ignoring the comment, Cooper continued by saying, 'And you'll never guess what we found?'

'Would I win a prize if I did?'

'Quite possibly,' he replied, removing an old colour

photograph from the file which he placed down on the desk for the suspect to see.

'Do you recognise this person?'

Mitchell's eyes flicked down briefly, but he didn't speak.

'She certainly is attractive,' continued Cooper, somewhat absently, as he picked it up to take a look for himself. 'For a fifteen year old schoolgirl, that is.'

Mitchell began staring at his hands again.

'So, do you know who she is, or not?'

'No comment,' came his muted response.

Turning the photograph over, Cooper said, 'OK, but I'm going to have to assume that you do, especially as on the back is written, *For my darling Gary*. That is your first name isn't it, Mr Mitchell? Gary?'

The man said nothing.

'We found it in a box up in your loft, along with some letters.'

Replacing the photograph on the table, Cooper delved back into the case file to pull out a small bundle of folded pieces of paper, some pink, some blue, all scrawled over with the same swirly handwriting.

Opening up the first one, he began to read.

'My darling, Gary. I can't stop thinking about you, especially the way you rub yourself up against my...'

'All right!' Mitchell exclaimed, his face flushing with embarrassed anger. 'Yes, I knew Claire Judson. So what? It was over forty bloody years ago!'

'Well, for a start, Mr Mitchell,' continued Cooper, 'from what we can make out from these letters, you were very obviously having sexual relations with her, which would have been fine had she not been only fifteen years old at the time. That, I'm afraid, makes you a child molester.'

'Look, it wasn't my fault! She told me she was eighteen! How was I supposed to know that she wasn't? I mean, just look at her, for Christ sake!'

Picking up the photograph again, Cooper said, 'To be honest, Mr Mitchell, I'd have to agree with you.'

Leaving Cooper to admire the girl, Tanner sat forward again to say, 'I assume you're now also willing to admit that you know where she was buried, and that you *have* visited her grave before?'

'OK, yes, I have, but only a couple of times.'

'Specifically?'

'Literally twice! Once after she was buried, and once more after the trial.'

'The trial where they acquitted the priest who'd been accused of having raped and murdered her - Martin Isaac?'

'If that's what his name was, then yes.'

'Are you honestly trying to tell us that you didn't know his name?'

'At the time I did, of course, but surprisingly, after forty-three years, I'd somehow managed to forget.'

'But you remember that it was exactly forty-three years ago?'

With a shrug, Mitchell said, 'I suppose it's not every day you find out that your girlfriend's been murdered.'

'Did you love her?' asked Tanner.

'We had good sex, if that's what you mean.'

'So, she was just another girl. One of many?'

'I suppose you could say that.'

'And yet, after all these years, you've still kept the letters she wrote to you?'

'In the loft, yes. But as I'm sure you've already

discovered, there must be a lifetime of crap up there.'

'Maybe, but I can tell you something we *didn't* find.'

'What's that?'

'Letters from any other girls. If she was just one of many, where are all the rest?'

'OK, look, I suppose you could say that Claire was my first love, but that doesn't mean I've spent every day since then pining after her. Life moves on. I got married, had children. I'm now a grandparent. As I said before, it was all a very long time ago.'

'Yes, of course. Maybe you can tell us when you first suspected that Martin Isaac, the priest who was acquitted of having raped and murdered the love of your life, was actually guilty?'

'The thought never crossed my mind.'

'So, you were happy to go along with the court's decision?'

'Of course.'

'Even though the only thing that saved him from having to spend a lifetime behind bars was the last-minute alibi produced by a couple of his fellow priests?'

'If he didn't do it, he didn't do it.'

'But you think he did, though, don't you? That's why you went back to her grave after the verdict, to swear you'd take revenge?'

Mitchell shifted uncomfortably in his seat.

Tanner allowed a heavy silence to descend on the room, before asking, 'What I really want to know is, how you found that letter.'

'What letter?'

'The one sent to the Cardinal, after the trial, signed by the very priests who'd given Martin Isaac the dodgy alibi, demanding he be excommunicated from the Church.'

'I've got no idea what you're talking about.'

'Don't you read the Norfolk Herald?'

'Only if I have to, which fortunately, I don't. I mean, it is utter rubbish.'

'Generally, I'd have to agree with you,' Tanner said, 'but recently they do seem to have been hitting the mark. For example, yesterday's front page story was about that letter I just mentioned. It said that it proved Martin Isaac was guilty all along, and that the Church had persuaded a couple of priests to provide alibis simply to save them from the embarrassment of having a priest on their books who was a child rapist, and a murderer to boot.'

'Well, as I said, I've never heard of the letter.'

'Yes, in much the same way that only five minutes ago you said you'd never heard of Claire Judson, and yet we've since learnt that she was the love of your life.'

'But I had a good reason for denying I knew Claire Judson, which was the same reason I didn't come forward at the trial. She lied to me about her age. Had I known she was only fifteen, I wouldn't have gone anywhere near her.'

'Unfortunately, Mr Mitchell, now that you've been caught lying to us once, it's going to be very difficult for us to believe anything you say from this point forward.'

'But I didn't know anything about the letter!'

'Can you at least admit to having known about what happened to the two priests?'

Mitchell glanced over at his lawyer, who just

shrugged back at him.

'I've heard about it, yes, but I had nothing to do with it.'

'Do you want to know what I think?'

'Not really,' he said, and reverted to staring back at his hands.

'I think you're telling the truth, in part at least. Claire Judson was your first love. But based on the fact that you've kept all her letters, as well as her photograph, plus the fact that we have an eye witness who says you've been placing flowers beside her grave every week for some considerable time, means that you're still in love with her, even after all these years.

'I also think that you've always believed Martin Isaac raped and murdered her. And when you were somehow able to unearth the letter sent to the Cardinal demanding Isaac be excommunicated from the Church, you considered that to be the proof you'd always been looking for. So you set out to avenge Claire's death, just as you'd promised you'd do after the trial, by first cutting the throat of the man responsible, then executing the priests who enabled him to be acquitted. And you did so whilst playing into the hands of the Norfolk Herald, and the types who read it, by making it look as if Martin Isaac was the evil satanic worshipper everyone thought he was, and that he'd raised himself from the dead to seek revenge on those who'd had him kicked out of the Church.'

'OK, look, I admit to having been in love with Claire, at least I was at the time. And yes, even after all these years, I've never forgotten her. But I've not been back to her grave since after the trial, and the idea that I could cut someone's throat, or do what the paper said had been done to those priests, I mean, good god! What sort of a monster could have done such a thing?'

'A monster like you, Mr Mitchell!' said Tanner, picking up the case file, standing up and walking out, leaving DI Cooper to close the session by leaning into the recording device to say, 'Interview suspended at 11:54.'

- CHAPTER THIRTY SEVEN -

AS COOPER CAUGHT up with him in the corridor, Tanner said, 'We need to know if Mitchell's DNA or prints can be matched to anything forensics have found at the murder scenes of Martin Isaac, Father Richard or Father Michael.'

'As well as at the cemetery, where Hannah Beal was found,' added Cooper.

'Of course, yes. All we need is one single piece of physical evidence to tie him to any of those locations, and we've got him!'

Bursting through the double doors, Tanner filed off towards his desk where he could see Jenny waiting for him, leaving Cooper to head for his own work station.

'How'd it go?' asked Jenny, as Tanner approached.

'Well, he *has* been carrying a torch for Claire Judson all these years. He admitted that much, at least.'

'But I assume he didn't own up to the murders?'

'Fat chance! The most we could get out of him was that he'd visited her grave before, but not nearly as often as Father Thomas told us he had. Talking of whom, is there any news from the medical centre?'

'They've said that his neck's been badly bruised, but there's no lasting damage. But as he may not be able to eat anything solid for a while, they're recommending that he stays there for a couple of days.'

Perching herself on the edge of Tanner's desk, she looked up at him to ask, 'So, what's next?'

'I've asked Cooper to chase forensics to find out if either Mitchell's DNA or prints match anything found at the various crime scenes.'

'And if they don't?'

'I'm fairly sure they will. It would be exceptionally difficult for him not to have left some sort of physical evidence behind, not after what he'd done to them. The problem is, it may take a while, and we don't have all that long to hold him before we'll need to go cap in hand to the magistrate to ask for an extension.'

'Don't we have enough evidence for one?'

'All we have at the moment is what we found up in his attic, which is purely circumstantial. So whilst we wait for forensics, I'm hoping we'll be able to sneak Father Thomas out of the medical centre to attend a line-up, to see if he can identify our man, and preferably within the next...' Tanner glanced down at his watch to add, '...sixteen and a half hours.'

'If he can, would that be enough to charge Mitchell?'

'We'd still need the physical evidence, but it would help any application for an extension. I don't suppose any of the neighbours surrounding St. Andrew's church said they saw anything suspicious? Unfamiliar cars parked up, or strangers hanging about?'

'None that have said so. But I've had an idea that may be worth a shot.'

'What's that?'

'You know how you were talking about re-opening Claire Judson's murder investigation, to see if it would shed light on any of this?'

'And how Forrester wasn't too keen on the idea. Yes, I remember.'

'Well, I was thinking that it may be beneficial for us to have a chat with old Tommy Mills, the DI you replaced when he retired. I know that he started working here in the seventies, so it's possible that he can still remember something about what happened. If he does, it would mean that we'd be able to find out some of the details, but without officially re-opening the case.'

'Now that, Jenny, is what I call a good idea. I don't suppose you know where he lives?'

'No, but it should be in the system, unless he's moved to Spain, of course.'

'Let's hope not. OK, see if you can dig out his address, and then give him a call to ask if he'd be happy for us to come over. Meanwhile, I'll have a chat with Forrester to fill him in on how we got on with Gary Mitchell.'

'No problem; but may I suggest you don't tell him that we're planning on seeing Tommy. I doubt speaking to an old colleague can be classed as re-opening a murder investigation, but I'm not sure he'd see it that way.'

'Don't worry. I'll keep it to myself; for now at least.'

- CHAPTER THIRTY EIGHT -

FORMER DETECTIVE INSPECTOR Tom Mills, or Tommy as he'd been affectionately known, had what many would consider to be the perfect retirement home. From the front drive, where Tanner parked, the house was nothing out of the ordinary, a single-storey dwelling with two dormer windows set into a sloping tiled roof. It was the location that made it special, and that was only apparent when he and Jenny were led through to the back of the house.

'Wow!' exclaimed Tanner, as he stepped through a large patio door onto a decked veranda, a mug of steaming hot coffee in hand.

Laid out in front of him was a peaceful stretch of the River Bure, which glided past with untroubled majestic beauty.

'That's quite a view.'

As he was guided towards a black wicker armchair, he added, 'And you have a sailing boat as well!', gesturing over towards a large dinghy moored up to a small dyke to the side of the house, one that was evidently much loved, judging by the way its smooth black hull and varnished wooden foredeck gleamed in the sunlight. 'It's a Wayfarer, isn't it?' he asked deliberately showing off his newly acquired knowledg

of all things nautical.

To Jenny, Tommy said, 'I thought you said he didn't know anything about boats?'

With the merest hint of a smile, she replied, 'I think that's the full extent of his knowledge.'

Turning to Tanner, Tommy said, 'It is a Wayfarer, yes. The Mark One version, to be precise, but I hear you have something a little larger?'

'Well, yes, but it has to double up as a home as well, so it needs to be. However, if I'm to be honest, I think I'd prefer the set up you have here.'

'Perhaps,' replied Tommy, as he gazed out over the river. 'Although the problem with living in an actual house is that the only way to change the view is to buy another one; whereas with yours, you can simply slip your moorings, go for a sail and take your pick.'

'That's true, I suppose,' agreed Tanner, 'although I can't say I've done as much, at least not yet.'

'I assume you can sail?'

'Not really. Jenny's had a go at teaching me, but I've proved a poor pupil, I'm afraid.'

'He's doing all right,' Jenny interjected, 'for a Londoner.'

As Tommy settled back into one of the empty chairs, he asked, 'So, anyway, Jenny tells me that you wanted to talk about the Claire Judson investigation.'

'If that's okay with you.'

'I assume this is in connection with what happened to Martin Isaac, and the two priests?'

'And possibly the girl at the cemetery as well.'

'I'll certainly do the best I can. What do you want to know?'

'Have you been reading what's been reported about

them in the Norfolk Herald?'

'I must admit to having scanned through some of the articles, but more for personal amusement than anything else.'

'OK, well, we started off with what were effectively two lines of enquiry,' began Tanner, making himself more comfortable by crossing one leg over the other. 'Our current theory is that someone close to Miss Judson, possibly an old boyfriend, thought Martin Isaac was guilty, despite having been proved innocent, and that the Church had persuaded a couple of local priests to give false alibis to ensure his acquittal. That theory's been backed up by a letter which the Herald was somehow able to dig up.'

'The one that listed the two priests as having asked for Martin Isaac to be excommunicated from the Church?'

'That's the one. We've seen the original copy, and we believe it to be genuine. So we're thinking that the murderer somehow found out about the letter *before* it was published by the paper, and came to the conclusion that it proved Isaac was guilty after all. That person then set about seeking vengeance for Miss Judson's murder by killing Isaac, and the two priests.'

'And what's the second theory?'

'That came about through the events surrounding Isaac's death. You probably don't know, but his body was removed from what was supposed to have been his final resting place.'

'That was during the storm, when the girl was killed at the cemetery?'

'That's right. But what you probably also don't know is that his DNA was discovered at the murder scenes of both Father Richard Illingworth and Father Michael Minshall.'

'I assume you're ruling out the possibility that he did actually manage to raise himself from the dead?' asked Tommy, a dry smile playing over his heavily weathered face.

'For now we are, yes,' Tanner said. 'However, if I see his undead corpse stacking shelves down the local supermarket, I may be forced to change my opinion on that.'

'So you think someone's been trying to make it look like Martin Isaac *did* raise himself from the dead to seek revenge on those who asked for him to be excommunicated?'

'Well, we were, but now we're thinking that the two are probably one and the same; that some very sick individual is taking revenge for Miss Judson's murder by making it look as if Martin Isaac has risen from the grave to do something similar.'

'Do you have any suspects, apart from the late Martin Isaac, of course?'

'We do have someone in custody, yes.'

'May I assume that it's the man Claire Judson was due to meet at the top of St. Andrew's church tower, as named in the paper?'

'Gary Mitchell,' nodded Tanner.

After a momentary pause, Tommy asked, 'Do you think it's him?'

'He has motive. We found some old love letters she'd written to him in a box up in his loft, along with a photograph of herself. And he's admitted to having held a torch for her all these years. We also have a witness who's stated that he'd been tending to her grave on a regular basis, and he has a history of violence.'

'But I take it you haven't charged him yet?'

'At the moment we're building a case against him, although we're beginning to run out of time.'

'So, how can I help?'

'We were wondering if there was anything you can remember about the murder of Claire Judson, and the subsequent trial; anything that might shed light on what's been going on in the here and now?'

'For example?'

'Well, for a start, did you think Martin Isaac was guilty?'

'We did at the time. But from what I can recall, there wasn't all that much in the way of physical evidence; but then again, we didn't have the luxury of DNA analysis.'

'Can you remember what evidence you did have?'

'Let me see,' he said, leaning back in his chair. 'I believe we found Isaac's fingerprints at the crime scene, and there were a couple of witnesses as well; a gardener who saw Claire running into the church, closely followed by Isaac, and someone else who saw her actually falling from the tower. I think it was a woman tending to a grave. She said that she thought she saw a priest with dark hair looking over the top, moments after she'd fallen.'

'Who she thought was Isaac?'

'She said it could have been him, but she was too far away to be sure.'

'But she did think it was a priest, though?'

'That she was sure of, yes, in that he was wearing a black cassock.'

'Was there anything else?'

'Not that I can recall. It doesn't sound like much, I know, but you have to remember that there was a huge amount of pressure on us to find the person responsible.'

'And what did Isaac have to say about it?'

'He never confessed, I remember that much.'

'Did he offer an alibi?'

'Not as such, no. He admitted to having been inside the church at the time. He even owned up to having seen Claire go inside, and followed her in shortly afterwards.'

'But he denied actually doing anything to her?'

'Vehemently, yes.'

With the conversation seeming to have come to a dead end, eventually Tanner asked, 'Can you think of anything else that may be of use to us?'

'Well, there was something, but nothing ever came of it.'

'What was that?'

'It was a theory being floated about; that he may have been covering up for someone.'

'Any idea who?'

'There was another set of prints found at the scene, those of an altar boy. But Isaac said he wasn't there at the time, and the boy's parents provided him with an alibi.'

'Then how come his prints were found at the crime scene?'

'Well, they were found on the ladder leading up to the top of the tower, and on the door. Some were also found on the decking, but Isaac said that he'd been helping him fix the tower's viewing platform a few days before, which was how his prints must have come to have been there.'

'I don't suppose you remember this altar boy's name?'

'I don't, no.'

'OK, what about after the trial, when Isaac was acquitted? Were any further attempts made to identify another suspect?'

'Not that I can recall, but you have to remember that the trial didn't take place until more than a year after the actual incident, and by the time it had finished, the world just seemed to have moved on.'

'But…why did it take so long to go to trial?'

'Because it didn't start out as being a murder investigation.'

'Sorry, but how'd you mean?'

'I thought you knew. Claire Judson didn't die from the fall, at least not straight away. She was unconscious and badly hurt, but she wasn't dead.'

After exchanging a surprised look with Jenny, Tanner turned back to say, 'So if she didn't die then, when did she?'

'Not until nearly a year afterwards.'

'Then how come she wasn't able to identify the person who'd assaulted her?'

'We never got the chance to ask her. She was left in a coma. She never regained consciousness.'

As Tanner and Jenny let that hitherto unknown information sink in for a moment, the sight of a sailing boat caught their eye.

After they'd watched it glide around a bend, its white sail spread out to the side as it drifted slowly downwind, Tanner eventually asked, 'I don't suppose you can remember the name of the hospital where she was looked after?'

'It was where everyone seems to end up around here.'

'And where's that?'

'Just down the road from the police station. Wroxham Medical Centre.'

- CHAPTER THIRTY NINE -

'NICE GUY,' TANNER said, as they walked back to the XJS, 'but I'm not sure he helped all that much. I mean, it was interesting, especially about how Claire Judson had been left in a coma, but not much more than that.'

'I'm surprised we hadn't figured that one out for ourselves,' observed Jenny, 'especially as we've got that scrapbook with all those old newspaper articles.'

As they reached the car, Jenny continued by asking, 'How about what he said about Martin Isaac covering up for someone?'

'Assuming Isaac was innocent, and it was this altar boy who Tommy mentioned, I can't see how it makes much difference to our current investigation.'

'Unless the altar boy found out that the priests had discovered it was him all along, and felt he needed to silence them?'

'Well, yes, I suppose, but if that was the case, why would he have gone to all the trouble of having them executed in such a public, vengeful fashion? Surely he'd have just put a plastic bag over their heads. And why kill Martin Isaac, and then try and make it look like he'd raised himself from the dead?'

The question was left hanging as they climbed into the car.

With the doors closed, and Tanner starting the engine, Jenny said, 'Maybe he didn't kill Martin Isaac? Maybe his intention had been to make it look like he was the one to kill the priests, but then Isaac killed himself before he had the chance?'

'So he had to change his plan,' added Tanner, following Jenny's line of thought. 'Which was when he came up with the idea of making it look like Martin Isaac had raised himself from the dead?'

Having reversed out of his parked position, Tanner slotted the Jag's chrome lever into forward drive to add, 'After all, I suppose it's unlikely he would have known Isaac was terminally ill, let alone that he was intending to take his own life.'

'And maybe the manner in which he did it - cutting his own throat on the high altar at St. Benet's - gave the killer the idea to have him supposedly rise up to seek retribution on those who'd had him excommunicated.'

As Tanner eased his car out of Tommy's drive and onto the quiet country lane, deep in thought, he added, 'And I suppose it could have been him who anonymously sent that letter to Kevin Griffiths, the freelance journalist.'

'It's possible,' said Jenny, with undisguised scepticism.

'Although not very likely,' Tanner was forced to agree.

Glancing down at his dashboard to see that it wasn't even five o'clock, he suggested, 'How about we head over to see how Father Thomas is doing, and ask if he's up for attending a line-up tomorrow?'

'You mean, at Wroxham Medical Centre, where

Tommy said Claire Judson had been cared for when she was in a coma?'

He shrugged. 'I can't help it if the Broads only seems to have one medical facility.'

Narrowing her eyes over at him, Jenny said, 'OK, but only on the condition that you don't go around openly asking people about Claire Judson.'

'I'd never dream of it!'

'And that you take me out for that meal you promised afterwards.'

'Deal!' agreed Tanner. 'We'll be able to chat more about all of this over dinner.'

- CHAPTER FORTY -

S TEPPING INTO THE tranquillity of Wroxham
Medical Centre's reception area, Tanner walked
straight up to the desk. 'We're here to see Father
Thomas, who was brought in here earlier this
morning.'

Checking her watch, the lady said, 'I'm sorry, our
visiting hours don't start again until six o'clock, but
you're welcome to wait until then,' and gestured over
towards a series of green fabric chairs lined up against
the far wall.

Glancing down at his watch to see that it was still
shy of half-past five, Tanner decided to pull out his
formal ID to say, 'We're actually from Norfolk Police.
I'm Detective Inspector Tanner, and this is my
colleague, Detective Constable Evans.'

With a stern frown, the lady studied both IDs from
over the rim of her glasses before chastising him by
saying, 'If you'd wanted to interview one of our
patients out of hours, then you should have called
ahead.'

'Sorry, I didn't know the rules. I'm still relatively
new here.'

'That's no excuse.'

'No, of course. I'll remember for next time. Is it
OK if we go through? We won't be long.'

With curt dismissiveness, she checked her monitor to say, 'He's in room 21, but you'll need to sign in first,' and pointed to a book left lying open on top of the desk.

Doing as he was told, Tanner signed the book before handing the pen over for Jenny to do the same. He then gazed about, looking for a sign to indicate which rooms were where. Not being able to find any, he leaned in to ask, 'Sorry to bother you again, but I don't suppose you could tell us where room 21 is?'

'Down that corridor, on the left,' the receptionist said, with a wave of her hand.

'Thanks again,' said Tanner, and with Jenny having finished signing herself in, he led the way they'd been directed.

Once they'd found the correct door, Tanner knocked quietly and waited for a moment. Not hearing a response, he eased it open to peer inside. Ahead of him was a single bed positioned squarely in the middle of a darkened private room, but the bed itself was lying empty, with the covers thrown back and the pillow dented.

'Father Thomas?' he called, as he crept inside; but there was no sign of him, or anyone else.

Turning to Jenny, he asked, 'This is room 21, isn't it?'

Checking the front of the door, Jenny replied, 'It is, yes. Maybe she gave us the wrong room number?'

Hearing someone approach from the corridor, she ducked her head out to see a nurse of retirement age tottering her way down towards them, leaning on the handles of a heavily ladened trolley as if it was a walking aid.

'Excuse me,' Jenny called. 'I don't suppose you know if this is the correct room for Father Thomas?'

Coming closer, the nurse asked, 'Sorry, what was the name again?'

'Father Thomas. He's a parish priest who was brought in here earlier today, suffering from a neck injury.'

Nodding her understanding, the nurse came up to meet them. 'I believe he checked himself out, just after lunch.'

Jenny shot Tanner a look of surprise, leaving him to say, 'We were led to believe that he'd be staying here for a couple of days.'

'I've not been told anything about that. All I know is that he told me that he was going to check out today, so that he could prepare for his sermon tomorrow.'

'But the receptionist thought he was still here.'

'If you're referring to Mary, she's only just come on duty, so she probably doesn't know. Now, if you'll excuse me.'

'Before you go,' said Tanner, squeezing past Jenny, deliberately avoiding her eye contact. 'I don't suppose you'd know where we'd be able to locate medical records concerning a former patient? She was treated here some years ago.'

Knowing what he was up to, Jenny cleared her throat, just loud enough for Tanner to hear, giving him reason to add, 'Should anyone have the need to find them, that is.'

Stopping again, the nurse asked, 'Going back to when?'

'Oh, I don't know. Say as far as 1976?'

'Well, this centre wasn't built until the eighties. As far as I know, all patient files pre-dating that were put into storage, but I've no idea where. You'd have to ask someone in administration.'

'I see. Yes, of course. And yourself, Nurse…?

'Nurse Peters.'

'I don't suppose you were working here at the time?'

'When this place was built?'

'No. Back in 1976.'

Jenny cleared her throat again, but more obviously that time.

'Are you all right, my dear?' asked the nurse, casting her eyes over her face with professional concern.

'I'm fine, thank you, but I really feel we must be on our way.'

'As should I, my dear. As should I.'

Before she set off again, Tanner asked, 'So, you weren't working here in 1976?'

'Oh, I was here a long time before that, young man.'

'Is there any chance you can remember a patient who we've been told was being looked after here at the time?'

'I doubt it. All I can remember about 1976 was how hot the summer was. We'd never had anything like it, before or since. They even had to turn the water off at the mains.'

'Her name was Claire Judson, if that helps. She was attacked at St. Andrew's church in Horning, and fell from the tower.'

'You mean that poor girl who was left in a coma?'

'That's the one. Do you remember much about her?'

'Only how sad the whole affair was. Imagine to have something like that happen to you, and at such a tender young age. And to then die giving birth, never to even see your child. Just sad. So very sad.'

With their mouths left hanging open, Tanner and Jenny stared round at each other, before Tanner turned back to say, 'You mean, she was pregnant?'

'That's right, and by all accounts, by the man who attacked her.'

Still reeling from the news, Tanner asked, 'But there was nothing about it in the newspapers.'

'Which I think was about the only good thing that came out of the whole affair. Imagine being brought up knowing that your father had raped and murdered your own mother! No. They kept his birth out of the papers, and hopefully made sure that he never knew anything about it.'

'So the child was a boy?'

'That's right, and a handsome one at that. I can still remember his cute little face.'

'Any chance you can remember his name?'

The nurse gazed up at the ceiling for a moment, before saying, 'You know, I'm sorry, but I can't. I'm not sure he was even given one, at least not when he was here.'

'And you say that *they* made sure he was kept out of the papers?'

'That's right.'

'May I ask who *they* were?'

'The authorities who dealt with the case, I suppose.'

'You mean, the police?'

'Them and the lawyers, yes. We were told very specifically not to talk to the press about anything we either saw or heard, *especially* about the child. And then, when he was born, and his mother died, a group of legal-looking gentlemen arrived with a nun, and they took him away.'

'You say the nun took the child?'

'The nun and the lawyers, yes.'

To Jenny, Tanner said, 'It must have been the Church's legal defence team.'

'Anyway,' continued the nurse, 'I really must be getting on now. Lots to do, you know.'

As she began rattling her trolley away, he called out after her, 'Thank you, Nurse Peters, you've been most helpful.'

Doubting she'd even heard him, he turned back to Jenny. 'I think we've just discovered a really big piece to this increasingly complicated puzzle. If Claire Judson's son had been told who his parents were, and what his father did, I think it could explain a lot.'

As he reached for his phone, Jenny asked, 'Do you think Alan Birch, the bookshop owner, would know anything about him?'

'If it *was* the Church's defence team who arranged for the child to be taken into care, then I'd be surprised if he doesn't. I'm going to call Forrester to give him an update. Then I suggest we head back to the station and have another chat with our Mr Birch.'

- CHAPTER FORTY ONE -

'DCI FORRESTER, IT'S DI Tanner here.'

'Tanner! Where the hell have you been?'

'Er…we're down the road, at Wroxham Medical Centre.'

'What on earth are you doing there? I've been trying to get hold of you for bloody ages!'

'Sorry, sir,' replied Tanner. 'I must have forgotten to take my phone off mute. We came to see if Father Thomas would be up for attending a line up.'

'Fair enough, I suppose. And is he?'

'Well, he's already checked himself out to prepare his sermon for tomorrow, so I'd have thought so.'

'OK, good. Anyway, I was trying to call to let you know that we've had news in from forensics. They've found Gary Mitchell's DNA at the scene where Father Thomas was hanged. I think that gives us the physical evidence we need to go ahead and charge him.'

Tanner relayed the information to Jenny, before replying, 'That's very interesting sir, but I was hoping we'd be able to delay that for a while.'

'Delay?'

'Yes, sir.'

'But why?'

'One of the nurses here has just told us something very interesting about Claire Judson.'

'What the hell are you doing talking to a nurse about Claire Judson?'

'I think her name just happened to come up in conversation, sir.'

'I see, and why do I find that somewhat hard to believe?'

Moving the conversation swiftly along, Tanner pushed on by saying, 'We've discovered that Miss Judson wasn't killed at St. Andrew's church as we first thought. She survived the fall from the tower to be left in a coma. She didn't actually die until nine months later. It was only then that it became a murder investigation.'

'And that's of interest, because…?'

'Because, sir, she was left pregnant by whoever it was who raped her. She died during the operation to deliver the baby.'

There was silence from the other end of the line, before Forrester eventually asked, 'I don't suppose this nurse you were talking to knows the name of the child?'

'Unfortunately not, sir, no, but she did remember that it was a boy, and from what she was saying, we believe he was taken into care by the Church. So we're about to head back to the station to ask Alan Birch about it. As he served on the Church's legal defence team during Martin Isaac's trial, we're hoping he'll know what happened to the child, and maybe what his name was as well.'

'OK, but there's no point looking for him here.'

'Sorry sir, but why's that?'

'I gave the order for him to be released.'

'You did…*what?*'

'Excuse me, Detective Inspector, but I really don't appreciate being spoken to like that.'

'Excuse *me*, sir, but as I'm the SIO for this investigation, you should have asked me first!'

'Just who the hell do you think you're talking to, Tanner? You answer to *me*, not the other way round!'

'That's all very well and good, sir, but you're the one who made me the SIO, which means that all decisions have to be run by me first, no matter who it is who's having to make them.'

'Then you'd better stop turning your bloody phone off, hadn't you?'

'I had it on mute, sir!'

'Either way, Tanner, if your phone doesn't ring, nobody can get through to you, can they?'

'And now you've gone and released a key witness whose life might be in danger.'

'I only released him when the physical evidence came through from forensics which proved Gary Mitchell *had* attempted to murder Father Thomas. And as Mitchell is still sat safe and sound inside a holding cell, I believe my decision was correct.'

'But only if Gary Mitchell did it!'

Tanner heard Forrester let out a heavy sigh, before saying, 'Listen, Tanner, you said it yourself. The guy had been holding a torch for Claire Judson for forty-three years. If he did come to the conclusion that Martin Isaac had been guilty of raping and murdering the teenage love of his life, then it isn't much of a stretch to see him seeking revenge on the man who he thought had done it, along with those who he felt responsible for having him acquitted, especially given his history of violence.'

'And I completely agree with you, sir, but that doesn't mean he actually did it though, does it.'

'But the physical evidence forensics found does!'

'Not if someone planted it there, in the exact same way they planted Martin Isaac's DNA on the two priests.'

There was a prolonged silence from the other end of the phone, before Forrester eventually said, 'So, what are you proposing?'

'We need to bring Alan Birch back in for questioning, not only to find out if he knows the name and whereabouts of Claire Judson's child, but also for his personal safety. If Claire's son does think that there was a Church-led conspiracy to have Martin Isaac acquitted, he could well have Alan Birch next on his list.'

'Very well, do it; but Gary Mitchell needs to remain in custody, and we can't hold him for much longer without charging him.'

'I understand, sir. All I'm asking is for more time to track down Claire Judson's son, and Alan Birch should be able to help us do that.'

'I suppose you'd better hurry up and find him then, hadn't you?'

- CHAPTER FORTY TWO -

A FTER TANNER PULLED his XJS onto the far kerb opposite Alan Birch's Victorian bookshop, Jenny stepped out to immediately know that something wasn't right.

'Can you smell that?'

'Smell what?' asked Tanner, following her gaze.

'Burning!' she stated, pointing up to one of the shop's top windows. 'Look!'

There, seeping out through a gap was a line of thick black smoke, steadily drifting up into the sky above.

'Shit!' said Tanner, as he flung himself around the car. 'Call control. We need the fire brigade, and an ambulance!'

Seeing how Jenny seemed mesmerised by the smoke as it weaved its way out from the window, he shouted, 'Now, Jen!' before launching himself over the road, heading for the entrance to the shop.

Jenny delved into her handbag, searching for her phone.

Just as her fingers wrapped themselves around it, the window she'd been staring at only moments before exploded, sending razor-sharp shards of glass spiralling out over the street like shrapnel.

As Jenny ducked away, Tanner took cover under the alcove above the shop's door, pressing himself against it as he did.

With shattered glass raining down on the pavement, he glanced over to make sure that Jenny was OK.

Relieved to see her heading for cover behind his car, he turned back to face the shop's door to peer through its window.

Inside, all seemed normal, until he looked up towards the ceiling. There, rippling its way over its surface like a swarm of bees was a layer of dense black smoke. As he followed it back towards the far end of the shop, just above the spiral staircase, he could see the bright flicker of orange flames.

Cupping his hands around his mouth, he bellowed, 'Mr Birch? Are you in there?'

For a moment he thought he heard the sound of someone calling back, but he couldn't be sure.

Peering inside again, he scanned the shop floor, desperately searching for signs of life. But the only movement came from the smoke spreading out over the ceiling, and the flames at the back, dancing around the top of the staircase.

Examining the door, he placed the palm of his hand flat against one of the square sections of glass. It was warm, but not hot. He tried the handle, but that was stone cold.

From behind him he heard Jenny shout, 'Don't you dare go in there, John! Do you hear me?'

Seeing her head poking up above one of the Jag's flying buttresses towards the rear, he called back, 'Did you get through to control?'

'Fire and ambulance are on their way.'

'How long?'

'They didn't say, but I can hear them.'

She was right. Now that he was listening for it, Tanner could just about make out the sound of a siren rolling in over the flat landscape, but it was a long way off.

He had to make a decision, and he had to do it quickly. Judging by the amount of smoke, if Alan Birch was trapped inside, by the time they arrived it would be too late. But if he *wasn't* inside, and Tanner had only imagined the voice, he'd be risking his life for nothing.

Calling back to Jenny, Tanner said, 'I think Alan's inside. I'm going to take a look.'

'No, John, *please*! It's too dangerous! Wait for the fire brigade!'

'I won't be long.'

'John, don't!'

But he'd made up his mind. He had to go now, before the whole place was ablaze.

Pushing the door open, a wave of heat came surging out at him, searing the inside of his nostrils as he breathed it in.

He took a step back, away from the door. The air inside was far hotter than he'd been expecting.

Bracing himself, he forged his way through the doorway, the bell ringing above his head, but this time more like a death knell than a cheerful welcome.

'Mr Birch?' he called, as a smothering blanket of heat wrapped itself around him. But all he could hear in response was the cracking of burning timber from somewhere out near the back.

Having taken a few cautious steps inside, he called out again, 'Mr Birch? Are you in here?'

Still nothing.

He glanced back through the open doorway to see

Jenny frantically gesturing for him to come out.

After raising his hands in a bid to placate her, he turned his attention back to the inside of the shop. It was then that he thought he saw something lying over the first few rungs of the spiral staircase, some sort of beige-coloured rug, or an off-cut from a carpet. Another step forward and he realised that it was neither. It was Alan Birch, stripped naked, his hands held above his head, secured to one of the vertical steel stanchions.

Throwing caution to the wind, Tanner tumbled his way inside, weaving his way past the many tables, all of which burgeoned with ancient books, like kindling awaiting the slightest touch of a flame.

The further inside he went, the more intense the heat, and the closer the deadly black smoke crept towards his head.

Keeping himself low to the floor he kept going, sucking gently at the burning hot oxygen-starved air as he did. Finally reaching the bookshop's owner, he stared down at him. He was lying still, as if dead, his eyes half-closed with what looked to be brown packing paper stuffed into his mouth.

Doing his best not to inhale the noxious fumes surrounding him, Tanner leant over the man's head. 'Mr Birch, are you OK?'

The man's eyes flickered open to stare imploringly into Tanner's. Then they rolled up towards where his hands were tied to the stanchion above.

Nodding his understanding, Tanner reached up to untie them, but instead of rope, he found that they had been bound by a thick plastic tie. He needed a knife, but he didn't have one.

Frantically he searched his pockets for his keys, hoping the serrated edge of one would be enough to cut the tie.

Tugging them out, he dared to suck in some of the poisonous air through his nose.

That was when he smelt it.

Petrol!

The man lying stark-naked beneath him reeked of the stuff.

Glancing up, Tanner saw the flames above were steadily creeping their way down the staircase, their intense heat warping the air in front of them. He knew he only had seconds before the temperature reached flashpoint, and the petrol the man was soaked in would ignite.

Using the key from his old London home he began hacking at the plastic tie. As he did, the hairs on the back of his hands began to singe, the sulphurous odour adding to the intoxicating mix of petrol and smoke. Only when he felt his skin burn did he wrenched them away.

One last try, he thought to himself.

Knowing it was going to hurt, he reached up again.

Doing his best to ignore the pain, he dragged the edge of the key hard against the plastic tie until it finally came away in his hands.

Dumping his keys back into his pocket, Tanner was about to grab hold of the man and drag him outside when it happened: the flashpoint had been reached.

As the man's hands burst into flames, a muffled scream tore through the paper stuffed inside his mouth.

Expecting Birch to leap up from the stairs to try

and escape the flames, Tanner pushed himself away, falling backwards as he did.

But the man didn't move.

As flames ripped over the length of his body, he remained where he was, stretched out over the first few rungs of stairs, his arms still held above his head.

Tanner stared out in horror as the motionless body began to blister and burn, all the while a deafening scream surging out through his open mouth, the inside of which was now ablaze, the paper stuffed inside burning bright.

Tanner watched in helpless agony as the flames began peeling away the man's lips, revealing two rows of crooked yellow teeth that seemed to grin down at him through a haze of shimmering heat.

It was too late. There was nothing he could do for the man now other than to pray that death didn't take long to move in to claim his mortal body.

Feeling his own face begin to burn, Tanner frantically kicked himself away. Rolling over onto his hands and knees he pushed himself up to stand on a pair of faltering feet, only to stagger sideways, crashing back down to the floor. With his lungs burning, choking at the toxic air he tried again. This time he made it as far as the nearest table, before falling against it, bringing the now smouldering books thundering down on top of him.

As his head began to spin, he stretched out his arms and tried to claw his way out. But then, from above his head came the agonising screech of twisting masonry, as it ripped and tore at the surrounding walls.

He didn't need to look up to know what it was. He already knew. It was the sound of the ceiling, about to give way.

- CHAPTER FORTY THREE -

WITH THE SOUND of crashing timber and wailing sirens filling his head, Tanner could feel someone heave him up by the back of his coat and begin dragging him along the floor, through the shop's door and out, all the way to the other side of the road. There he was dropped into the hands of a couple of waiting paramedics, who eased him down onto the back of their ambulance to begin tending to his burns.

Tanner blinked open his eyes to see Jenny come running over towards him. As she crouched down in front of him, fighting back the tears, she said, 'Jesus, John. I thought I'd lost you.'

Through a rasping voice, Tanner replied, 'Birch. Alan Birch.'

'Was he inside?'

Tanner nodded. 'I couldn't save him. I thought I could, but... I was too late.'

'Nobody could have done any more.'

'I'd cut the tie, but the petrol. It was all over him. And then - and then it caught, and I just watched him. I just sat there and watched him.'

To the paramedics, Jenny asked, 'Is he going to be all right?'

'Looks like he's inhaled a fair amount of smoke,'

replied the nearest. 'He's also sustained minor burns to the back of his hands along with lacerations to his face, but he should be fine, yes.'

'And he didn't move,' continued Tanner. 'Even when he was burning, he didn't move. Then his mouth was on fire, and he grinned. He was grinning at me, Jen, as he was burning.'

Concerned with what they were hearing, one of the paramedics said, 'I'd better give him a sedative. Then I think it would be sensible for us to take him to the medical centre.'

Sending them a look of intense concern, Jenny asked, 'But he'll be OK though, yes?'

'He should be, but it does sound like he's been through a lot. Better to have him in overnight, just in case.'

As the paramedic began fitting an oxygen mask over his mouth, Tanner yanked it away, stared deep into Jenny's eyes, and said, 'My car, Jen?'

'Yes, your car. What about it?'

'Is it all right?'

With a smile that burst with emotion, Jenny said, 'Yes, John! Your bloody car's fine, for fuck's sake!'

Re-fitting the mask, the medic looked at her and said, 'We'd better take him. You can come with us if you like?'

'I'd like that,' she replied. 'Thank you.'

- CHAPTER FORTY FOUR -

Sunday, 7th July

'SORRY I'M LATE,' croaked Tanner, the following morning, as he laid two bandaged hands down on the back of Jenny's chair to squeeze his way past.

Jenny spun round to glare at him and ask, 'Tell me you're not being serious?'

'I'm fine,' said Tanner, wincing with pain as he eased himself down into his chair.

'Yes,' she said, watching as he fumbled to turn his computer on, 'you certainly look fine, apart from maybe the bandages covering your hands, and the plasters stuck all over your face.'

'Apparently, looking like a multiple burns victim is all the rage these days,' replied Tanner, as he logged himself in. 'Didn't you know?'

'I suppose you read that in Cosmo?'

'Men's Health, actually,' he corrected. 'Anyway, I've been awake since six o'clock this morning and I've got bugger all else to do.'

'At least tell me you didn't drive in?'

'Well, I would've done, but I've got no idea where my car is, so I got a taxi.'

'That's something, I suppose.'

'Speaking of which, I don't suppose you know where it is?'

'It's parked around the back.'

'Still in one piece, I hope?'

'Bad news, I'm afraid. Apparently, just after we left in the ambulance, it caught fire and blew up. Sorry about that.'

'I do hope you're joking?'

'Unfortunately, I am.'

'One day you're going to like my car so much that you'll be wanting one for yourself.'

'Somehow, I doubt that. Anyway, putting your 1980's TV mini-series of a car to one side for the moment, may I ask what you're doing here, exactly?'

'I thought I'd pop in to see how everything's going.'

'Well, you'll be pleased to hear that everything's going just fine, so you can pop straight back to your hospital bed. I'll even be happy enough to give you a lift.'

Ignoring her offer, Tanner looked down towards the other end of the office. 'Is he in?'

'Assuming you're referring to DCI Forrester, then yes, he is. Why?'

Heaving himself back to his feet, he said, 'I'll tell you later,' before staggering around the desks to make a slow beeline for his superior's office.

Reaching his door, Tanner gave it a tentative knock.

Hearing the call to enter, he eased it open and poked his head around to say, 'Sorry to bother you, sir, but I was wondering if you had a moment?'

Looking up with a start, Forrester said, 'Tanner! What the hell are you doing here?'

'The doctor gave me the all-clear, sir.'

'Really? From all accounts, you barely made it out of that bookshop alive.'

'It wasn't that bad, sir.'

'Judging by the state of you, it was probably worse.'

'Just some minor burns. Anyway, I wanted to say that I've been thinking things over, about the investigation, and I feel that as things stand at the moment, we have no choice but to re-open the Claire Judson case.'

'Sorry, I thought you already had?'

'Er…I meant officially, sir. It's obvious now that Gary Mitchell is innocent. There's no way he could have attacked Alan Birch, not when he was locked up in one of our holding cells.'

'Surprisingly, Tanner, I'd somehow managed to figure that one out for myself, which was why we let him go last night.'

'Oh, sorry. I didn't know.'

'Well, I would have asked you first, of course, had you not just been dragged out of a burning building and driven away in an ambulance. And before you ask, yes, I have arranged police protection for Father Thomas, but this time we've posted men outside his front and back door, not just parked idly outside his house.'

Still standing in front of the DCI's desk, Tanner shifted uneasily from one foot to the other, before eventually saying, 'I'd also like to speak with the Bishop of Norfolk again, sir.'

'Please god, tell me you're joking?' demanded Forrester, scowling at him over his desk.

'Not at all, sir. We still need to find Claire Judson's son, and the only person who may have been able to confirm his identity was the person I saw burnt to death yesterday.'

'Yes, quite, but why does that give you cause to speak with the bishop, *again*?' asked Forrester, with a heavy emphasis placed on the last word.

'For the same reason as before, sir. It's the Church connection. If what the nurse said is correct, that Claire Judson's son was taken into care by them, then there's a good chance that the bishop's office will have access to records kept on file somewhere, which will hopefully provide a name, and possibly even tell us his whereabouts.'

Forrester thought for a moment, before eventually saying, 'OK, you have my permission to contact his office, but *not* the bishop himself. There's no reason why he should personally know anything about this, and with what happened the last time you spoke to him, I don't want him bothered again.'

'You mean…apart from the fact that he *personally* held a funeral service for an excommunicated, self-confessed devil worshipper who, according to the coroner's office at least, took his own life; meaning that by Catholic standards he'd have gone straight to hell, and therefore had no place being given any sort of a church send off, let alone one in Norfolk Cathedral?'

'Seriously, Tanner, if I receive so much as a text message from Head Office saying that you've been attempting to speak with the bishop again, and for no other reason than he presided over that funeral, forget being suspended, I'll have you thrown off the bloody Force! Do you understand?'

'With respect, sir, over the last few days I've seen a priest crucified, another impaled, one nearly hanged to death, and a former Church defence lawyer burnt alive, right in front of my eyes. Frankly, I don't give a fuck who I have to speak to in order to find out who did it!'

With a darkening face, Forrester sprang up from his chair. '*But I do, Tanner!* And if you *dare* speak to me like that again, you'll be off the fucking Force, whether you've questioned the bishop or not!'

The sudden shock of being yelled at sent Tanner reeling. As he stumbled, he grabbed hold of the top of one of the chairs to try and stop himself from falling, only to bring it crashing down on top of him.

'Jesus Christ!' exclaimed Forrester, as he launched himself around his desk to come to Tanner's aid.

Pulling the chair off of him, he helped him back to his feet to ask, 'Are you OK?'

'I'm fine. Just a bit dizzy. That's all.'

As he eased him down into the chair, Forrester said, 'Look, it's glaringly obvious to anyone with half a brain that you're in no fit state to be back at work.'

'I'm fine, sir. Really!'

'Like hell you are!'

Moving back to the other side of his desk, Forrester picked up his phone, saying, 'I'm having you taken back to the medical centre, and that's my final word on the matter.'

With one of his bandaged hands pressed against the side of his head, Tanner said, '*After* I've found Claire Judson's son.'

'No, Tanner!'

'But he's the one who's behind all this; I know he is!'

'That's as may be, but I'm afraid you're not going to be the one who finds him. I'll get Cooper to cover it.'

'*Cooper?*'

'Yes, Cooper!'

Feeling his head starting to spin again, Tanner conceded by saying, 'OK, but at least allow me to contact the bishop's office.'

Holding the receiver in his hand, Forrester scowled at him. 'You don't give up, do you?'

'I can't let this one go, sir. Not after what I saw happen to Alan Birch.'

Forrester replaced the receiver back into its cradle, sat back down and cast an eye over his more senior detective inspector; in particular the stitches on his forehead, the taped gauze covering his left cheek bone, and the bandages wrapped around his hands.

'OK, I'll give you permission to contact the bishop's office, but only by email, and I'll need to approve whatever it is that you write before it's sent off. How about that?'

'I suppose that'll have to do.'

'But if they *are* able to identify who Claire Judson's son is, then the whole thing will have to be handed over to Cooper, and you're going to be checking yourself back into the medical centre. Agreed?'

'And if they're unable to identify him?'

'Then I suppose we'll be back to square one.'

'And what about me?'

'I'll have to have a chat to your doctor about that. It will be for him to decide if you're fit to return to active duty. However, at this precise moment, even from a layman's perspective, it's pretty bloody obvious that you're not up to it, not by a long way.'

- CHAPTER FORTY FIVE -

WITH FORRESTER DECIDING to give DI Cooper the order to officially re-open the forty-three year old investigation into the rape and murder of Claire Judson, Tanner sat down with Jenny to compose an email to be sent to the Bishop of Norfolk's office, requesting any historical documents held with regard to both the trial of Martin Isaac, along with the identity and location of Claire Judson's son.

After it had been drafted, approved by Forrester, and sent to the general enquiries email address for the Diocese of Norfolk, Forrester told Jenny to drive Tanner back to the medical centre, which Tanner was happy to agree to; or so it seemed until he sat in the passenger seat of Jenny's Golf.

'How about we go and see how Father Thomas is doing?' he asked, sending her an oh-so-innocent grin.

'Do I have to remind you that I'm under orders to take you back to the medical centre?'

'Yes, but it wasn't an order, as such. It was more of a suggestion. Besides, St. Andrew's is on the way.'

'It's in completely the opposite direction.'

'Not if you take the long way round.'

'Based on that logic, anywhere is on the way if you take the long way round.'

'Exactly!'

She pulled a face at him, but didn't argue. Reversing out of the parking bay, she asked, 'What have you got against hospitals, anyway?'

'Nothing in particular. I just don't like spending my time having to look at an endless number of posters advertising a wide variety of god-awful diseases, ones that if I don't already have, I've apparently got an above average chance of developing. Besides, as I keep telling everyone, I'm fine!'

'Forrester told me you keeled over in his office.'

'Apart from that.'

Coming to a halt at the car park's exit, looking left and right, she said, 'If Forrester's watching from his office and I turn left, he'll know that I'm not taking you to the medical centre.'

Swivelling around in his seat, Tanner looked behind them, towards Forrester's window.

'Is he watching?' asked Jenny.

'Uh-huh.'

Turning back around, he said, 'You'd better turn right, but you can do a u-turn when we're out of his sight, and head back the other way.'

'But what if he's still watching when I drive past?'

'Then it's a good job your car looks almost exactly the same as everyone else's.'

- CHAPTER FORTY SIX -

AFTER TAKING A minor detour for the
benefit of DCI Forrester, about half an hour
later Jenny pulled up behind a squad car
parked directly outside Father Thomas's house, next
door to St. Andrew's church.

Seeing the car was empty, as they climbed out,
Jenny said, 'At least they're not sat inside, enjoying an
early afternoon snooze.'

Looking over at the house, Tanner said, 'But they're
not guarding the front door either,' and broke into a
run.

Reaching the house, he rang the bell before peering
through the letter box to call out, 'Father Thomas! Are
you in there?'

There was no response, just a cold still silence.

'He must be up at the church,' Jenny said.

'Let's hope so,' replied Tanner, and together they
set off up the path that led up towards St. Andrew's.

The moment the church's heavily fortified entrance
came into view, they reined themselves in to continue
up the hill in a more sedate, leisurely fashion.

In front of the door, pacing up and down, was the
welcome sight of a uniformed constable.

'We were beginning to wonder where you were,'
said Tanner, with some relief, though a little out of

breath.

'Don't worry, sir,' the young constable replied. 'Father Thomas is inside. He's just packing up after the Sunday service.'

Tanner had completely forgotten about that. Had he remembered, he'd have told him to cancel it.

'Did it go all right?'

'What, the service? Yes, it was fine, sir. Kind of nice, actually.'

'And Father Thomas? Is he OK?'

'Well, his voice is a bit hoarse, but apart from that, he seems well enough.'

Taking in Tanner's bandaged hands and face, the constable went on to ask, 'And how about you, sir?'

'Me?' questioned Tanner, surprised to have been asked.

'Yes, sir. We were told what happened; and your face...'

'Nothing for you to concern yourself with, Constable. It's Father Thomas you need to worry about.'

'Yes, sir. We've been ordered not to let him out of our sight.'

'And yet here you are, standing outside his church, where you can't see him?'

'Er...yes sir, but Constable Higgins is inside.'

'OK, fair enough, but keep your eyes open!'

'Absolutely, sir,' the young man replied, standing to attention.

Brushing past him, Tanner and Jenny headed inside the Church to see Father Thomas at the top of the very pulpit where they'd found him hanging only the day before. Thankfully, this time around he was standing at the top, leaning over the lectern, looking down with a pen in his hand.

A quick glance over to the right side of the church revealed the other constable, propping up one of the ancient stone walls.

Seeing Tanner and Jenny walk in, the young constable straightened to nod over a greeting.

'Oh, hello, you two,' came the cheerful yet rasping voice of Father Thomas, looking up to see who was approaching.

'Good afternoon, Father,' said Tanner, his voice equally strained. 'We just thought we'd stop by to make sure that you were OK.'

'As you can see,' the priest replied, glancing over at the constable by the far wall, 'I'm being well guarded. Hold on. Let me come down and say hello to you properly.'

With that, he pocketed the pen and carefully made his way down the pulpit's wooden steps, which were as steep as they were narrow.

Watching the way he was having to cling onto the hand rails, Tanner said, 'We can still put you up in a safe house, if you'd prefer?'

'No, no. I feel quite looked after, thank you. A little too much, to be honest.'

'I must admit, we thought you'd be staying at the medical centre for a while longer.'

Stepping safely onto the floor, as he began making his way over towards them, the priest replied, 'I can't say that I've ever had a particularly good relationship with hospitals. Too many posters advertising too many diseases for my liking.'

Glancing at Jenny, Tanner said, 'See. It's not just

me.'

'And besides, I had a service to prepare for.'

As he approached, he took in the state of Tanner's face and hands to say, 'Goodness! What on earth has happened to you?'

Glancing down, Tanner replied, 'It looks worse than it is.'

'Your face doesn't, surely! Shouldn't you be in hospital yourself?'

With a grim smile, Tanner replied, 'Too many posters.'

As his face brightened with amusement, extending a hand, Father Thomas said, 'I never had a chance to thank you for yesterday.'

Taking it with his own bandaged one, Tanner gave it a careful shake. 'Anyone in my position would have done the same.'

'But it wasn't anyone, though, was it? It was you! If you hadn't come along when you had, I'm fairly sure I wouldn't be standing before you today.'

Feeling a twinge of embarrassment, Tanner replied, 'But I was, and you're OK.'

After they'd exchanged smiles, the priest's face darkened as he said, 'I heard you were able to apprehend the man who'd done that to me, but that you've since released him. Is that true?'

'Well, yes, but I was going to ask you about that. Are you absolutely sure it was Gary Mitchell who attacked you?'

'It was definitely him,' he replied. 'The same man who's been visiting Claire's grave.'

'Yes, but are you sure that the man you've seen outside in the graveyard was Gary Mitchell?'

'Oh, I see what you mean. Well, when you put it like that, I suppose it's possible that I could have been mistaken. But if it wasn't him, who else would it have been?'

'We've found out something rather interesting,' continued Tanner, 'from a nurse, over at Wroxham Medical Centre. Something about Claire Judson.'

'Oh yes, do tell.'

'She survived the fall from the tower.'

'She survived? But I thought…'

'She was left in a coma, a condition from which she never recovered.'

'I didn't know that.'

'There was something else we discovered as well. When she was taken into care, she was pregnant.'

With a look of astonishment, Father Thomas repeated, 'Pregnant?'

'And the father of the baby was believed to be the person who'd attacked her. Furthermore, Claire lived long enough to give birth, to a boy. We believe it may be Claire Judson's son who's been visiting her grave, and is subsequently behind the attacks against you and the other priests.'

'But, surely, if such a child existed, it would have been reported in the papers?'

'The powers that be decided to keep it out of the media which, at the time at least, was probably a sensible decision.'

'Do you know who the child is?'

'Not yet, no. The person we thought might know has unfortunately been -' Tanner was about to say killed, but not wishing to alarm Father Thomas any more than was necessary, instead said, '- has passed away.'

'I'm very sorry to hear that.'

'But don't worry,' added Tanner. 'I'm not going to stop until I've found him.'

'No, I can see that.'

'We've already reached out to the Norfolk Diocese, hoping that they may have some answers for us.'

'What makes you think they'd know anything about it?'

'We believe Claire's son was taken into care by the Church, so we're hoping they'll have a record of his name; possibly where we'll be able to find him as well. However, in the meantime, you need to make sure you stay close to the officers who've been assigned to keep an eye on you.'

'Of course, yes, although I must admit that I was hoping to be able to bring you over a little something this evening, by way of a thank you.'

'That's very kind of you, Father, but I'm not sure that would be a good idea. Not yet, at any rate. Maybe it would be better if I was to pop by to pick it up from you?'

Looking a little aggrieved, Father Thomas said, 'I am allowed out, aren't I?'

'Well, yes, but...'

'Tell you what. How about if I was to bring it over to you under police escort?' He looked over at the uniformed constable, who had returned to propping up the church wall.

Tanner said, 'I suppose that would be all right.'

'Good. Now, whereabouts do you live?'

'Actually, I live on board a boat.'

'A boat?'

'A floating one, yes,' he said, with an embarrassed smile.

'How on earth did you end up living on board a boat?'

'It's a long story, one which I'll gladly tell when you come around.'

'Well, I'm intrigued.'

'It's nothing fancy, the boat that is. Just an old Norfolk cruising yacht. It's called *Seascape*. You'll be able to find it opposite the marina in Ranworth.'

'OK, well, I still have to finish up here, and then I've a few other things I need to attend to. Sunday's obviously my busiest day, but I'll try to pop around with it later this evening, if that's convenient?'

'I look forward to it,' Tanner assured him. 'Anyway, we'd better be off. But remember; make sure to stay close to the two constables at all times.'

'I will.'

'And you've still got my number?'

Tapping his hand against his breast pocket, with an appreciative smile he replied, 'I've got your card, and my phone's right here.'

'Good. Well, goodbye for now, Father.'

With that, Tanner and Jenny turned to make their way out of the church.

- CHAPTER FORTY SEVEN -

ONCE THEY'D STEPPED outside, and had passed the constable still standing beside the entrance, Jenny said quietly, 'I thought I was taking you back to Wroxham Medical Centre; and yet there you were, planning your evening's social engagements.'

'Well, yes, but I really am feeling much better now.'

'But even so…?'

'Besides,' continued Tanner, 'I'll sleep better in my own bed.' Seeing the concerned look on her face, he added, 'Look, if my head starts spinning again, or if any part of my body begins to hurt any more than it already is, I'll give you a call and you can drive me over. How does that sound?'

As they entered the cemetery, heading for the car, she said, 'And what about Father Thomas?'

'What about him?'

'Do you really think it's safe for him to come round to see you?'

'As long as he has the police escort, I can't see it being a problem.'

'But he can still identify the man who tried to kill him.'

'Yes, but we'd need to catch whoever it is before he'd be able to do that.'

Stopping dead in her tracks, Jenny grabbed hold of Tanner's arm and glared at him. 'I sincerely hope you're not thinking about using Father Thomas as bait?'

'Look, if the man wants to bring me round a gift, who am I to say no?'

'You are, aren't you?'

'OK, I'd be lying if I said the thought hadn't crossed my mind, but he'll be coming with police protection, and will be on board my boat with me. Whoever's doing this would be mad to try anything.'

'Without wanting to state the obvious, whoever's doing this is a psychotic serial killer. By definition, he *is* mad!'

Hearing his phone ring, he dug it out to see Forrester's name.

'Bugger! He must have found out I'm not back under medical supervision.'

'Or maybe he has news on the investigation?'

He hesitated for a moment, but decided that he'd better take the call.

'Tanner speaking!'

'Tanner, it's Forrester.'

'Yes, sir.'

'I assume you've checked yourself back into Wroxham Medical Centre?'

'Just about, sir, yes.'

'What do you mean, just about?'

'Er...we had to make a slight detour, but Jenny's about to drive me over there now.'

Overhearing the conversation, Jenny scowled at Tanner for telling such a blatant lie to their superior officer.

'Well, fair enough,' continued Forrester. 'Anyway, I just wanted to let you know that I had a call from Superintendent Whitaker again. I'm afraid the bishop's been back in touch.'

'Not about that email, surely?'

'Unfortunately, yes.'

'What did he say?'

'He wanted to make another official complaint: that you, personally, were harassing him.'

'Seriously?'

'I'm afraid so. But don't worry. I told Whitaker that I'd both approved *and* authorised the enquiry.'

'Did the bishop say anything about Martin Isaac's trial documents, or if they knew the identity of Claire Judson's son?'

'Apparently, he said they had no such records, and if they had, they would have been thrown away years ago.'

'That sounds to me like they didn't even bother to look.'

'Who knows, but it does mean that that particular avenue is closed.'

'It also means that we're back to square one again.'

'Not quite. Cooper and Gilbert have just arrived back from Head Office. They managed to dig out Miss Judson's old case files from storage. Hopefully they're going to find something in there that may shed some light on all of this.'

'Well, that's something, I suppose. Can you ask Cooper to keep me posted?'

'Will do, but only if I feel it's important. For now I want you to get all the rest you can.'

With the call ending, Tanner turned to Jenny to ask,

'Did you hear that?'

'Something about the Bishop of Norfolk not being too happy about our enquiry.'

'He called Superintendent Whitaker to make another complaint. Can you believe that? Fortunately, Forrester's backing me up this time, but honestly, I've got no idea why the man's being so deliberately unhelpful. It's almost as if he's...'

'...got something to hide,' finished Jenny, as the two of them stared at each other. 'You don't think...?' she continued.

Tanner cast his mind back to his first attempt to question the bishop, just after Martin Isaac's funeral. 'If it is Claire Judson's son who's behind all this, then we're looking for someone who's forty-three years old.'

'Nearer Forty-two,' corrected Jenny.

'Either way, the Bishop of Norfolk is far older than that; or at least he looks it.'

'Maybe we should do a quick background check on him?'

Tanner laughed. 'That's hilarious, Jen. Nice one!'

'What?'

'One minute you're telling me to steer well clear of the guy, and the next you're saying we should do a background check on him.'

Shrugging her shoulders, Jenny replied, 'He's behaving suspiciously, so why not? He wouldn't have to know. It's not as if we need his permission.'

'No, but somehow I don't think Forrester will see it that way. Besides, even if he does have something to hide, in all fairness, who doesn't? Whatever it is will probably involve something like tax evasion, or having an unnatural interest in children.'

'Or it could be that he's a forty-two year old serial killer who just happens to look twenty years older than he actually is.'

'Yes, but highly unlikely.'

Seeing Jenny pouting rather obviously, Tanner thought it best to add, 'Look, if he was younger, then it would make more sense, but he's not even close. I really think we need to be concentrating on suspects who are at least the right sort of age.'

'Like who? Everyone on our original list is dead!'

'Kevin Griffiths isn't.'

'The reporter?'

'Could be.'

'But he's far too young, surely?'

'Maybe he looks younger than he is, in the same way that the bishop might look older? Anyway, with Alan Birch dead, and the Norfolk Diocese not being particularly helpful, we're going to have to think of another way to approach this.'

They walked in silence for a while, until they came to the end of the graveyard. As they stepped onto the path that led down to the road where they'd parked, Jenny announced, 'I've got an idea.'

Before Tanner had a chance to ask her what it was, she turned around and started to jog back up the path, calling back, 'I'll meet you at the car. I won't be long.'

A few minutes later, as Tanner rested up against the passenger door of the Golf, Jenny re-appeared at the end of the path, her handbag in one hand, a plastic bag in the other, and a particularly smug expression stamped all over her face.

'What's in the bag?' called out Tanner, as she reached the road.

Crossing over, she pulled out her car keys to say, 'A hunch!'

'Your lunch?' queried Tanner, raising an eyebrow.

'I said a hunch! Now, am I taking you back to your boat, or have you changed your mind and are looking for a lift back to the medical centre?'

'Boat please!' requested Tanner, and slid with some relief into the passenger seat.

- CHAPTER FORTY EIGHT -

L YING PROPPED UP in his yacht's small but cosy cabin bed, immersed in the latest John Grisham novel, Tanner was about to get up to turn the oil lamp on to counteract the diminishing light from a fast setting sun, when he heard a familiar voice calling from outside.

'Hello? Is anyone home?'

It was Father Thomas.

Glancing at his watch to see that it was gone half past nine, surprised he'd come so late, Tanner called back, 'Just coming!' and rolled himself off the bed.

'Sorry about the time,' came the priest's voice again, as Tanner ducked out into the cockpit. 'One of my more elderly church members popped round for a bit of a chat, which went on a little longer than I'd hoped.'

Lifting the canvas awning covering the entrance, Tanner looked out at Father Thomas. He was standing on the grass bank wearing a nondescript dark grey waterproof jacket and carrying what appeared to be two bottles of homemade beer, one in his hand, the other tucked under his arm.

'It's not too late, is it?' asked the priest, with a concerned frown.

'Not at all!' said Tanner. 'It's not as if I was halfway through watching a film, or anything. No TV.'

As he rolled up the canvas flap to create a doorway, he added, 'No electricity either, for that matter.'

'How on earth do you survive?'

Standing back to allow the priest to climb on board, Tanner said, 'I've found books make a good substitute for television, and you get used to the rest. The hardest part is not being able to charge things up, like my phone, for example. So I try to turn it off every now and again to save the battery; which reminds me.' With that, he ducked back inside the cabin to return a moment later, phone in hand, as its familiar start-up tune chimed out.

'Well, this is certainly cosy!' exclaimed the priest, with a pleasant smile.

Casting an eye over Tanner's various bandages, he asked, 'How are your hands?'

'Oh, fine. How's your neck?'

'Much better, thank you.'

An awkward silence followed, before Father Thomas said, 'Here, I bought you this,' and handed Tanner the bottle of beer he'd been holding in his hand. 'Nothing special. Just something by way of a thank you.'

Taking the bottle, Tanner thanked him to look down and read out what the label said.

'Thursday, 9th May.'

'Not the most imaginative of titles,' admitted the priest, 'but it certainly packs quite a punch.'

Holding it up to what was left of the light, Tanner thought it looked a little cloudy for his liking, but not wishing to appear rude, he said, 'Looks great!' and placed both the bottle and his phone down on the table. Spinning around, he lifted up the bench seat behind him to begin rummaging inside the cabinet underneath for something to use to drink it from.

'I don't have any pint glasses, I'm afraid,' he said, standing up with two tumblers in hand, ones he normally reserved for his preferred cocktail of rum and coke.

'Not a problem,' replied the priest, pulling the bottle out from under his arm to remove its swing-top rubber cap and begin pouring himself out a glass.

As Tanner tugged open his own bottle he glanced out of the rectangular opening in the canvas awning. 'I assume our two constables followed you over here?'

'I left them parking up, just outside the marina,' the priest replied, before raising his glass to say, 'To your good health!'

'Cheers!' responded Tanner, taking a cautious sip.

Pleasantly surprised to discover that it tasted far better than it looked, Tanner downed half the glass, just as his phone pinged, telling him he'd received a voicemail.

'Excuse me for just a moment,' he said, retrieving his phone from the table to begin accessing its messages.

Discovering that it had been left by DCI Forrester, several hours before, Tanner kicked himself for having missed it.

Continuing to drink from his glass, he sat back to listen to Forrester tell him that the old case files they'd found buried deep inside Headquarters had born fruit. Although they'd yet to discover the identity of Claire Judson's son, they'd managed to unearth a sperm sample that had been collected from within Claire's body at the time, on which they'd had forensics do some DNA sampling. The message finished by saying that they'd found a match, and for Tanner to call him as soon as possible.

Raising an intrigued eyebrow, Tanner removed the phone from his ear.

'News?' enquired Father Thomas, as he picked up Tanner's bottle to refill his host's glass.

'It's my boss,' replied Tanner, reaching for it with an uncoordinated hand. Remarkably, the priest's homebrew was already having an effect. 'Do you mind if I give him a quick call?'

'By all means,' replied Father Thomas, offering him a thin smile.

As he waited for Forrester to pick up, Tanner took another large drink from his glass. 'Sir, it's Tanner,' he said, when he heard the familiar response, the words slurring ever so slightly.

'Did you get my message?'

'I did, sir, yes.'

'You're not going to believe what name came up from that DNA result.'

'Try me!'

'Fredrick Simpson!'

'Sorry, sir, but I'm not sure that I'm familiar with the name.'

'Otherwise known as your Grace, Tanner.'

'You mean…the Bishop of Norfolk?'

'The one and only!'

'But…how?'

'DS Gilbert ran a background check on him. He was the altar boy at St. Andrew's, all those years ago.'

Thinking back to what old Tommy had told them, Tanner asked, 'But didn't his parents say that he was with them at the time of Claire Judson's assault?'

'Evidently they were lying. Hardly the first time misguided parents have done so in order to try and protect a child.'

'But Martin Isaac also said that he wasn't there.'

'Then he must have been covering up for him as well. Furthermore, we've discovered that it wasn't the only occasion he'd been suspected of rape. There were two other school girls, during the Eighties, which was why we had his DNA on file.'

'And what happened with those?'

'The same thing as with Martin Isaac. The Church moved in and provided him with a rock solid alibi. Neither case even made it to court.'

'And now he's the Bishop of Norfolk!'

'So it would appear. It also justifies your reasons for having been suspicious of him.'

After pausing for a moment to let all that sink in, Tanner asked, 'So, what happens now?'

'With someone who holds such a high office, I'm not taking any chances. We're going to get a second opinion on the DNA. Then I've asked Cooper to see if the other girls who'd accused him of sexual assault are still around. If they're still prepared to testify against him, only then would I seek the approval of Head Office before bringing him in for questioning.'

'Makes sense. What about the other aspect? The identity of Claire Judson's son?'

'At the moment we're still drawing a blank on that one, although DS Cooper told me that DC Evans had brought in some possible evidence. We're still waiting to hear back from forensics on that.'

Assuming he was referring to what Jenny had found

back at the church, and had kept hidden from him in the plastic bag, Tanner asked, 'May I ask what it was that she brought in?'

'Cooper didn't say; just that it was a long shot. Anyway, what have the doctors said?'

'About me?' he said, remembering that as far as Forrester knew, he was tucked up in bed at Wroxham Medical Centre, and not downing a bottle of some of the strongest beer he'd ever had the opportunity to drink with one of the victims from the investigation. 'They said I'm fine, and that I just need some more rest.'

'You sound half asleep as it is. I assume they've got you on medication?'

'Something like that.'

'OK, well, I'd better let you go. Maybe give me a call tomorrow morning to let me know how you're doing.'

'Will do, sir.'

As the call ended, Father Thomas looked over at Tanner. 'What was all that about?'

'Just work,' Tanner answered, with curt dismissiveness, as he wondered how much he'd inadvertently said out loud that maybe he shouldn't have.

Feeling his head beginning to spin, but in a pleasant way for a change, he retrieved his glass from the table. 'This is certainly strong stuff!'

'Stronger than you think.'

'No kidding!' agreed Tanner, and was about to take another sip when he thought it might be sensible for him to slow down a little.

As Tanner leaned back against the cockpit's

wooden side, swirling what was left inside the glass around in his hand, Father Thomas leaned forward to place his elbows on the table to say, 'You know, I've spent just about my entire life thinking that it was Martin Isaac who raped and murdered Claire Judson.'

Finding himself struggling to focus on the priest, even though he was sitting directly in front of him, Tanner said, 'I'm afraid it was indiscreet of me to have had that conversation in your presence. I hope you'll be able to treat what you heard with a degree of confidence.'

'What, that the Bishop of Norfolk was the man who attacked and raped my mother, when she was only fifteen years old, before throwing her from the top of St. Andrew's tower, effectively murdering her in the process?'

Tanner's heart jumped inside his chest. With his vision blurring and his head spinning in a more sickening manner, desperately hoping that he'd simply misheard the priest, he said, 'Sorry - what did you say?'

'And I must admit that I'd been convinced of it,' continued the priest, as if Tanner hadn't spoken, 'especially when Father Richard stepped into my confessional to admit that the Church had told him and Father Michael to provide Martin Isaac with a false alibi, all in an attempt to cover up what they thought he'd done. And when he admitted to me about the letter they'd all sent to the Cardinal, well...'

With it finally dawning on Tanner that not only was the priest sitting opposite him Claire Judson's son, but was also the serial killer they'd spent all this time searching for, an all-consuming fear began creeping its way into the darkest corners of his mind; even more so when he realised that he'd been drugged, and that he was therefore the next intended target.

Adrenaline surged through Tanner's veins, accelerating his heart to dangerous levels. Only able to think fight or flight, choosing the latter he threw himself over the table, heading for the canvas opening. But the drugs had done their work. The moment he was on his feet, they gave way underneath him, sending him crashing headfirst into the cabin to land hard against the side of his bed.

Watching with casual amusement, Father Thomas crossed one leg over the other, leaned back against the cockpit's wooden side, and with his drink in hand, continued the conversation as if Tanner was still sitting across the table from him.

'But now you're telling me that it wasn't Martin Isaac after all; it was his Grace, the Bishop of Norfolk! Now there's a turn-up for the books. Imagine: my father, a bishop! Who'd have thought it?'

Hearing Tanner mumble and groan as he tried to push himself up, Father Thomas said, 'Anyway,' and finished his drink with one swift gulp to place the empty glass back down on the table. Standing up, he stepped over to the cabin doorway.

'It looks to me like someone's had a little too much to drink.'

Crouching down, he enjoyed a quiet moment watching Tanner clawing at the bedsheets, trying to haul himself up.

'Before I leave you to sleep it off, I do have one more tiny little gift for you. Actually, it's probably more like two.'

With that, he reached inside his coat to carefully

remove a hypodermic needle. After removing its protective lid, he flicked at the liquid inside, lifting any air bubbles trapped within.

'If you think the Ketamine I used in your beer was strong, wait till you feel the effects of this one!'

Pulling down one of Tanner's socks to expose the skin underneath, he inserted the needle deep into Tanner's ankle.

'No doubt you'll be interested to know that this is called Succinylcholine, or at least I think that's how it's pronounced.'

As he began to ease the plunger down, watching the liquid slowly disappear into Tanner's body, he explained what the drug would do to him.

'It's what scientists call a neuromuscular paralytic drug. Basically, it paralyses the nerve endings whilst allowing the brain to function as normal. It has proved to be the perfect tool for my recent endeavours. Not only has it enabled me to torture and kill those involved in the rape and murder of my mother, and in the most painful ways I could think of, but none of them were able to put up too much of a fuss as I did. To be honest, I'm not sure how I'd have coped without it, not on my own. Another benefit, of course, is that it's remarkably difficult to trace. Someone would have to know what they were looking for in order to find it. Apparently, enzymes in the body start to break down the drug almost immediately, leaving virtually no evidence behind. However, there is one slight drawback. It does have a tendency to affect the muscles used for breathing. So to prevent death from asphyxia, you have to use just the right amount.'

With the liquid gone, Father Thomas removed the

needle to say, 'There, that should do it. Now, all I have to do is fetch a few more items from the car, and I'll be off to pay a rather belated visit to my father, the Bishop of Norfolk.'

- CHAPTER FORTY NINE -

TANNER AWOKE FROM some darkly disturbing dream as if he'd been asleep for a week. As his mind fought to separate the real from the imagined, he began to recall what had happened, and what Father Thomas had been saying to him.

Had all that been a dream?

A single blink of his eyes was enough for him to know that it hadn't.

He was lying face down between the two narrow beds inside his cabin. His arms were tied behind his back and he could feel something secured over his mouth. But what was far worse than either of those were the nauseous fumes of petrol, stinging his eyes and catching at the back of his throat.

He tried twisting round, but he didn't seem able to. Although he could feel his arms and legs, try as he might, he couldn't move them; not one inch. They just felt heavy and dead, like useless slabs of meat, lying out on a butcher's table.

That was when he heard a sound that sent a wave of panic rampaging through his mind. It was the sharp crackle of fire.

He desperately tried to look around, to see where it was coming from, but he couldn't even move his head.

He could barely swivel his eyes. But it didn't matter. He knew what was burning: the coach roof, less than a metre above him.

Is this how I'm going to die? To be burnt alive, like Alan Birch?

As smoke seeped in under the lip of the roof he could feel the heat from the unseen fire, scorching the tender damaged skin of his face.

Got to move! Can't die here! I've got to move!

Doing his best to bring his rising panic under control, he focused his mind on his legs. If he could just bring his knees up towards his chest, he'd be able to turn himself the other way.

He felt a tingling sensation in his toes. They moved! They definitely moved! The same feeling began to creep into his hands.

Whatever it was that the psychotic priest had injected him with was beginning to wear off.

He rolled his eyes up towards the ceiling. The smoke was thicker, the air was hotter, but he still had time. He *must* still have time!

He focused his mind again on his legs, urging his knees up towards his chest.

They twitched, but had they moved?

He forced his head down to look along the length of his body.

They had! His legs were bending. He could even open and close his hands.

He was going to make it. It was going to be close, but he knew then that he was going to make it.

That was when he saw the mud weight; the 10kg lump of solid steel used by Norfolk Broad's boaters as an anchor. It was nestled against his stomach, a rope looped around both it and his waist. He'd be lucky if he could lift his own body weight, let alone that as well.

As all hope for his survival slipped away, he let his head fall back against the hard wooden floor. Doing his best to remain calm, he closed his eyes and started to pray - as best as he knew how - asking God for the strength and courage to endure what at that point he felt was going to be inevitable.

- CHAPTER FIFTY -

I T WAS DARK by the time Jenny drove into Ranworth village. She'd been desperately trying to get hold of Tanner on his phone for the last twenty minutes, as had Forrester and Cooper. Neither had they been able to get in touch with the two police constables who were supposed to have been guarding Father Thomas, which wasn't good; not with what they'd discovered from the evidence Jenny had brought in earlier that day.

With the sound of sirens wailing in the distance, skidding to a halt outside Ranworth Marina, Jenny leapt out of her car and began sprinting towards where Tanner's boat was supposed to be moored. She'd seen the ominous glow from a fire lighting up the night's sky as soon as she'd passed the Maltster's pub, but as bad as her fears were as to what that meant, what she found was far worse. Not only was the top of Tanner's boat ablaze, it wasn't on its mooring. Whoever had set fire to it must have untied it as well, as it was steadily drifting out, away from the bank, making slow but steady progress towards the middle of Malthouse Broad.

Reaching the edge of the bank she didn't stop. Ditching her handbag on the grass verge, she launched herself off the siding, plunging headfirst into the cold dark water below.

As soon as her head broke free, she began ploughing her way over the surface, arm over arm, as fast as she could, heading out towards the burning boat. She'd seen from the car that the cockpit was clear of flames, and as she wasn't able to spy anyone in there, she had to assume that Tanner was either lying on the floor or, more likely, locked inside the cabin. If she could just reach the boat in time, hopefully she'd be able to drag him off before the fire consumed it in its entirety. It was going to be a long shot, but she had to try.

As she swam up to the hull, she could feel the heat from the fire.

Taking hold of one of the lines that held the nearest fender in place, she first submerged her head under water to give her maximum protection from the flames, before lifting herself up and over the side, to tumble down, first onto the bench seat, then onto the cockpit's floor.

A quick glance around told her that Tanner wasn't there, but the cabin doors were firmly closed. He must have been locked inside.

Keeping herself as low to the floor as possible, she spun around until her feet were facing the twin cabin doors. Even lying flat, the heat from the boom burning above was so intense, she could see it evaporating the water from her clothes, right in front of her eyes.

With a surge of adrenaline she kicked at the doors, splintering the lock and flinging them both inwards.

Flipping round, she peered into the blackness beyond.

Seeing a shadowy figure lying curled up on the floor, she lifted her voice above the noise of the fire to call out, 'John?'

From within the darkness she saw a head turn to face her, its mouth covered by tape.

It was Tanner!

Finding his feet, she took a firm hold of his ankles and said, 'I'm going to try and pull you out!'

Seeing him nod, she began tugging at his legs, as Tanner did his best to lever himself out using his elbows.

'Jesus Christ, John! How much do you weigh?' she asked, before clenching her teeth together and heaving at his legs with all her might.

As he gradually slid out of the cabin, the moment his shoulders were clear of the door, she rolled him onto his back, took hold of the lapels of his jacket and said to his face, 'I'm going to drag you overboard!'

Hearing that, Tanner's eyes widened with fear. As he started shaking his head furiously from side to side, he used his chin to point down towards his stomach.

That was when Jenny saw something she instantly recognised. A mud weight, secured around his waist by the rope normally used to fasten it to the bow of the boat.

'Shit!' she said.

Then she smelt the petrol.

Fighting against a rising tide of panic, she realised that if she dragged him overboard with the mud weight still attached, she'd be saving him from being burnt alive only to be drowned about a minute later. There was no way she'd be able to swim all the way back to the shore with both him and the mud weight, not when Tanner's hands were bound as well.

Acutely aware of the fire raging above their heads, she found the knot that secured the mud weight and began tugging at it desperately, but the rope was wet with petrol, and kept slipping through her fingers.

When the sulphurous smell of burning hair caught in her nose, she knew they had a matter of seconds before the petrol ignited and they'd both go up. She had no choice. They had to get off the boat.

Ripping the gaffer tape off Tanner's mouth, she said, 'We're going over the side!'

'But the weight?' questioned Tanner, finally able to speak.

With the reflection from the flames above dancing in his eyes, she said, 'Don't worry. I'm not going to let you go.'

With that, she scrambled onto the bench seat, then up and over the side, dragging Tanner along with her.

Plunging down into the cold murky depths of Malthouse Broad, they disappeared under the surface. But before going over, Jenny had taken hold of the same fender rope she'd used to climb on board, and with her other hand still latched on to the front of Tanner's jacket, she heaved both herself and him up until their heads burst out through the water.

'Got ya!' she said, as Tanner began sucking in great lungfuls of air.

Looking over towards the bank, Jenny could see the flash of emergency lights ricocheting off of distant trees, but whichever service it was, they weren't there yet.

'We'll be safe enough here,' she said, before turning to look up at the flames above. But the way they were burning, with even more ferocity than they had been before, did little to allay her fears.

Following her gaze, Tanner said, 'You mean, before the boat begins to sink?'

Jenny stared back towards the shore, trying to judge the distance, and if it would be possible for her to swim back with both Tanner *and* the mud weight. But deep down she knew she wouldn't, not with Tanner's hands still bound behind his back.

Knowing what she was thinking, Tanner asked, 'Is there any way you can untie me?'

'Unfortunately, I've only got two hands, one of which is holding you; the other the boat.'

'So, that's a no then?'

'Well, it's not a yes, if that's what you mean.'

A moment passed, before Tanner said, 'When the time comes, Jen, and the boat starts to go down, you're going to have to promise me something.'

'What's that?'

'That you'll leave me here, and swim back to the shore on your own.'

'No problem.'

'Oh, OK. Well…that's good, I suppose.'

'Sorry, I should have paused for a moment there, shouldn't I?'

'It would have been nice if you'd at least pretended to give it some thought, yes.'

'Hold on. I think I've got an idea.'

With that, she wrapped her legs around his waist to hook her feet together in front of him. With one of her hands now free, she reached down under the water, found the knot that was holding the mud weight in place, and began trying to prise it loose. But if she was unable to untie it with two hands earlier, being able to do so with one was proving impossible.

'Fuck it!' she eventually said, beginning to struggle for breath. 'It's no use. I can't untie the damned thing!'

'Need a hand?' came a voice from out of the darkness.

Turning their heads, they saw a stocky middle-aged man sitting inside a wooden rowing boat, slipping silently through the water towards them.

'You could say that,' said Jenny, beaming a huge smile over the water towards him.

As the boat slid to a halt about ten feet away, the man called out, 'I can't get much closer, I'm afraid. Can you swim over?'

'We can't, no,' said Jenny. 'My friend has a mud weight tied around his waist.'

With a confused look, the man asked, 'He wasn't trying anything silly, was he?'

'Other than entertaining a psychotic serial killer, I don't think so, no.'

Staring at the burning yacht behind them, his look of bemused confusion turned to one of acute concern. 'It's beginning to go down,' he said. 'I can try and get a little closer, if that would help?'

'Probably not,' said Jenny. 'His hands are tied together as well. Could you maybe hold out an oar for me, and then pull us over?'

'OK. Hold on. Let me try and get a little closer first.'

Already feeling the intense heat against the side of his face, the man pulled gently on his oars before lifting one out of the rowlocks to swing over for her to grab.

With her legs still locked around Tanner's waist, with her free hand she took hold of the oar, where it joined the paddle. As soon as she felt she had a firm enough grip, she said to Tanner, 'Are you ready?'

'Not really,' he replied.

Forced to assume that he was being his normal sarcastic self, she said, 'OK, take a deep breath.'

As they both did, she let go of the fender rope.

The moment she did, they slid silently beneath the surface, leaving the man in the boat to begin pulling in the half-submerged oar.

As it gradually emerged from the blackness beneath, seeing that she was still holding on to the end, with one hand he took hold of her wrist. When he saw her let go of the oar, he threw it down into the bottom of his boat and leaned over the side to continue to pull both her and the man up until their heads broke free of the surface, gasping for air.

'Are you all right?' he asked, staring down at the two of them.

Seeing them nod as they blinked the water out of their eyes, he began heaving at the man's body, until his top half was hanging over the edge of the boat. Once the woman had handed him the mud weight, he continued to pull the rest of the man in, until he rolled safely over the side to end up lying in the bottom like a dead wet fish.

After he'd done the same for the woman, he wrestled the oar back in its rowlock, spun the boat around and began rowing them away from the burning remains of what was left of Tanner's floating home, making speedy headway for the safety of Malthouse Broad's moorings.

- CHAPTER FIFTY ONE -

S THEY WERE rowed towards the moorings, Jenny busied herself with the ropes that had been used to bind Tanner, starting with the one securing him to the mud weight, before tackling the other used to hold his hands behind his back.

Once free, he sat up straight to begin massaging his wrists. As he did, he studied Jenny's face. 'How did you know?'

'What? That Father Thomas was going to try and burn you alive? I can't say that I did. But after we worked out that he must have been the one behind all of this, I thought he might have a go, especially after what you'd told him earlier.'

'What was that?'

'That you'd never give up until you found out who killed Alan Birch, and the two priests.'

'OK, but how did you know it was him?'

'It was what I went back for, after we left St. Andrew's church. Something that, according to you at least, is virtually invisible to the male of the species; well, what you put into them is.'

'Sorry, I'm not with you.'

'The vase beside Claire Judson's grave. I realised that whoever had been leaving the flowers there must have been her son.'

'And that the vase would have his prints all over it,' concluded Tanner, feeling a little stupid for not having thought of that himself.

'But I can't say I had any idea that they'd end up belonging to Father Thomas. Fortunately, we had his prints on file, after forensics had requested them when he was at Wroxham Medical Centre to eliminate them from the scene at St. Andrew's.'

'After he'd pretended to have been attacked and hanged by the neck,' interjected Tanner.

'It was only when we did a background check on him,' continued Jenny, 'and discovered who his mother was, and that he'd been adopted by a Church orphanage when he was born, that I believed it.'

Tanner took a moment to allow that to sink in, before asking, 'I assume he's not been caught yet?'

'Not yet, no, but Cooper and Gilbert are waiting for him at his home, along with a couple of uniform.'

'I doubt he'll be going back there.'

'Why not?'

'He's got unfinished business with his father, the Bishop of Norfolk.'

'But how could he know about him? We only found out ourselves a couple of hours ago.'

'Because I told him,' said Tanner, feeling even more stupid. 'He was sitting directly opposite me when Forrester phoned. Of all the people he's wanted to take revenge on, it's his father who's the most important. He'll be heading straight over there. I guarantee it, so we're just going to have to get to him first.'

'OK, but you're not going anywhere. As soon as we make land, I'll get the word out to have the bishop placed under protection. As for you, John Tanner, you're going straight back to the medical centre, even if I have to drive you there myself!'

- CHAPTER FIFTY TWO -

B Y THE TIME they'd been rowed safely into Ranworth's moorings, a number of emergency vehicles had arrived, including a fire engine, an ambulance, and a couple of squad cars.

As they heaped thanks on their rescuer, Tanner and Jenny were both wrapped in foil blankets by waiting paramedics. They were then led away to be checked over. As soon as she was cleared, Jenny relayed Tanner's news to DCI Forrester via one of the attending constables' radios, that they had good reason to believe Father Thomas knew the true identity of his father, and could well be on his way up to Norwich to seek him out.

Once they'd each given a full statement about what had happened on board the boat, after promising the paramedics that she was going to drive him to Wroxham Medical Centre herself, they were eventually allowed to be on their way. It was only when Jenny was turning into the medical centre's car park, half an hour later, that she got a call from Cooper.

Pulling up, she picked up the phone to answer it. After a brief one-sided conversation, she put it away to turn to Tanner and say, 'That was Cooper. He's not at his home.'

'Who's not at his home?'

'The bishop. One of his neighbours saw him getting into someone else's car, but he wasn't on his own. Someone was helping him.'

'Shit! That means Father Thomas has him.'

'That's what everyone's assuming,' continued Jenny. 'A county-wide search is underway for his car. Cooper said that he and Gilbert are heading over to St. Andrew's church, to see if he's taken him there, and Forrester is driving up to Norfolk Cathedral, to liaise with units from HQ.'

'I doubt he'll go to either,' said Tanner. 'They're both too obvious, and he's not going to risk being caught; not when he's so close to finishing what he set out to do.'

'But where else would he take him?'

With a cold blank expression, Tanner turned to stare out of the passenger side window. 'He made a mistake the first time. He thought Martin Isaac was his father. But now he knows who it really is, I think he's going to try and correct that mistake at the same place he made it.'

'You mean…?

'Where all this began. At the ruins of St. Benet's.'

- CHAPTER FIFTY THREE -

WITH JUST ABOUT everyone else from Wroxham Police Station either racing over to St. Andrew's church, or making their way up to Norfolk Cathedral, Tanner and Jenny knew they'd been left with little choice. If Tanner was right, and Father Thomas was taking his biological father, the Bishop of Norfolk, to St. Benet's Abbey to torture and execute him, then they were going to have to go there on their own. Even though they'd both been nearly burned alive and half-drowned only a couple of hours earlier, they felt they had no choice.

Jenny threw the car into reverse. With wheels spinning on the gravel, they sped out, heading for Ludham, and the ruined abbey beyond.

Less than twenty minutes later, Jenny was tearing down the narrow track that led down towards the banks of the River Bure, where what was left of St Benet's Abbey lay. As the car jumped and jolted its way down the uneven surface, with a plume of dust kicked up by the tyres rising into the blackness behind them, it wasn't long before the headlights caught the fluorescent yellow of a car's number plate, parked up at the end.

'Is that his car?' asked Jenny, keeping her attention focused on the road.

'It looks like it,' confirmed Tanner, peering out through the windscreen.

The moment they were near enough to be certain, Tanner borrowed Jenny's phone to let Cooper and Gilbert know, and to ask them to come as quickly as they could.

Reaching the end of the track, Jenny deliberately hand-braked the car to a halt to leave it blocking the road, so cutting off the priest's only means of escape.

Jumping out, they raced over towards the abbey's ruined tower gateway, beyond which a near full moon rose above a bank of brightly illuminated clouds.

Diving through the gap between the fence and the long-disused mill, they hurried through the field on leaden legs, following what they could see of the footpath that they knew led to the ruins of St. Benet's Abbey.

It was only when they reached the first misaligned outcrops of weather-worn stone that marked the entrance to the former medieval church, that they saw Father Thomas. He was kneeling at the base of the tall wooden cross that was set in stone, just beyond the high altar. Above him, the body of a fat naked man was nailed to the cross, tape flattened over his mouth, blood dripping from his wrists and feet.

Seeing them approach, the Bishop of Norfolk raised his eyes to send them a look of pure desperation. As tears ran down over his face, they could hear what must be pleas for help, but the words themselves were unintelligible. The gaffer tape was making sure of that.

Coming to a standstill, Tanner called out, 'Father Thomas, it's Detective Inspector Tanner and Detective

Constable Evans, Norfolk Police!'

Stopping where they were, they watched as the priest bowed his head and crossed his chest before standing to turn and face them.

'Inspector Tanner,' he said, a thin leering smile spreading out over his deceivingly affable face. 'I see you survived the house warming party I went to such lengths to throw for you. And little Jenny Evans as well. How sweet.'

'Father Thomas,' continued Tanner, 'you're under arrest for the...'

'Not yet I'm not!' he interrupted. 'I've unfinished business with my father here. But don't worry, I'm nearly done.'

Seeing something catch the light of the moon, held down by his side, Tanner called again, 'This is over, Father. Drop the knife, and step away from the bishop.'

'I'd love to oblige, really I would. But it's not a knife, so regretfully, I can't. Sorry about that.'

As the psychotic priest held up his hand, Tanner saw that the man was right; it wasn't a knife. What it was, however, was potentially far more lethal.

'I must admit,' the priest continued, 'that I was about to break my father's legs with the hammer I used to nail him up there, before enjoying a few pleasant hours watching him die from asphyxiation. But when I heard your car pull up, I decided to douse him in petrol instead.'

He held aloft a chrome plated Zippo lighter. 'Of course, being burned alive won't take him nearly as long to die, but on the plus side, it will at least be considerably more painful.'

'Father Thomas,' said Tanner, as he began to edge his way forward, 'I need you to place the lighter on the ground and raise your hands above your head.'

'Or what? You'll shoot me?'

'There's armed back-up on the way,' Tanner warned, even though he knew that there wasn't.

The priest's gaze roamed over the flat moonlit landscape that encircled them. After inhaling deeply through his nose, he said, 'You know, one of the many things I love about the Broads is its vast open space. I've always found it to be somewhere you can happily lose yourself. It also just happens to be a place you can see something coming from over a mile away. Three miles, to be exact. And as I can't see a single flashing blue light, not even beyond the horizon, if they are coming, which I doubt, they've got some serious distance to cover before they get here.

'So, I suppose that means it's just the four of us: you two, myself, and my over-stuffed father here. So I suggest you sit the fuck down and let me finish dealing with the man who raped and murdered my mother.'

With that, in one swift motion, he flicked open the lid of the lighter and rolled the circular flint with his thumb.

Seeing it spark into life, as a threatening flame began to dance at the end of Father Thomas's now extended arm, the bishop behind began tugging painfully at each of the thick steel nails that had been driven through his wrists, sobbing and squealing as he did.

With his hands held out in front of him, Tanner took another few steps forward.

'Don't do it, Father. You might be able to get away

with what you did to the others, but if you murder the Bishop of Norfolk, right in front of two police officers, there'll be no turning back.'

'I suggest you keep your distance, Inspector,' warned the priest. 'I think it's unlikely that a quick dip in Malthouse Broad would have rid you of all that petrol I poured over you earlier.'

Tanner had almost forgotten about that. The priest was right. Despite having been completely immersed in water, his clothes would still have more than enough petrol for him to go up like a human torch, were he to come in contact with the naked flame that flickered with such menacing portent at the end of Father Thomas's arm. The noxious fumes which drifted up from his clothes were enough for him to know that.

Deciding on a different tack, Tanner said, 'And there's nowhere for you to run. We've blocked your car in, and you won't get far on foot.'

As the priest began edging his way back from the base of the cross, glancing behind him as he did, he said, 'You don't seriously think that I'd have been stupid enough to come all the way out here without some sort of a plan as to how I was going to get out again, other than climbing back into my car?'

It was then that Tanner remembered the river.

With his eyes fixed firmly on the Zippo lighter held at the end of the priest's still outstretched arm, Tanner crept ever nearer to the base of the crucifix, until he was standing directly beneath it.

'You do realise that I've only got to drop this, and you'll be going up in flames, along with our friend here.'

'And *you* don't seem to realise what will happen if

you do. I can assure you, Father Thomas, that the prison service doesn't take at all kindly to those convicted of killing policemen, and I can't imagine what half the inmates would think of someone who'd been banged-up for murdering various members of the clergy. So unless you really want to spend every day for the rest of your life being beaten in the morning and gang-raped at night, I'd strongly recommend that you extinguish that lighter and turn yourself in.'

'I'm afraid it's too late for that now, Inspector. Far too late.'

With that, he tossed the burning lighter over towards the base of the cross, directly at Tanner's feet, and took a backwards step, turning his head to look behind him as he did.

As the lighter came down, in desperation Tanner kicked out at it with his foot, catching its corner and sending it arcing back towards the priest.

Seeing it come flying back at him from out of the corner of his eye, the priest made an instinctive grab for it. Missing it by inches, it landed against his chest to slide down his front. As it went, flames sprang up over his coat, where he must have inadvertently spilt petrol during his evening's various nefarious activities.

With flames climbing his black clerical shirt to begin licking at his face, he stumbled backwards, frantically trying to douse them with his hands. But his coat sleeves must also have had traces of petrol on them, as they too caught fire. Within a matter of seconds, the entire top half of his body was consumed by a raging inferno.

With Tanner's own clothes still reeking of petrol, he could do nothing but stand there and watch, as the priest began spinning around in circles before charging down the incline, heading for the River Bure, limbs flailing, head screaming.

As Jenny came sprinting up to Tanner's side, she asked, 'Can't we do something?'

'He'll reach the river soon enough,' replied Tanner, with detached dispassion.

'But he'll be dead by then.'

'For his sake, hopefully, yes.'

- EPILOGUE -

THE FOLLOWING WEEKEND, with the summer's sun warming their shoulders, Tanner and Jenny stood arm-in-arm as they looked respectfully down at Claire Judson's headstone.

'This was a really sweet idea of yours, Jen,' he said, turning to look at her.

Unlinking her arm from his, she knelt to place a colourful bouquet of flowers within the glass vase that stood empty on the stone's marble plinth.

'I thought it was the least we could do,' she said, taking a moment to arrange them into place. 'Besides, I'm not sure that there's anyone left to remember her.'

'Apart from maybe Gary Mitchell,' remarked Tanner.

A moment's silence followed, after which Jenny said, 'Did I tell you that it's looking increasingly likely that Father Thomas is going to pull through?'

'You didn't, no.'

Tanner was still officially on sick-leave, and had subsequently been relying on Jenny to keep him updated with any news.

'Although I'm not sure if that's good or bad,' he added. 'I don't suppose he's said anything about what he did with Martin Isaac's body, or even *if* he did anything with Martin Isaac's body?'

'Well, he's still breathing through a tube.'

'So, that's a no then?'

Without feeling the need to answer, she stood back up to smooth down her summer dress. 'One thing I do know. If he does survive, he won't be tending to his mother's grave anymore.'

'Probably not,' agreed Tanner. 'How about the bishop?'

'I'm not sure he ever did.'

'I meant, if he's admitted to having murdered Claire Judson?'

'Not yet, no. Just the rape. He's still adamant that she fell.'

'He could be telling the truth, I suppose. But even if he is, he'd still be guilty of constructive manslaughter.'

'Which is…?'

'It's when someone murders without intent, but does so in the course of committing a crime. So even if she fell off the church tower when she was trying to get away from him, which I think is plausible, he could still be found guilty of having killed her. What did Forrester charge him with again?'

'Only for the rape of a child, and assault and battery.'

Tanner raised an eyebrow.

Seeing him do so, Jenny asked, 'You don't agree?'

'Yes, of course, but he should have gone with the manslaughter charge as well; after all, the medical records are there, as are the original witness statements, along with the physical evidence.'

'There's something else he admitted to.'

'What was that?'

'He paid for Martin Isaac's funeral, as well as his tomb.'

'Did he say why?'

'Not that I know of, but I presume out of guilt for Isaac having taken the fall for what happened to Claire. However, there's one thing I do know.'

'And that is?'

'The Church are going to need to find themselves another bishop.'

Taking in their surroundings, and in particular the way St. Andrew's church tower stood against the azure blue sky, Jenny breathed in the warm summer air, saying, 'It makes for a good resting place, don't you think?'

'It does,' agreed Tanner, 'although I'm not sure I'd like to be buried within view of where my life effectively came to an end.'

'No, I suppose not.'

After another moment of silence passed, Tanner glanced down at his watch to say, 'Anyway, I need to get going. I'm supposed to be helping drag out what's left of my boat for the insurers to look at.'

'You're lucky you had it insured.'

'I can't say that lucky's the word I'd have chosen.'

'Well, you're not dead, so you are in that respect.'

'Did I ever thank you for saving my life?'

'Not that I can remember.'

'OK, then I suppose I should, at some stage, at least.'

They both smiled over at each other in mutual understanding, before Jenny asked, 'Do you think they'll pay up?'

'Who? The insurers? They bloody well better! It wasn't as if I set fire to the thing on purpose.'

'No, but Father Thomas did.'

'I suppose I'll have to read through the small print, to see if there's anything in there about them covering for a fire caused by a psychotic serial-killing priest. But assuming there isn't, I'm just going to have to wait and see what they say, and be grateful that there's a Travelodge down the road where I can stay.'

'It's hardly ideal, though.'

'No, but it's only until I can find something more permanent.'

After a moment's pause, Jenny piped up with, 'If you like, you could always crash at my place?'

'Thanks, Jen, but I wouldn't want to impose.'

'You wouldn't be,' she replied, before turning to gaze up into his eyes. 'To be honest, I'd like you to.'

Tanner thought about it for a moment. 'Well, I've already booked and paid for tonight, but... How about tomorrow?'

'Sounds good,' she said.

Encircling her arm through his again, with the uplifting sound of birdsong filling the air, she gave it an affectionate squeeze to add, 'And then, maybe we could have a chat about us buying a boat together?'

A LETER FROM DAVID

I just wanted to say a huge thank you for deciding to read *St. Benet's*. If you enjoyed it, I'd be really grateful if you could leave a review on Amazon, or mention it to your friends and family. Word-of-mouth recommendations are just so important to an author's success, and doing so will help new readers discover my work.

It would be great to hear from you as well, either on Facebook, Twitter, Goodreads or via my website. There are plenty more books to come, so I sincerely hope you'll be able to join me for what I promise will be an exciting adventure!

David-Blake.com
facebook.com/DavidBlakeAuthor
facebook.com/groups/DavidBlakeAuthor
twitter.com/DavidDBlake

ABOUT THE AUTHOR

David Blake is an international bestselling author who lives in North London. At time of going to print he has written sixteen books, along with a collection of short stories. He's currently working on his seventeenth, *Moorings*, which is the next in his series of crime fiction thrillers, after *Broadland*, *St. Benet's*, and *Moorings*. When not writing, David likes to spend his time mucking about in boats, often in the Norfolk Broads, where his crime fiction books are based.

www.David-Blake.com

MOORINGS

A DI Tanner Mystery

Book Three

A war veteran murdered in his home, a property developer with links to organised crime, and an old family secret that seems unwilling to stay dead.

When Harry Falcon, a wealthy boatyard owner and highly decorated World War Two veteran, is found drowned in his bath, DI John Tanner and DC Jenny Evans start by questioning his two sons, each with a motive for wanting him dead.

But when the elder son is found with his head smashed in under a toppled yacht, and that the younger son has been talking to a local property developer, one who'd spent months trying to buy the yard from his father, the investigation soon leads them towards a dark and dangerous secret, one which nobody can quite believe.

- PROLOGUE -

Sunday, 6th October

THE SUDDEN SOUND of the cattle shed's door being rattled from the outside made Harry Falcon's heart jump with a start.

Unwilling to move, he remained motionless for a few seconds, straining his ears for further sounds. Hearing boots being scuffed against the ground outside, he slowly sank himself into the water trough he was hiding in until his ears lay just above the surface.

Lying face down on top of him was the stinking corpse of a dead German soldier, its cold bristly face pressed firmly against his own; a pair of rubbery lips gently touching his ear.

The soldier was one of many he'd butchered a few days before, in and around the French farmyard. Since then he'd been using the farm to take shelter, plundering the soldiers' medical supplies to tend to his many wounds whilst gorging himself on their food. He knew it wouldn't be long before another troop came sniffing about, but with a bullet wound to his leg and only a few rounds of ammunition left, he'd had no choice but to remain where he was. If everything went according to plan, it shouldn't be long before the allied forces arrived, the ones he and his long dead members of the SAS had been sent behind enemy lines to help clear the way for.

The cattle shed's door rattled again. Then came the sound of German voices. From what he could make out, there were at least three of them, maybe four. As to what they were saying, he'd no idea.

He remained where he was, as still as the corpse lying on top of him. Should the soldiers force their way in, he thought it was unlikely they'd lift up the body to peer underneath; at least he hoped to God they wouldn't.

The voices continued, but thankfully the shed door itself was left alone.

After what felt like hours the voices began trailing away to be replaced by the sound of a truck's doors being opened and closed, presumably the same one he'd seen being driven up to the farm a few minutes earlier. Then came the noise of the diesel's engine being turned over before rumbling into life.

Harry waited in earnest for it to drive off, but it didn't. It just stayed where it was, the engine left ticking over.

Becoming increasingly desperate to shove the decomposing corpse off to begin clawing his way out of the trough's freezing cold water, he muttered to his long-dead enemy, 'What are they waiting for?'

The soldier's face twitched in response.

Shock mixed with repulsion as he screwed his eyes closed and turned his head away, his mind racing to understand how its nerve endings could still be active. He'd seen dead people twitch before - many times, but only in the brief moments following death. This one had been killed three days before! And there was no question that he was dead. Apart from the stiffness of his joints, and of course the smell, he knew he was because he'd slit the man's throat himself, holding a quietening hand over his mouth until he'd felt his life force ebb slowly away.

As Harry's heart began pounding deep inside his chest, every sinew of his body was screaming at him to push the disgusting rotting corpse off and climb out; but his mind refused to obey. Until the truck had gone he had no choice, he *had* to remain where he was.

Then something truly terrifying happened. He felt a breath of stale air escape the body's decaying lungs to brush against his ear, whispering out a name as it did. And it wasn't just any name. It was his!

Fractured thoughts exploded inside his mind, leaving his body convulsing under the rotting corpse, desperate to shove it off. But the more he tried, the more it seemed to force him back down.

'Harry,' it whispered again, its flaccid head flopping against the side of his face.

Kicking and punching, Harry tried to force it away, but every time he thought he'd been able to roll it off, somehow it managed to fall back down.

'Harry, my love,' came the voice again. 'I'm not finished with you yet.'

'Get the fuck off me!' he screamed, pushing up against it with all his might.

With the weight finally feeling as if it had fallen away, for a moment he thought he'd done it. But when he dared to open his eyes, he saw he'd done no such thing. The body was now sitting directly on top of him, smiling. But what had been the rotting corpse of a dead German soldier had somehow transformed itself into a beautiful naked young woman, one with luminous blue eyes, full red lips, flowing auburn hair and a pair of mesmerising white breasts which heaved up and down as she took in a series of deep, passionate breaths.

Harry's mind began to tear itself into two; one half still desperate to claw itself away, the other left longing for the pleasures this beautiful temptress seemed to be offering.

As the woman rested her hands gently down on his chest, she stared deep into his eyes, and with a voice full of enticing promise, bent her head to say, 'This one's on me.' She then leaned forward as if to kiss him, but instead she raised up her hips to push down hard on his chest, forcing his head to plunge under the water's cold, unwelcoming surface.

Waking with a start, Harry gasped at the air, his hands clawing at nothing more sinister than a bath full of lukewarm water.

Darting his eyes about, it took him a few moments to remember where he was - at home in his bath, and that he'd been having a nightmare, the same one that had been darkening his sleep every night for the past few weeks.

As the water he'd been wrestling with returned to its natural placid state, so did the peaceful serenity of the bathroom he was in.

Grateful for being alive, he took a moment to stare down at his body as it lay stretched out before him, just under the water. What he saw left him feeling old and depressed. What had once been a lean, strong and athletic physique was now nothing more than a skeleton wrapped in pale sagging skin.

A creaking noise came from out in the hall.

Blinking his eyes open, he stared over at the closed bathroom door to listen. His hearing wasn't as good as it used to be, but it was far better than most people's his age. But all he could hear was the sound of dripping water coming from the tap just a few inches above his feet.

He was about to rest his head back down against the bath's smooth curved end when the sound came again. He knew what it was. It was the creaking noise of someone coming up the stairs.

'Hello?' he called out, wondering who could have been wandering around his house at such an hour. It was then that he realised he'd didn't have a clue what time it was, and stole a glance over towards a large carriage clock that he kept on the shelf above the sink. But there was no way he could see what it said, not from where he was lying.

Trying to remember what time he'd taken the bath, he heaved himself into a sitting position. Had it been before dinner, or after? Looking out of the bathroom window only told him that it was dark outside, but as it was October, all that meant was that it was sometime after six.

Remembering he'd left his watch on the chair by the bath, he drew his hand out of the water. After leaving it to drip for a moment, he reached over to retrieve it. It had been a gift from his wife, decades before, and he never liked to be too far away from it.

Bringing it to within just a few inches from his eyes, he squinted at it to try and see what it said. But it had been a long time since he'd been able to, at least not with any accuracy. As far as he could make out it was either five minutes to seven, or half-past eleven. Which one, he wasn't sure.

Hearing another sound from out in the hallway, he replaced the watch to call out, 'Phillip? Is that you?'

Phillip was the name of his elder son. He lived in a small cottage just down the road. He'd often come around unannounced, although not normally quite so late.

He stopped again to listen.

After about a minute of not being able to hear

anything other than the steadily dripping tap, he began to question whether he *had* heard the sound of someone walking up the stairs. It could easily have been just the noise of the water pipes expanding as the central heating turned itself on.

A thought crept into his mind which made his heart jolt hard in his chest.

Did I lock the back door?

Like so many things recently, he simply couldn't remember.

Then he definitely *did* hear something. The weight of a foot creaking a floorboard, directly outside.

It must be Phillip, he thought, and began the slow, painful process of heaving himself out of the bath. But he'd only managed to lift his pelvis up when someone opened the door and stepped inside.

Plonking himself back down, he glared over to be greeted by the sight of a complete stranger, smiling over at him.

'Who the hell are you?' he demanded, his heart beginning to race.

The stranger's smile fell immediately away to be replaced by a look of disappointed irritation. 'Don't be daft. You know who I am.'

'I've never seen you before in my life!' the old man insisted. 'And if you don't get the hell out of my house, I'm calling the police!'

Ignoring the remarks, the seemingly unwelcome visitor glanced around the larger than average bathroom to ask, 'Where's your towel?'

'I don't want a towel! I want you out of my house!'

'I see. So you want to go to bed soaking wet, do you?'

Furious at being talked to as if he was a five-year old child, the old man shouted, 'Of course I don't! But there's no way I'm having someone I don't know stand there and watch me get out!'

'As I've said, you already know who I am.'

'Well, you're not my Phillip, I know that much!'

Stepping over to the bath, the visitor leant over to dip a hand into the water. 'Good God! It's stone cold! How long have you been in here for? You must be freezing!' and reached out for the hot water tap to begin frantically twisting it around.

As steaming hot water began to pour out, thundering down into the bath below, the old man shouted, 'None of your damned business!'

'Well, don't worry. We'll soon get the temperature up. Now then, let's see if we can get you back in. Then I'll go on the hunt for that missing towel of yours.'

With the old man left muttering out a series of protests about being physically manhandled by a complete stranger, a guiding hand was placed onto a bony shoulder to ease him gently down, until his head was resting back against the end of the bath. Laying the other hand on the opposite shoulder, the visitor stared down at him to say, 'Now, if you relax, this shouldn't take too long,' and pushed down hard, so that his head slipped off the edge to plunge into the water below.